Andy and the Extroverts

Andy and the Extroverts

JESSICA K. FOSTER

NEW YORK LOS ANGELES

This is a work of fiction. Names, characters, places, and incidents are either products of the author's imagination or, if real, are used fictitiously.

Jacket design by Rejenne Pavon

Interior book design by A Raven Design

ISBN#: 978-1-960724-10-6 (pbk)
ISBN#: 978-1-960724-11-3 (ebook)

Published by Winding Road Stories
www.windingroadstories.com

To my fourth-grade teacher
Mrs. Maureen Marlette,
the first person to tell me I should write a book.
Thank you so much for believing in me.
This is for you.

1

SAY SOMETHING REAL

The last day of junior year was a wreck.

Teachers didn't care. Students didn't care. Even the custodians didn't care—I hadn't seen Mr. Breyer once today. Locker cleanout was the only reason they made us show up, and I'd already purged mine yesterday. Now, if I didn't pretend to take stuff home, I'd look overprepared in the worst way.

After the final bell rang, I braved the narrow hall, dodging sharp shoulders and squeezing through holes in friend groups. A few guys from the lacrosse team laughed as they punched and shoved each other near the bathrooms, so I lowered my eyes and hugged the wall to stay out of their way.

Of course, there were no adults in sight to break it up. They were probably hunkering in their darkened rooms, counting down the seconds until the halls cleared and they could celebrate surviving us another year.

I was almost to my locker when a familiar set of shoes blocked my path. I stopped dead in my tracks. I knew those shoes. I'd been staring at different versions of their pristine white perfection since the end of freshman year.

"Hey, Andrea." Eric Phan's dark eyes lowered as mine rose to meet his. He flashed me a shy smile.

I forgot how to breathe for a second. *Oh my God.*

"Hi, Eric," he whispered encouragingly when I didn't say anything.

My lips twitched. This was why my crush on him was bigger than the Atlantic. "Hi, Eric," I said in a strangled voice.

He adjusted his wire rimmed glasses. "Just wanted to return this." His fingers brushed mine as he slipped a black mechanical pencil into my limp hand.

Sparks erupted all over my body.

"Thanks for letting me borrow it."

I attempted to smile, but my lips wouldn't move. *Eric is looking at me.* Like, really looking, not just skimming over me to find someone else. This morning was the highlight of my year when he forgot to bring a pencil to fill out his history book card. I'd gathered every speck of courage I had and tapped him on the shoulder to hand him mine. After, it didn't seem real, like it even happened. I was never that brave.

He probably had a million summer plans waiting for him on the other side of the school doors, yet he decided to track me down to return the cheap thing? It was so calm, caring, smart. And those glasses! When he used his finger to push them into place during class, the subtle action plucked every nerve ending in my body. At least I had good taste when I chose a daydream boyfriend. Eric was everything awesome in one studious package.

"No problem," I whispered to my shoes.

Say something real. Right now. Anything. But my heart slammed an uneven rhythm and my throat dried up. *I can't.*

"Have a great summer, Andrea," he said.

Everyone called me Andy, but Eric could call me anything he wanted. The low rumble of his voice kept me up at night. Like, a lot.

He turned and strode down the hall, taking his messy hair and perfect manners with him.

I leaned my forehead on the cool metal of my dented locker and closed my eyes in disgust. Just because he returned a stupid pencil didn't mean he liked me. Could I be any more pathetic?

Forget it.

I opened my locker and stared inside it for about three seconds before I stopped pretending to care about this year. Slamming it, I merged into the crowd of kids flowing toward the cracked cement of the parking lot, the pencil still clenched in my fist.

At least I'd be able to go home and start on the stack of romance books on my dresser without homework getting in the way. For a couple hundred pages, I could be the girl a guy would notice, would care about. I could live in a time of social etiquette and manners, where lives were lived out loud instead of through text and tech. I'd get to be confident, beautiful, reckless.

People at school raised their eyebrows when they saw the covers of my novels, but I didn't care. Everyone could shove it.

Except maybe Eric.

Like every summer, I'd spend my days checking in overdue books at the library while wondering "What if?" What if I said hello first? What if I sat on the side of the cafeteria closer to him? Been like the girls in my books and made him notice me by having a witty comeback in class or a cool quirk? *What if...*

My flip flops scuffed against the uneven sidewalk on my way home. Just because he was soft-spoken didn't mean we belonged together. Just because he stood up for me last year in a group project when everyone tried to make me do all the work didn't mean we'd be good as boyfriend and girlfriend. This wasn't a cheesy movie where he'd spot me from across the room and realize that even though I had on the same black T-shirt and holey jeans I always wore, I was suddenly gorgeous.

This wasn't one of my romance novels where we'd enter into a marriage of convenience on page ten, fall for each other by the end of the book, and live out the rest of our days in Love with a capital L. Even though I may have imagined exactly that before I went to bed last night.

I unlatched the gate to the white picket fence in front of my house and smiled as I bent to pick up garden shears, gloves, and a half-empty can of sparkling water off the lawn. Mom must've gotten bored enough to ruin the bushes again. It didn't look like she'd gotten too far, but the one on the left side of the walk drooped a little, the branches much more uneven than they were this morning.

When I pushed through the front door, the June humidity gave way to a wave of air conditioning and an uber-strong smell of cinnamon. The Christmas playlist blasted as I set the garden tools on the counter. She must be happy today. Michael Bublé and Bing Crosby were reserved for only her best moods. Mom danced around the kitchen, which was filled with pie, cookies, and some sort of bread.

Her frizzy head tilted in my direction when I entered. I nodded and grabbed a mug from the cupboard. Mom always made a fresh pot of coffee right before I came home from school, and she never cared how much of it I drank. That was love.

She set a plate of chocolate chip muffins on the breakfast bar. My favorite.

I set down my pencil and slid onto a stool.

"Alexa, turn down the music." A cheery rendition of *Walking in a Winter Wonderland* backed off a few decibels. "How was your last day of school, honey?" She sniffed the air and opened the oven to check her progress.

I was right: apple pie. I never could figure out how she baked without timers.

Mom glanced at me when I didn't answer.

I shrugged one shoulder and grabbed a muffin.

She frowned, stepping around the breakfast bar with her arms outstretched. "What's wrong?"

I batted her hug away before she could smear flour all over my shirt.

She huffed her disapproval as she wiped her hands on a dishtowel. Waiting.

"My day was okay. Do you want me to finish the bushes?" Put them out of their misery, maybe.

"I need to talk to you, Andy."

I took a small bite of muffin.

"Andrea." *Whoa.* Full name and direct eye contact—a lot of it.

But baking equaled happy. She couldn't be Christmas Song Mom and Serious Mom at the same time. It was physically impossible. "Why are you making all this stuff?" Diversion probably wouldn't work if she was Andrea-ing me, but maybe I could get her to talk about her pie instead.

"It's for church. I have to get them done before my next shift." She scanned the kitchen like she just now noticed it looked like she'd slaughtered Frosty the Snowman in here. Flour covered every surface. "Did you try to make any plans with friends for the summer like we talked about?"

I picked a chocolate chip out of the muffin and set it aside. She put too many in. I liked the muffin part better.

"I'm serious, honey. Didn't we talk about you reaching out to Brynn again?"

I shrugged. Brynn didn't have time for someone like me anymore. Co-captain of the tennis team, treasurer of student council, the one flute player to make it to state solo and ensemble. Her social life had exploded in cool and interesting directions, whereas mine... had not.

It didn't keep me from missing her. We could still be hanging out next to her pool or going shopping for stupid plastic bracelets if she had time for that kind of thing. But it wasn't going to happen.

Mom hummed sympathetically. "I get it, Andy. I remember when I was a kid..."

I glared at her. If she started talking about her high school days as queen of the popular girls again, I was out. School wasn't like that anymore. We didn't even do prom queen and king at ours. And why couldn't she see we were polar opposites? She married *Dad*. She had to like something about quiet people.

"You've been so withdrawn." She made her I'm-Concerned face. "I know I've said it before, but I'm worried. Maybe you should go see Dr. Santos again."

The name of my counselor made me swallow hard. She was great, but I'd convinced Mom that I should take a break from therapy this summer. Digging through feelings always left me exhausted.

"I'm applying to colleges like you wanted me to." I gripped my coffee mug tighter. "And I see people—Joan said I could work part time in the library again this summer."

Actually, Joan let me sit in the back room fixing the spines on books and laminating things ninety percent of the time, and the rest of my hours were spent in monk-like silence checking in books from the turn-in slot, but Mom didn't need to know that.

"I sit with people at lunch." *Kind of.* At the same table, anyway. "No one is mean to me." They'd have to notice me to be mean. I took a sip of my coffee. "I don't need to talk to Dr. Santos."

"Look at me." She had a gooey smudge of batter on her cheek. Her apron lay on the floor behind her, sopping up a spill. "I should be grounding you for staying out past curfew or talking back. I should be taking away your phone because you spend too much time on social media or telling you to keep it down during slumber parties, but I'm not." She wrung her hands. "I'm glad you have the library, but you avoid all talk about college, and you're so smart, honey. And after all those hours we spent teaching you to parallel park? You still haven't signed up for the final road test—you're going to be a senior. You should be excited! This isn't normal."

Nothing like surviving a whole school year just to be told how much you sucked when you got home. "Everywhere I need to go is walkable." And so, I didn't want to think about college. Who did? I had a whole year to prepare myself. We'd had this conversation a million times before. What did she expect me to say? Sorry?

Mom hung her head, a tactic she used when she didn't want me to see her face. What would her expression have revealed? Anger? Sadness? No matter what, her message came across loud and clear. I was a disappointment.

Eventually, she pushed back from the counter and returned to her food prep. Fine with me. This wasn't our best conversation, and my books were calling.

"Do you still have that duffel I got you last year?" Mom asked.

I narrowed my eyes. "Why?"

"A spot opened up at camp today, and I nabbed it for you."

An atomic bomb went off in my chest. My vision of a calm summer, page-flipping in the backyard disintegrated. Camp. Tons of people. Cheesy team building. With tons of people. No wonder she wanted to hide her face.

"Church camp?" I whispered. At least at church camp everyone got to read alone during devotional time. I could maybe handle that. Tell them I needed more time for prayer.

"No. It opened a few years ago. It's called…" She flipped through a few papers on the breakfast bar. "Follow the Leader. Ha! That's clever."

I choked on a stray chocolate chip. "What?" She did not just sign me up for *leadership camp*.

Mom must've heard the terror in my voice because hers softened. "You used to love camp as a kid. Remember when we sent you to that one at the lake? When we picked you up, you cried and told us how much we were ruining your life by bringing you back home."

She might have had a point if I hadn't been seven. Everyone got along at seven.

I clutched my ceramic mug so hard my knuckles turned white. *Stay calm.* I would rather fall into a pit of poison-tipped spikes than go to a leadership camp. I would rather swim the English Channel in a hurricane. I would rather—

She pointed a wooden spoon at me. "Stop. Breathe."

But I couldn't. My mug clattered onto the countertop, coffee sloshing over the side to mix with the mess she'd made. "I'm too old for camp," I gasped.

She touched my hand.

This wasn't happening. I just needed a second! A second to not have to try so hard all the time. I didn't fit in at school, but I *always* fit in here. My house was my safe place, and she wanted to take it from me. She wanted to take me away from my books and send me into a new group of strangers, another place where I'd be expected to "participate." Not just that but *lead* something. I couldn't lead anything.

"Honey, we've talked about this. About baby steps."

Yeah, baby steps. Key word *baby*. This wasn't a baby step. This was a monstrous step.

She turned to pull the pie from the oven with a dishtowel. "The brochure says it's specifically for 'high school students looking to expand their interpersonal and leadership skills.' It'll be good for you. Break you out of your shell. You need…" She paused in fanning the pie to gather herself. "Well anyway, you leave tomorrow."

"Tomorrow? Are you trying to get rid of me?" I couldn't jump from dealing with people at school to dealing with people at camp. I couldn't believe she put me on a waiting list.

She crossed the kitchen and lifted my chin, forcing me to meet her eyes. They were the same color as mine: a moody, serious grey.

"Never." After a long pause, she let go of my face and cleared her throat. "Now help me clean up, will you? Before your father thinks these goodies are for him." She gave me a warm smile, and I slid off the stool to do her bidding.

This was so not over.

When Dad came home later that night, I was ready by the time he got to his study. So was Mom.

The second he turned his big puppy dog eyes on her, she handed him a cookie. It was the cookie that did it. He wouldn't listen to me complain while Mom bribed him like that. I still took a stab at it when he sat down in his leather chair.

As soon as I stopped talking, he looked to her for help. "Well, uh…"

She gestured to me with an annoyed hand. Why was he scrunching down in his chair like he was the one who—

"You knew about this?" Betrayal sliced through me, and I blinked back tears.

He picked at a piece of lint on his shirt. He totally did. This couldn't be happening.

"Can't you… er, just take some books with you?" He forced a smile through his scruffy beard.

That was *so* not the point! "I want to stay home."

He sighed and rubbed his palms on the thighs of his pants like he'd rather be anywhere but here.

"I have a job! I'm making money for college. Please, Dad," I whispered. "Don't make me go."

He blew out a breath. I recognized a look of defeat when I saw one. He was going to cave. *Take that, Mom!*

She crossed her arms. "I talked to Joan in the grocery store earlier today, and she said your job will be waiting for you when you get back."

My hands shook as I glared at her. She had no right!

"Paul," Mom said sharply. "You know why we're doing this."

His eyes darted to her, and he frowned. "Andy, it's not the whole summer. Your mom's right. You have to learn how to work with people. It's a life skill. We don't want you to feel isolated when you leave for college." Wow, that was scripted. The one person who should've gotten it, who should've been on my side. He couldn't even look at me as he opened his book.

I deflated. No one got to Dad after he started reading, even if he'd read every book in the study a hundred times.

"Really, Andrea, you're making such a big deal out of this." Mom sighed. "Look what you're doing to your poor father."

Like him hiding behind a hardcover was a new thing.

I marched to my room and collapsed on my bed. I didn't even have the heart to choose my first romance novel of the summer.

Mom peeked her head in after a few minutes. "Honey, it's going to be great. I know you don't want to go, but I think... I just know you're going to love it."

I turned my head away from her. "This is my room. You could at least knock."

Without another word, she pulled my duffel out from under my bed. I stared at the ceiling, because there was no way I was going to help her pack. If she thought she knew best, she could choose what underwear I wore, too. When she threw my bathing suit on the top, I snorted. Like I would go swimming.

As soon as she left, I shoved as many books as I could into the outside pockets of the duffel and fumed in silence until sleep swallowed me whole.

2

CAMP KILL ME NOW

Mom said nothing until we pulled into a Starbucks drive-thru on the way to camp the next morning. "I'll take a tall Chai and a venti Caramel Macchiato. Extra whipped cream."

If she was trying to butter me up, it wasn't working. All venti proved was that she knew she was in the wrong. And all her stupid whipped cream meant was that she thought she could fix it.

I still took the coffee.

We headed into the wooded foothills of the Green Mountains. She didn't talk, but I could tell my silence bugged her from the way her fingers drummed against the steering wheel.

I hid behind the lenses of my oversized sunglasses and sipped my coffee as she navigated around the corners of country roads. It didn't take long to wait her out.

"The bake sale's tomorrow. We're raising money for Mr. Carlton's barn that burned down last week."

I stared at the twisting road as it wound through the ancient pines. I loved Mr. Carlton, and she knew it. He let me read in the corner during Sunday school instead of memorize Bible verses the whole year I had him.

"The ladies said it was a shame you wouldn't be helping, but I told them where you were going."

I said nothing. This was supposed to make me feel *better*?

"Andy."

Nope. I was stone. She wouldn't get anything from me.

We turned onto another road, this one less smooth. Where was this camp? Psycho-killer country? I sipped my coffee again. In fact, every time she asked me anything, I took a huge, scalding gulp.

By the time we got to the entrance of Camp Kill Me Now, my body buzzed with caffeine and dread, and Mom looked more frazzled than ever.

When we drove into the packed roundabout, she teared up. Why was she about to cry when she was the one forcing me to do this? If I refused to get out, would she make me? The image of my mom hauling me out of the car by my arm made my stomach squirm, so I did what I always did: what I was told.

We got out of the van and with one Pilates-toned arm, she pulled my bag from the trunk and plunked it down in front of me. Dust mushroomed around it, and we watched it settle. She was waiting for me to break down, to tell her it was okay, that I'd be okay. I wouldn't. Other teens flowed around us, dragging luggage and pillows, talking to each other casually the way she wanted me to talk to her now.

Two weeks. She was leaving me here for two weeks.

We never fought for more than an hour or two. It killed both of us, but she only had herself to blame. I couldn't do this, and she knew it.

She pulled me into a hug. "I love you."

"Don't love me like this," I whispered into her hair. I grimaced under my sunglasses, my hand on the strap of my duffle.

She didn't hear me. She'd already released me and climbed back into the van. My fingers squeezed my coffee like it was a buoy and I'd just fallen off the Titanic.

Mom rolled down the passenger's side window. "I know you're going to find yourself here. You've got this!" She gave me a big thumbs up.

Did she have to be so loud? It was like those parents who screamed, "Don't do drugs!" to their kids. Like that would change anything.

She hadn't listened earlier, so I didn't bother to say anything now. Her mouth turned down when she got the hint, and she pulled out of the parking lot. It was easy to imagine her cranking up the radio as she sped away from this godforsaken place. She'd be able to relax now that I was being transformed into a person more like her than Dad. Who told their teenager they wanted them to get in trouble?

My mom, that's who.

Well, she could get a text from me a hundred times a day until she came back and took me home.

I breathed deeply the way Dr. Santos taught me, taking in the smell of wet grass and pine trees. If I didn't turn around, I could almost pretend I was in my backyard after a heavy rain. This summer was supposed to be *mine*.

Eventually, I turned my attention to the campground. It was exactly what I expected: counselors barely older than me bustled around wearing safari vests with a million pockets, checking laminated lists, and ushering campers down narrow paths and into their cottages. One of the buildings peeked through the woods in the distance. Thank the Lord for small miracles. A window unit air conditioner dripped condensation on the grass below. At least it would be cool. Ish.

"Hello there, camper!" A red-haired counselor with freckles and a wide smile popped up in front of me. She held out her hand, but mine were full. Coffee before everything. She withdrew hers like it was no big deal. "I'm Suzie! Welcome to Camp Follow the Leader, where teens become tenacious! What's your name? Let me help you find your bunk."

I sighed. And now I had to talk to people. "Andy Stevens."

"What was that?" She cupped her ear with her hand. A bit unnecessary.

"Stevens." I cleared my throat. "Andy Stevens."

She scanned her list. "I don't have an Andy—Andrea! There you are. You're in the Beaver Cottage with me! Isn't that lucky? We're right over there." She waved in the direction of literally all the cottages.

I nodded and hoisted my bag over one shoulder. I could lie down on the dusty ground and refuse to move until Mom came back to get me, but the scene that would cause wouldn't be worth it.

Seeming content, Suzie turned and started in on a guy who had just stepped out of a green minivan. "Hello there, camper! Welcome to..."

I lugged my book-filled bag about twenty feet and plopped it next to a picnic table in front of a clump of cottages. I did my best not to look lost as I scanned the names nearest me. Fox Cottage. Bear Cottage. Porcupine Cottage. *Crap.* Nervously, I tipped my coffee up to my lips, but ended up sucking air. It was empty.

"Hello there, camper," a masculine voice behind me mocked.

Suzie's head whipped around. How did she even hear him from so far away?

He chuckled, happy she'd caught him making fun of her.

Her spine stiffened, and she turned up her nose with dramatic flair before returning to her task of greeting new campers. All she needed was a big sign pointing to him that read "Mortal Enemy." I wasn't surprised. That's what happened when you were in people's faces all the time.

I heaved my bag over my shoulder and turned to the guy. The last thing I needed was to get in the middle of whatever drama they had going on.

His sunglasses mirrored mine. He wore his hair short on the sides, but longer on top and perfectly styled, like he'd spent an hour on it. His thin waist tapered into frayed cargo shorts. A nametag gracing his left pec labeled him as Tyler. He gave off a seriously hot vibe. For a second, I could imagine him in one of my books, hair tousled and in full pirate get up, his crooked smile charming all the wenches in the port taverns. There'd be a noblewoman, of course, kidnapped for ransom, and—wait. *A nametag?*

"Are you a counselor?" I asked in horror.

"I am. Do you want help with your bag?" He stepped toward me, and my palms began to sweat.

"Um sure." Then I remembered my books. "Wait, you probably don't want to do that. I mean..." I whispered.

"It's fine." He pulled my bag off my shoulder, swaying under the weight. "What the... what do you have in here?"

"Books." *Kill me now.*

"What? I'm sorry, you speak really softly."

My mouth dried up, and I couldn't say it again. Not louder, anyway. I gave a helpless shrug.

He pushed his sunglasses to the top of his head, exposing ice blue eyes. His mouth curled into a gentle smile. "Cottage?"

I'd been here all of ten seconds, and already I was being treated like I was a five-year-old. How pathetic did I look? "Beaver."

He whistled, long and low. "You've got Suzie. Spirit with a capital S."

I gathered that.

We walked together toward the other side of camp in silence. After a bit, he said, "You're such a loudmouth."

I huffed. Very funny.

He hoisted my bag onto the top step of Beaver Cottage. I wanted it to look crappy, to be a total shack. If I told my mom this place was a fire hazard, maybe she'd come get me. Except it wasn't. It was quaint, cute. Stable. The dark green roof looked relatively new, and someone had stained the wooden porch recently.

My sunglasses slipped down my nose, loose with sweat from our short trek. Counselor Tyler reached up and caught them before they toppled from my face.

"Thanks," I muttered as he handed them to me.

He moved back a bit. "Woah, your eyes are silver? Intense."

"Thanks," I repeated. It intimidated me to talk to someone so attractive, but I was raised with manners. If someone helped or complimented you, you said thank you. He dragged my butt to the right place and saved me from the humiliation of appearing lost while I attempted to find the cottage myself. I actually was thankful.

"Anytime." He started back down the stairs. "Nice to meet you!" he called as I pulled my bag into the cottage.

I shut the door behind me, happy to end that awkwardness.

Inside, girls chatted and threw their crap onto the bunk beds that lined the walls. The noise alone was overwhelming, not to mention the fact I looked like a total weirdo walking in circles looking for a bed that didn't have a pillow or sleeping bag already on it. Nothing was assigned as far as I could tell, and it appeared that I was the last one to arrive. That meant…

Freckled Suzie popped into the cottage like some kind of manic jack-in-the-box and made a beeline for her bed. "Well, then." She smiled so wide I could see way more of her gums than seemed possible. "Looks like you're with me, Camper Andrea. I'm a bottom bunk gal, myself." She gestured to where she'd already set up her space, complete with a fluffy pink comforter and assorted pictures of an equally freckled family.

Just great.

3

VOLUNTEER OR VICTIM

How did Suzie get here so fast? Did the cottage have a back door? It was obvious by the way she blinked at me that she expected me to jump for joy. I couldn't give her that.

"Okay," I mumbled.

She pulled a hot pink bucket out from under her bed. "I'll relieve you of your tech."

Seriously? How was I going to harass Mom into taking me home? Or stalk Eric's social media? He always posted the cutest robotics team pictures. They did all their best work during the summer. Maybe this year I'd finally comment on one. Maybe this time I'd show up in the crowd to cheer him on and our eyes would meet, and… I mean, probably not, but there wouldn't even be a chance of it if she took my phone like some kind of technology thief. Not to mention my music, my Kindle app, my—

She shook the bucket, and the other phones smashed together in protest. So, she'd already taken everyone else's?

Girls unpacked and talked all around me; none of them sat empty-handed, going through withdrawal. Maybe they were hiding their pain under their smiles. Well, who cared what they were doing? This was my *phone*.

"Um, no thanks," I said politely.

Her smile turned up a notch. "Camper Andrea, those are the rules. Technology distracts you from the ultimate goal of this camp. It pulls your mind out of the leadership zone."

There was no way that was a real thing. I wanted to argue with her, tell her she could pry my phone from my cold, dead hands, but of course I didn't. Arguing with people was pointless. It's not like anyone changed their mind.

I dug my phone out of my pocket and pressed the power button. As the screen faded, it took with it my last sliver of hope for escape. Mom had to be halfway home by now, windows open, living her best life. Never mind that cutting off technology was the beginning of every crappy horror movie ever. I set my phone in the bucket, careful not to scuff it.

"Now the leadership can begin!" she crowed. "If you need to contact your parents, there's always the phone shack. There's a free payphone in there, super cute! You won't need it, though. No one ever does." She flounced away, and I tuned out her chirpy voice as she used the same lines on a girl one bunk over.

Yeah, being cut off from the outside would be super thrilling. How could I get out of this now? I couldn't spend every second at a payphone. Maybe I could try to get kicked out of camp?

I snorted. Yeah, like I was brave enough to challenge authority. No, now I had to hunker down and pray this place didn't kill me. For two whole weeks. My stomach rolled as I crawled up the ladder to my bed, trying to avoid splinters.

A bunch of the girls left to check out the bathroom. One bathroom. As in communal. Their shrieks of disgust echoed through the open door as I struggled with my bag. Where did they think they were going this summer, a five-star hotel?

I held a rung with one hand as I tried to push the duffel over the ledge of the bunk bed. Wow, it was high. I closed my eyes in annoyance. If the camp had signs somewhere, I could've found my cottage earlier and been able to sleep closer to the ground.

As I hung on for dear life halfway between the floor and my bunk, I knew it would make more sense to climb up the rest of the ladder to put the bag down, but I wasn't ready for that right now. I needed to psych myself up first.

And the bag wouldn't budge. *Crap.* Too many books. It teetered on the ledge of the bunk with the shaky support of my right hand. One of my feet slipped from the wooden slat, and I barely had time to brace for a painful impact with the dirty floor.

Except a gentle push against the bag helped me right myself before I tanked. With the help of a pair of muscular arms, I rolled my duffel onto my bed.

Sweating, I stepped down to the safety of the floor.

"Hey, thanks," I said to my rescuer when my feet were steady.

The girl's eyes sparkled with humor. She was beautiful in a tall, sporty way. She wore a tank top and running shorts, her blonde hair pulled back into a sleek braid. "Sure," she said, scratching her long, slender nose. "Are you new this year?"

I dropped my eyes to the floor, realizing I'd been staring. "Yeah."

"And you lugged that heavy thing all the way here?" She pulled off her backpack and kicked it toward the next bunk. "What's in there, anyway? Bricks?"

I blinked. That was two questions. Which one did she want me to answer? "Books."

She cocked her head to the side. "Cool."

Silence stretched between us as she waited.

"Uh, I had some help," I admitted. This place already required ten times the amount of talking I was willing to do. My eyes darted to the door.

"Ooh, don't tell me! I want to guess. Suzie?"

I shook my head, sweat beading on my upper lip. I shouldn't have said anything.

"You're blushing! Was it a boy? This changes things. Who would be Mr. Helpful?" She tapped her fingers against the bedpost. "Pete?"

I shot her a blank look. "It was another counselor."

"Hmm." She started ticking off names on her fingers. "Dan... Jamie... no, Tyler! Ooh, don't let Suzie find out. She had a thing for him last year."

I nodded. I didn't need any drama with the most vocal person around.

"Camper Paige!" Suzie's shrill voice rang out.

The girl's eyes widened. "Do you think she heard me?"

Suzie materialized in front of us. "Camper Paige, Camper Andrea. Perfect." She handed each of us a pink sticker in the shape of a beaver. "These go on your bunk posts so we can all get to know each other's names."

I touched the tail of my beaver where a big cursive "Andrea" was feathered with silver glitter glue across it. Andrea, not Andy. I didn't have a choice in what this sticker said any more than I had a choice to come to this camp.

Paige slapped her sticker on her post, then pulled a pillow out of her bag and flung it on the bed. "Ugh, I'm so not in the mood to do this right now."

Suzie arched an eyebrow. She opened her mouth like she might reprimand Paige, but then turned her head when a dark-skinned girl walked by. "Camper Jordan!" She waved another sticker. "This goes on your camp bunk!" she sing-songed as she bounced over to her.

I placed my beaver on the post of my bed. "It's Andy," I told the sticker. Why my name was suddenly so important to me, I didn't know. Maybe I didn't want to change into Leadership Andrea. There was nothing wrong with Bookworm Andy.

"Has anyone told you that you have zero poker face, Andy?" Paige asked.

Huh?

"Come on, you don't think all of us are here by choice, do you?" she teased.

That was exactly what I thought.

"I mean, I am now. But my first year?" She chuckled. "Let me show you what I mean." She started for the front door.

What other choice did I have? Stay in the cottage with Suzie the phone stealer? Please. I followed Paige out of the cottage.

We descended the wooden stairs of the porch and Paige marched us down a side path, our feet crunching over dirt and gravel as we passed a dozen identical log cabins. She gestured to a tree about a hundred yards into the woods, and I craned my neck to peer around it. Three guys huddled together passing around a thin vape pen. One of them coughed hard, bracing his hand on the ground. *Weed.*

"Definitely Victims with a capital V, though they take it a little far," she said. "They don't want to be here, and they want everyone to know it."

A thin shaggy-haired guy leaned around the tree. "Paige! Come over here!"

She shook her head, grinning.

He gave her a hooded look, but whether it was because he was trying to be sexy or because he was high was unclear.

Paige gestured to a group of girls who were practicing flips and cartwheels next to a clearing that had a cement basketball court. "Obviously Volunteers. You can figure everyone out by their attitude. You're totally primed to go one of two ways."

Obviously. She'd only outlined two ways.

"Victim or Convert. I'm a Convert." She flipped back her braid and grinned. She sure did smile a lot.

I didn't get it. Why was she being so nice to me? Maybe she felt bad because I had to bunk up with Suzie. Or because I had no sense of balance. Did I care? It had been so long since a girl my age went out of her way to say anything to me. I was fine on my own, of course. It was just... Brynn was the last person to talk to me like this, and maybe I missed having a person. A little. I didn't want to think about Brynn, though, or how easily she'd been absorbed into the popular group while I was stuck being me.

A game of four on four escalated on the basketball court. The guys argued about a foul, not even noticing the cheerleaders vying for their attention. At the trailhead, a muscular guy and a girl in yoga pants checked out the maps. On one of cottage's steps, a group had gathered around Counselor Tyler as he strummed an acoustic guitar.

Of course, he played guitar. Everyone here was a caricature of a person, so exaggerated they may as well be extras in a teen rom-com.

Maybe Paige could see the differences, but I couldn't. Pretty much everyone here looked like a Volunteer to me.

She stared at me, her eyebrows raised, waiting for me to say something.

I wasn't naive enough to think she'd turn into my best friend forever, but maybe if I told her the truth, we could hang out once or twice. I needed a distraction.

"I didn't want to come," I admitted. And no way was I converting to anything, but I didn't say that.

She shrugged, apparently content with my one small sentence. "I figured. So, what kinds of books do you read, Andy?"

Was she—? She was. She was actually trying to get to know me.

I jutted out my chin, ready for her to make fun of me. "Romance."

A sly smile crossed her lips as a group of guys passed by us, two of them holding Nerf footballs. "Oh, I bet we can find you some of that."

I snorted. Not likely.

She looked to me in surprise, then threw her head back and laughed. "We're going to get along great if you're half as sarcastic as I think you are."

This time it was my turn to raise my eyebrows.

A bell rang long and loud and grating, followed by a chipper voice announcing through an intercom that it was time to eat.

Paige grabbed my hand. "Come on!" Like good little cult members, we sprinted to the cafeteria together.

4

THE HALLMARK OF A GOOD LEADER

"Heya, campers!" a curly-haired blonde woman yelled from the dining room stage. Did she forget she had a microphone attached to her vest? My ears were on the verge of bleeding.

"Heya!" the campers yelled back. I lifted my eyebrows; even Paige joined in, shrugging helplessly at me.

I eyed my gloopy macaroni and mixed salad. Even my pint-sized milk carton had a dented corner. Where was the coffee? Maybe they only put it out in the morning. Figured.

"You're all here for one reason. What's that reason, campers?" the blonde shouted, holding her hand to her ear like she couldn't hear us.

"Leadership!" they chorused.

"I can't hear you!"

Sure, you can.

The lady's smile froze when she looked at me, so when everyone yelled "leadership" again, I mouthed the word, dying a little inside.

She nodded as if this satisfied her. Cult might not be a strong enough word for this place.

"For those of you new this summer, I'm Dana, your camp director."

"The leader of leadership camp. Fantastic," I muttered.

"We have some fun activities ahead of us, all tailored to develop your leadership skills. Every exercise will help you become a better person for your family, your school, and your community. Since I've got you all here, your first task starts now!"

And there went my appetite.

"I want you to pick up your trays and mix with the table next to yours. Counselors will help you find your partners. That's right, ladies and gentlemen—boys and girls should sit next to each other. Boys, get to know the girl to your left, because it will come in handy in the next challenge!" She beamed at us like talking to each other was the most original activity ever.

My stomach sank. What if this was how the whole camp went? They'd lure me in with crappy food and spring some talky, boy-meets-girl scenario on me every time? I could *not* do this.

I stood to leave, but Suzie popped up in front of me like a happy little whack-a-mole, dividing our group in half right between Paige and me. And even though it wasn't like we were friends or anything, when Paige left me and a bunch of boys started weaving into our table, I mouthed *help me!* at her.

She threw her hands in the air. "You've got this," she said before Suzie shooed her away. Like I needed a hype woman. What I needed was an escape.

I scanned the ugly yellow wall across from me, desperately searching for a bathroom to hide in when a tall, sandy-haired guy sat down beside me, slapping his overloaded tray next to mine. My pulse hammered in my throat as he chuckled at something Tyler said. He bore a striking resemblance to his counselor. Cousin, maybe? Brother? Or it could be that everyone had the same stupid haircut this summer, since most of the guys looked like they were recently kicked out of a boy band.

Tyler backed away and the guy finally turned to me. "Hey, I'm Lucas. Looks like we need to get to know each other."

An extrovert. Big surprise. Where were all the Victims Paige promised me? I narrowed my eyes at the back of her head. Had she been lying to make me feel better?

Lucas held out his hand, and I stared at it for a moment before slipping mine into it. He practically crushed my fingers as we shook.

"What's your name?" His smile was dialed all the way up like he was on a commercial. I was sure his mouth to head ratio had to be off since I could see all the way to his molars when he grinned. From his grin to his flawless nose, to the twinkle in his eye, every bit of him screamed Class President. If he were in a romance novel, he'd be clean-cut main character for sure.

It was a dangerous brand of hot to me. I'd always loved those kinds of heroes the best.

"I'm Andy," I said, my breath catching. *Don't act stupid, don't act stupid, don't act stupid.* Why did he have to be the exact kind of cute I loved so much?

"You have a pretty voice, and whoa. Your eyes are cool."

"Thanks," I said automatically. Crap, I should probably return the compliment. That's how it worked, right? "You have nice, uh, hair." *Real smooth.*

He smothered a laugh. "Thanks. Do you mind?" He pointed his fork to his pile of slop. "I'm starving."

I gestured for him to go ahead. For the next couple minutes, quiet talking and chewing filled the cafeteria. It was almost peaceful.

"Aren't you going to eat anything?" he said around a mouthful of pasta.

I returned my attention to the processed macaroni and wilted salad, then speared a cucumber. Vegetables couldn't cause food poisoning, right?

As I chewed, he interrogated.

"Do you like it here? What's your cottage? Do you like your counselor? Is this your first year?"

His questions were easy enough to handle, as they could all be answered with shrugs or a simple yes or no. Then it was my turn.

He looked at me expectantly, and I blanked entirely. When he braced his head on his hand like that, blinking those deep blue eyes at me, I couldn't think.

"Is Tyler your brother?" The words escaped my mouth before I could call them back.

He raised an eyebrow. "You know Tyler?"

I shook my head, flipping my hair down to cover my flaming face.

"He's my brother, but you should probably pick someone else to crush on," he said, peering under my hair. "He's private about it, but he just got engaged."

My breath whooshed out of my lungs. "No, uh... you just um, you sort of look alike," I stammered.

Lucas nudged my shoulder with his. "It's cool, Andy. You're so easy!"

We both fell silent as the double meaning sank in, and this time, it was his turn to blush.

I couldn't help the nervous giggle that spilled out of my mouth. It was great to not be the only awkward one in this conversation.

"I knew you could smile! Maybe that should be my mission this summer." He squinted at me in a playful way. The knot in my stomach that had twisted me up since the moment Mom drove away unraveled slightly.

"Maybe it should be," I said to the table. This was the closest I'd ever gotten to flirting in my entire life. How was this happening? I couldn't even look at Eric, and here I was encouraging this guy I didn't even know.

Lucas caught my eye, and I froze. I didn't often make direct eye contact. It was so personal—intimate. The pressure of his gaze was intense and kind at the same time. My mouth went dry.

"Maybe it is," he said. "Do you—"

A blast of feedback cut him off and we both shifted our attention to the stage where Dana ignored the fact she had just punctured our eardrums. "Campers, it's time for your counselors to lead you back to the cottages where your two teams will get a chance to bond since you'll be paired the rest of camp for bigger leadership opportunities. Because great leaders are awesome listeners and speakers, today you will get to make a short speech about your partner!" Her yelling might be enthusiasm for her "awesome" activity, but it still made me want to cover my ears.

Then it sank in. I had to talk. In front of a crowd. It didn't matter if it was the whole camp, two cottages, or just two people. I couldn't fade into the background when they made it a partner activity.

"Why the hell..." I whispered. My bite of cucumber sat heavy in my stomach. When I got in front of everyone I was going to pass out, or cry, or worse. I didn't know anything about Lucas except that he had a brother and was cute. I couldn't say I'd daydreamed about us together as leads in a romance novel. I pressed my hands flat against the table, seconds away from a heart attack.

Lucas patted my arm. "Don't worry. We've got this," he whispered, biting his lip to keep from laughing. Probably at me.

I swatted his hand away. I couldn't concentrate on my panic with him so close.

"Public speaking is the hallmark of a good leader. We all need this very important skill!" Dana boomed. If she kept this up, she'd lose her voice. How could anyone so small be so deafening?

I sighed.

Lucas gave me a cheesy thumbs up. *Perfect.*

5

DON'T DO IT

Suzie shepherded us outside, and the walk back to the Beaver cottage was tense and full of nausea. Thankfully, Lucas didn't try to hype me up. Maybe he sensed it would send me over the edge. I was highly aware of how he hovered near me, giving off major protective vibes even though he didn't know me at all.

"It may seem a bit quick, but this place is about pushing outside your comfort zone," Counselor Tyler said as we trudged up a hill. Was it that obvious I was about to lose it? I couldn't tell what he was thinking, since his eyes were once again covered with those reflective sunglasses.

Like I could talk. Mine were firmly in place, too.

Suzie and Tyler gestured to the porch of the Beaver cottage, and we all jammed together on the steps to wait for their instructions. I found myself squished between Paige and Lucas. When we sat, I pressed my legs into Paige's so hard that she flinched. She looked from Lucas to me and smiled a knowing smile. I knew it was obvious, but I couldn't even look at him when we were this close together, let alone touch his body to sit next to him.

Tyler spoke to the group, but I couldn't hear it over the roar of the blood in my ears. They didn't even warm us up to anything leadershippy. Just straight into public speaking. The first set of pairs stood up and faced us. Each explained the other with a smile, like this was the easiest thing in the world. I blew out a shallow breath as my heart ratcheted up another level. This, right here, was why I didn't want to be at this camp. No one in their right mind did public speaking for *fun*.

Next to me, Lucas fed me whispered information about his family (divorced parents, one sibling), his dog (a terrier named Nana after the dog from *Peter Pan*), his passion for D&D (he was a master of dungeons or something), the number of girlfriends he had (six, which was high?), and more.

I tried to pay attention, to memorize what he said, but I was the worst sponge ever. Even an awkward guy with braces and glasses too small for his face squared his shoulders and talked to us in a quiet but firm voice, making eye contact with most of us, then centering on a point above our heads.

Two by two they proceeded in order of who sat closest to the front of the steps. Three pairs left until our turn. Two pairs. One.

When the applause faded for the pair in front of us, I stumbled to my feet, and Lucas caught my hand to steady me. Tingles spread through my arm, and I jerked back. My eyes snapped to his, but he just smiled.

"Okay, Luke," Tyler said. "Take it away."

My fingers curled into fists, my knuckles stretching the skin until it was as white as the bones beneath it.

Lucas glanced at me, then stepped forward. "This is Andy. She likes to read. She's an introvert. Introverts can be great leaders because they lead by example and are amazing listeners. Her soft voice is really calming. She and Paige are already friends. She's also an only child?" He raised his eyebrows at me. How did he figure out all of that stuff so quick?

I nodded, but even that small movement took a huge effort. I was dead—I had to be. Coffee overload maybe. This had to be one of the inner circles of hell.

"Okay, Camper Andrea. Your turn," Suzie chirped.

I could've slugged her. I didn't remember anything about Lucas. What could I say? He was taller than me?

"Lucas has a dog and Tyler is his brother. He eats a lot," I blurted out.

Next to me, Lucas shook with silent laughter, but Suzie frowned.

"I'm sorry, Camper Andrea. Can you be a little louder for us?" She forced a wide smile. She probably meant to be encouraging, but it came off fake. Everyone here was so fake.

Lucas whispered his dog's name to me again.

Tyler raised his eyebrows and mumbled something to Suzie. She shrugged.

Panic welled within me, and I clasped my hands together. "And his dog's name is Nana, but like, not because she's their Nana." *Oh my God, shut up.* "Peter Pan," I said a little louder. My whole body shook, but I was trying. *Happy, Mom? I'm trying.* Even if it was only to keep myself from complete humiliation. They were *not* going to make me repeat myself. The other campers' eyes crawled all over me, judging me.

Lucas reached over and took my hand, making me jump about a mile into the air.

"And my dog is my best friend," he added. "That's pretty much all I talked her ear off about on the way here." He laughed. Then he guided us into a bow.

And I don't know if it was because he was so cute, or because of the cheesy bow, or because they totally had to, but the other campers clapped, and suddenly it was over.

I ripped my hand from his and squeezed next to the rough wooden rail this time so I wouldn't run the risk of touching him.

"It's okay," Paige whispered to me as she stood. "It's over."

I leaned against the railing and closed my eyes.

"Breathe," Lucas murmured from his spot.

Hot tears pricked at the backs of my eyes, and I shook my head. It was one thing for Paige to comfort me. The fact that Lucas felt bad for me was beyond embarrassing.

Thankfully, Paige and her partner Jonas were the last to present. She spoke with ease and confidence. I didn't have to open my eyes to know she'd smile in all the right places, but I did, anyway. Jonas blushed a bright shade of pink when it was his turn, obviously interested in more than their speech, but she didn't so much as blink his way after they were done.

What must it be like, being so outgoing and fun that guys wanting you was an everyday thing? She was like Jane in *Pride and Prejudice,* straight up fabulous in every way I'd never be.

Thankfully, the counselors stopped torturing us after that and told us we could "hang out" and unpack. I'm not sure where they thought we were going to unpack, since there weren't any drawers. All we could hope to do was organize our suitcases and put a sleeping bag on the bed.

At least I could escape Lucas. I couldn't stand to do anything else that might make me look pathetic. All I needed was to trip and fall on my face in front of him. I slipped by him and into the cottage before he had a chance to notice. Once inside, my body sagged. Eventually the adrenaline faded, leaving me exhausted.

Sitting at the one rickety table in the corner of the Beaver cottage, I chewed my way through the sandwiches Suzie snagged for us and devoured three chapters of my first romance this summer. The story was slightly unbelievable, but those were the best kinds of books. So far, Mieka's loving father had trained her in swordsmanship. He'd probably die in a chapter or two. Couldn't let the main character feel too comfortable.

Comfortable was a foreign concept to me too as I punched my pillow after lights out. I'd counted to three before vaulting up the ladder as fast as possible with my eyes closed. Once on top, I was better. I'd fall asleep if I wasn't lying in the dark, listening to all kinds of nature that didn't exist in the suburbs. I couldn't even hear myself think over all the bugs buzzing and chirping. Why didn't they just eat each other and get it over with?

"Hey, Andy." The whisper came from the top bunk next to mine. *Paige.*

I moved my pillow to the other side of the bed so our heads would be closer. "Yeah?"

"You did okay today." She was being nice—so nice that tears

pricked my eyes. I wanted to forget the way I choked on every word in front of them.

"No, I didn't."

"Okay, it kind of sucked." Paige paused and the crickets chirped over the silence in their annoying vermin way. "Lucas seems to like you."

I bit my lip, glad she couldn't see my face in the darkness of the cottage. Lucas was… well. My mom would say he was a very nice boy.

"You like him?"

I'd shrug, but she wouldn't be able to see it. "I don't know." The way he helped me with the speech, how he didn't seem to judge me? I found it impossible not to like him when he was a knight in shining armor masquerading as a teenager.

"Don't do it, Andy." Her voice was harsh, like the crack of a whip.

A girl in another bunk snorted in her sleep and rolled over.

"What?"

"You're going to get hurt. He's like… major league," she said uneasily. After the way she handled herself during her speech earlier, it threw me.

"What do you mean?"

She sighed loudly. "Like, he's really experienced."

Yeah, I knew that. Six girlfriends. It didn't take a genius to see what she was getting at. There may as well be a big stamp on my forehead that read VIRGIN. It didn't matter. He'd wedged the door open by saving me during the speech. "Will you be mad if I kind of like him?" I whispered back. "I'm not saying I do," I backpedaled. "But you know… if I do…" It made no sense aloud, but I hoped she knew what I meant.

A camper rustled in their sleeping bag. I held my breath, waiting for Paige to speak.

"Who could resist? In any case," she said in a lighter tone, "you and I are going to be besties this summer. Bros before hoes."

I suppressed a giggle. "You can't say that. We're not guys."

"Then sisters before misters. It's not as fun." Her voice rose.

"Why do they get to be misters and we have to be hoes in the same kind of saying? You ever wonder about that? You ever wonder—"

"You ever wonder why people are talking after lights out and keeping their counselor and the rest of the cottage awake when we have a full day tomorrow?" Suzie was a lot less forgiving when her sleep was interrupted.

"Yeah," came a girl's voice from the other side of the cottage. "Shut up."

"Camper Emma, that's not very nice." Counselor voice was back.

"Ugh," Emma moaned. Her sleeping bag crinkled as she shifted, and then silence.

I closed my eyes and waited for the embarrassment to wash over me like it did every time I got called out for something.

It didn't come.

Was it because Paige was becoming my person in this horrible camp? Maybe it was because it had been a long time since someone tried to know me, talk to me.

Brynn's face flashed in front of me, but I forced the image away.

Maybe my therapist was right. Maybe I was kind of… lonely.

6

MERMAID TOWELS AND SWIM TESTS

Where was all that chirping coming from? And why was it so bri—Oh. I pulled off my purple sleeping bag, breathing in the obnoxious scent of sleep and pine. I was at a leadership camp. One with a really annoying—

"Good morning, Beavers! Breakfast is in an hour, so you have a bit of time to yourselves. Use that free time wisely, friends!"

I could not handle Suzie without caffeine.

A group of girls rushed to be the first into the communal bathroom as I staggered down the ladder, rubbing sleep from my eyes and fishing around in my bag for toothpaste and a toothbrush. The fuzz on my teeth reminded me I'd forgotten to brush them last night—so gross.

Sound came from literally everywhere as I shuffled to the bathroom.

"Can you braid my hair?" one girl asked another, snapping a hairband onto the handle of a brush.

"I have to pee."

"Ugh. I did not sleep well at all. Someone here snores."

"I wonder if the boys are up yet."

I couldn't follow who said what. My mornings at home had not prepared me for this. I was an only child, and everything was silent. No one talked until their coffee cups were half drained. Not even Mom.

"Morning, Sunshine," Paige said with a smirk when I snagged a sink in the bathroom.

I glared at her through the reflection in the mirror as I brushed my teeth. She sounded so much like Suzie that it took effort to stop myself from flipping her off. How many days were left of this torture? Thirteen? I was going to die.

Coffee would make me nicer.

"Not a morning person, huh?"

I rinsed my toothbrush. Until today, I didn't know anyone was. I thought you were either caffeinated or uncaffeinated. Before I could put together a sentence saying as much, we returned to the main room and found half the cottage empty. A majority of the girls were headed down to the lake to take the dreaded swim test, if their boisterous conversations could be believed. No way in hell was I joining them. Not without coffee.

"I don't know," I said to Paige when she turned her doe eyes on me. "I'm not feeling very swimmy." I hated to disappoint her, but I'd rather crawl back into bed than dip one big toe into a frigid Vermont lake.

"Look, if you don't do it, some happy counselor might make you their project." She pointed to my bag. "Suit up."

"I wouldn't put it past Suzie," I muttered. If I had to take the test anyway and everyone else was doing it right now, I didn't want to be the only one taking it later, but it was like eight in the morning or some other ridiculous hour. And… what about coffee?

"Without your swim test, you won't be able to do the slip and slide," she wheedled. "Or go on the Blob."

I had no desire to be jettisoned off an inflated bag, which knowing me, would end with a painfully ungraceful belly flop. The slip and slide, however… I'd seen it yesterday. A brief glimpse as we'd trudged into the cottage after speeches. It was little more than a black plastic tarp, but it was massive. At least ten feet wide, it stretched all the way down a huge hill and ended overtop of the shallow part of the lake. Hoses had been hooked up to stream water over the slick surface. I pictured myself rocketing down it, screaming. There was no world in which that wouldn't be equally terrifying and fun.

Paige squealed when I grabbed my bag and unzipped it. "You'll love it!"

Waking up on the coffee-less side of the bed was nothing in the face of her enthusiasm. It was contagious. After a minute or so of her pep-talk, I began to think that maybe I didn't hate swimming. Maybe I just thought I did. I'd gotten a great night's sleep after talking to Paige, and it couldn't be as bad as public speaking, right?

"You know how to swim, yeah?" she asked as we turned our backs to give each other privacy while changing.

"Yeah. I just wonder what the test's like. I'm not a lifeguard or whatever."

That was an understatement. I had maybe two years of swimming instruction during elementary school. I wouldn't drown if I fell off a boat, but I had zero buoyancy. I sighed and pulled out the suit my mom packed for me.

"Oh, they have lifeguards here."

"What? Then why do we have to take a test?"

"So we can swim out past the kiddie rope and watch the guys be dorks on the floating dock. Why else? Okay, I'm ready."

I finished shimmying into my suit and turned around.

We both burst into laughter.

"Why are you wearing that?" She snorted. "It looks like your dad picked it out."

I looked down at my sensible one piece. It was a sporty brand, basic. Blue. "Because I'm actually swimming?" I gestured to her hot pink string bikini. "How are you going to swim in that?"

She frowned, as if now realizing her chest was only covered by tortilla chip-sized triangles. "I hope it doesn't fall off."

"No kidding."

"Okay, double knot the strings for me and let's go."

I huffed as I did what she asked, but I couldn't help a small smile.

Paige would take the test with me, and she was totally nice so far. I'd be okay. Probably.

She picked up a fluffy towel with stripes that matched her bathing suit and slung it over her shoulder.

I grabbed my threadbare Little Mermaid towel.

When we stepped outside, goosebumps rose on my bare arms and legs. It was maybe sixty-five degrees, and though most would hesitate to dive into a frigid lake in this weather, that was New England. If it wasn't snowing, it was summer.

We joined the long stream of other campers who wanted to get the test out of the way. All the boys wore board shorts. Life was easy if you were a guy. But the girls… most of them wore skimpy bikinis like Paige's. Even curvy girls wore suits that showed off their assets. I must have missed the memo. It was like walking into a music video. All these girls needed now was slippery tanning oil spread on them by muscular playboys. Good for them. I wouldn't sacrifice comfort for wardrobe malfunctions.

Lucas sidled up to us, looking all calm and sporty in his black shorts that rode low on his hips. "Hey, ladies."

"Hey." I averted my eyes from the V that disappeared below the waistband of his trunks. My heart rate ratcheted up to a million beats a minute. Talk about hotness overload.

"Okay, Andy, I'll see ya later." Paige waved to a couple girls near the lifeguard tower and skipped over. About ten pairs of male eyes watched her bounce all the way there.

I could've died. What happened to her pep talk? She hadn't taken the test yet, and she was already bailing on me? Now, it looked like Lucas and I were walking together.

He squinted after Paige before refocusing on me. "You doing the swim test today?"

"Mmhm." My stomach clenched. It was like his voice had two modes: public speaker and deliciously intimate one-on-one Lucas. Self-conscious, I resisted the urge to cover my body, even though I wore more fabric than anyone else in a twenty-foot radius.

"You don't say much, Andy."

"There isn't much to say," I mumbled. The sun peeking out from behind the clouds had nothing to do with how sweaty my hands were right now.

He chuckled. "You're funny."

I wish.

A long, loud scream of a guy being catapulted off the Blob echoed across the water.

We got in line with the other million kids who wanted to pass the swim test, even though Lucas already wore a band around his left wrist. Did he think my ultra-conservative swimsuit was lame? I mean, of course he did. So why was he talking to me instead of the bikini girls?

"I like it," he said.

Wait, what? I snapped out of my self-pity.

"That you're a good listener." He winked at me and shoved his hands in the pockets of his swim shorts.

I should've hated it, should have been annoyed at how cheesy it was.

But I wasn't. It was cute.

"Thanks for yesterday," I mumbled again and toed the ground.

He laughed. "I don't know what you're talking about." Then he ran down the dock, way ahead of the rope no one was supposed to pass and did a cannonball off the end. Two counselors yelled at him from the shore, but he ignored them, flipping back his wet hair like an Instagram model. His head blended into all the other wet heads in the lake after about ten seconds.

I shuffled forward as the next group jumped off the dock and into the water. Now that Paige and Lucas were gone, all I had to keep me company was my nerves. Why was I doing this again? I didn't plan to swim every spare moment I was here.

The line bunched up behind me, and I took a few steps forward. I couldn't be the only Victim here who didn't want to swim. I craned my neck around to scan the beach. Every wrist I spied had a blue wristband attached to it.

Fine.

It took a while to get to the front of the line, which gave me plenty of time to figure out how the test worked. I would swim out to a floating dock past where I could touch. There'd be a lifeguard in the water and one on the dock. At the dock, I'd have to tread water for sixty seconds, and then swim back to the dock we were now standing on without a flotation device. Easy enough if you were a good swimmer.

I was just okay.

I tried to figure out how quickly everyone would swim out to that stupid red platform. If they were fast, and I was forced to keep up, would I have enough energy left to tread water and get back?

My turn came sooner than I wanted. I slid into the frigid water with the others and listened to the instructions. Put an arm up if we need help. Don't kick each other. *Ya think?*

Then we were off. Before we left the dock, I almost drowned in the splashing from everyone's kicking, but then that was no longer a problem because I fell behind. By a lot.

Dana was one of the lifeguards in the water. She kept herself off to the side, between me and the rest of the group ahead, holding onto one of those red flotation devices.

My doggy paddling was nothing in the wake of the trained swimming in front of me. Their strong strokes made my paddling seem even more wimpy. What had I been doing with my life? I should have been at the pool for the past six years preparing for this one moment.

"You got this, Andy!" Paige yelled from the shore.

Thanks a lot. Draw all the attention to the slow girl.

"Yeah, Partner! You can do it!" A masculine voice rang out. I opened my mouth in surprise and inhaled a mouthful of fishy water. Of course, Lucas was witnessing this disaster.

"Camper in the blue, you okay?" Dana called, paddling back to me.

I gave her a thumbs up while coughing out the brackish water like it was my job.

I sped up, but by the time I made it to the dock, people were headed back, having treaded water for their full minute already.

The lifeguard on the dock held a stopwatch and nodded at me when my time started.

It was just me, Dana, and the string bean of a dude on the raft as I tried to keep my head above water in any kind of graceful way. It lapped at my face and invaded my nostrils as I began to sink. My mouth dipped below the surface.

The lifeguard arched an eyebrow. "You okay?"

I kicked frantically underwater, but my legs were giving out. "Fine," I managed to gasp at him.

If this was one of my books, the hero would jump in and save me. No, if this was one of my books, the main character would kick this swimming test's butt.

I paddled for all I was worth, but the lifeguard frowned, then jerked his head to Dana.

She approached me from behind. "If you need to grab the dock, grab it," she said. "Then I can take you back."

I gritted my teeth. "I'm fine."

The guy clicked the stopwatch. "Time."

I turned my body back toward the shore. Why was it such a long swim? It was going to take me forever.

My shoulders ached and my knees cracked more than once on my swim back to the rope. I was acutely aware of how each second of my struggle held up the next group, but at least this time I wasn't being splashed to death. The roar of water in my ears and my own gasps were deafening, but I could do this. I hadn't seen a single camper fail before me, and though I knew statistically not everyone would pass the test, I wasn't going to let it beat me. I just wasn't.

As soon as my feet hit the ground again, I breathed a sigh of relief, but Dana walked out of the water behind me, her face serious. Whatever. I did what they told me.

She climbed onto the dock with me, then looked at my name on the roster. "Andrea—"

"Andy."

One of the guys waiting in line held out a hand for a high five and I slapped it with my wet one, grinning. I did it!

"Andy," she corrected herself, then hesitated. "Are you planning on doing a lot of deep-water swimming this summer?"

I stared at her as she wrung out her ponytail.

"I think..." She planted her hands on her hips but not in a mean way. She almost looked sorry.

My exhausted body caved in defeat. "I'm not hugely into swimming," I said.

She nodded.

"I doubt I'll be here a ton." I didn't want to be here at *all*.

"And when you are—"

"I'll wear a life jacket if I need to."

She gave me a wide smile. "That sounds great, Andy." She grabbed the blue wristband I'd earned from the tackle box on the ground and snapped it onto my wrist. As she used the scissors to cut the extra plastic off, she raised her voice to a grating volume and addressed the entire line behind me. "Even if you pass this test, you are still more than welcome to use the life jackets if you plan on an extended stay in deep water. You are also required to wear one when you use the Blob."

Wow. Way to totally call me out in front of everyone. It's like when a teacher looked over your shoulder in class and then yelled out the problem you botched on your paper so no one would do what you did. They never said your name, but everyone knew—they always knew. I swallowed hard at the pitying looks aimed at me by the other swimmers in line. As soon as I got home, I planned to pour all Mom's favorite vanilla creamer down the drain.

Dana released my wrist, and I stumbled back on wobbly legs. Even though most people stuck around to swim off the shore, I'd had enough for one day. I didn't care if Paige, or even Lucas was waiting for me. I wasn't the heroine in a romance novel. I'd been shipped off to this horrible place where even when I did something right, I couldn't measure up. Where the hell was the coffee?

7

WHAT DO YOU MEAN, THERE'S NO COFFEE?

I scanned the dingy walls of the cafeteria twice, but all I found was one table of juice, water, and hot cocoa. Hot cocoa, but no coffee? There wasn't even the smell of it in the air. I might've been able to live on the scent of a coffee bean at this point. I couldn't do this without coffee! How could anyone else? Yet everywhere I looked, I saw smiling faces and zero coffee. None.

It was unnatural. It was inhuman. I swiveled my head again, hoping I'd just missed the coffee station. It had to be hiding in a corner or something.

"Good morning, Loudmouth."

I turned.

Tyler. Holding a Styrofoam cup that smelled like coffee. With creamer. He would tell me where I could get the liquid that allowed me to live. It would require speaking, but desperate times called for annoying measures.

"I need some of that." I pointed to his cup. My head pounded from withdrawal and embarrassment from the swimming disaster. I didn't care what I had to do. I was getting some freaking coffee.

"I think this is the loudest I've heard you, Andy." A teasing smile spread across his lips, and for once he didn't have on sunglasses. He had the same disarming blue eyes his brother had, but I would not be distracted.

I stared at him from under the brim of my baseball cap.

"There's no coffee for campers," he explained.

I narrowed my eyes as he took a sip in front of me. Was he joking?

"Caffeine interferes with your natural leadership skills."

That made zero sense. These human bouncy balls might not need caffeine, but I did. *So* bad. "You're leading us, and you get coffee."

"True." He fought a smile as he combed back his dark hair with one hand. "I don't know what to tell you."

Then I did something I would not be proud of later. I reached for his cup.

He laughed, holding it away from me. "Seriously?"

I lunged at him, knocking my hat loose. "You don't understand," I pleaded as he held the cup above my head. "I can't do this without coffee." I leaned over him, our chests pressing together as my fingers brushed the bottom of the cup. Just one more inch and I could get it. One more inch and everything would be bearable. I couldn't let the coffee leave the room without me.

"Camper Andrea!" Suzie's voice pierced through the din of the cafeteria.

I froze, one hand grasping Tyler's shirt and the other stretching toward his cup. Campers all around us had stopped their morning activities to watch the scene we were making. *Crap, crap, crap!*

Tyler laughed again as I slid off him. Let me die. Let me die right now but let them serve coffee at my funeral. They can pour it into my casket.

I turned toward a chortling Paige, but before I could sit next to her, Tyler pressed his coffee cup into my hand. "Sometimes I need it to do this, too," he whispered. Suzie's eyes narrowed, and she jerked her head at him from across the room.

He held his hands up innocently, then followed her, retreating to a door labeled "staff." Probably the room with the staff-only coffee maker.

Like I cared. I had coffee. I took an enormous gulp, and my brain cells settled in.

"What was that?" Paige shrieked in my ear.

"I need coffee." Obviously. What was she drinking? Water? Oh my God, she was. These people weren't real.

"You must really like… coffee."

Uh, yeah. It was the only thing standing between me and going all *Psycho* on these people. Forcing me to talk, to swim, to… I shuddered to think what was next.

"It's coffee." I took another gulp.

"Would you jump on me too if I could get you a cup?" Lucas joked from across the table.

I sighed. Only a lukewarm sip remained. "If you can keep me up to my ears in coffee, you can have whatever you want."

"Andy!" Paige shrieked again.

"Promises, promises," Lucas drawled as he took his empty tray to the trash.

I downed the rest of it. Then I processed what I'd just said. "Did I just…" The blood drained from my face.

"Yeah," Paige said.

"Oh my—"

"God. Yeah. Also—Andy, I can *hear* you." Her eyes were wide.

"What?" I mumbled as I readjusted my hat. Of course, she could. How else had we been talking to each other?

"And now it's gone." She frowned. "Coffee's the key?"

I shrugged.

She shot me an amused smile. "You're hilarious."

8

NEVER HAVE I EVER

Not ten minutes into my scrambled eggs and sausage, Dana's hyperactive voice filled the cafeteria. "Heya!"

"Heya..." The campers were much less enthusiastic than yesterday. Could it be because they pushed us out of bed and then wouldn't let us have coffee at eight in the freakin' morning?

"I can't hear you!"

"Heya!" the campers said a little louder.

"Yesterday we threw you into the deep end." Dana's voice blared through the cafeteria speakers, as grating as ever. "Today, we're going to slow it down, let you get to know one another."

Or the inside of a book. Please? I needed alone time.

"We're going to concentrate on some cottage team building!"

I sawed my sausage into small pieces, pretending it was Dana's legs. Or Suzie's. Any loud person who liked activities.

"When you're finished eating, please return to your cottages where your counselor will have a list waiting for you!"

Paige laughed. "You're going to love this."

Not likely.

I trudged back to the cottage and the girls circled up on the dingy floor with Suzie, who held a pink list. Couldn't be a normal color. Had to be pink.

For a long second, I stood beside the closed circle of girls, not knowing where to sit. This always happened to me when I arrived late. It was too awkward to ask someone to scoot over.

"Andy! Over here!" Paige moved over.

Oh, thank God. I scurried over and sat cross-legged next to her in the now droopy circle.

"What should we do first, girls?" Suzie trilled.

"Truth or Dare!" one girl shouted.

"BS!" said another.

"Seven Minutes in Heaven!" Paige cried.

I snorted.

Suzie's smile unscrewed a smidge. "How about Bingo?"

Everyone groaned.

"Or how about we go around the circle and introduce ourselves and our favorite—" Boos drowned her out.

"Poker!" A girl burst out laughing. I mean, it was kind of funny. They really had Suzie's number.

"I'm sure there's a middle ground somewhere here, girls. One that doesn't involve gambling or swearwords."

Everyone fell silent. Ah, here was the leadership part. We had to be okay with a middle decision even though it wasn't what anyone wanted. Compromise for the sake of compromise. I was learning so much already.

"Never Have I Ever," Paige said.

Suzie opened her mouth to object.

"But you can shoot down the questions if you don't like them," Paige added.

Suzie cocked her head to the side like the ditzy poodle she was, then nodded. "Deal." A huge smile broke out over her face. "See how easy that was? Camper Paige, you can start us out."

I'd seen this game before. You put up five fingers and for everything you did that someone had "never," you put a finger down. The last person with a finger up won. It was a game about people taking joy in being daredevils and everyone making fun of the inexperienced "winner". That's why I never played.

"Never Have I Ever..." Paige paused for dramatic effect. "Gone skydiving."

One girl put her finger down.

The next girl went. "Never Have I Ever kissed a boy during summer camp." A few fingers went down, including Paige's. She ducked her head when I tried to make eye contact with her. So that's what made her into a Convert.

It was Suzie's turn. "Never Have I Ever... hmm." The silence stretched. Come on, there had to be billions of things someone like Suzie Sunshine had never done. She laughed. "Eaten steak."

Pretty much all of us put fingers down. At least I could do this one.

"Are you a vegetarian or?" a girl with braces asked.

"Vegan." She shrugged. "It's a family thing."

The game continued, and I put a finger down for playing a sport. That one year of track and field finally came in handy. But then it was my turn.

"Camper Andrea. What have you never done?" Suzie asked.

Everything. Nothing. I couldn't think. Talking to Lucas had been torture because he was a boy, but I could nod and shake my head and he got it. It was one-on-one. Eleven sets of blinking eyes now studied my every move. "I've never..."

"You have to say Never Have I Ever," she corrected.

I lost what I was going to say. "Pass."

A deep-voiced girl across the circle butted in. "You can't just—"

"Now Camper Denise, this exercise is about getting to know people, getting comfortable. As a leader or boss, would you criticize an employee who looked so scared?" Suzie gestured to me.

Heat flooded my face, and I pulled my hat low over my eyes.

"Well, no, I—"

"Exactly. Camper Andrea is allowed to pass. She can participate by showing us the fingers she puts down until she's comfortable enough to speak. Right, Camper Andrea?"

It's Andy. I nodded, ever so happy to have been made into an example for the group. Like that wasn't more embarrassing than being called out. The swimming test, and now this? They should be paying me for this crap.

"Never Have I Ever…" the next girl said, and on it went. Suzie didn't throw out another freebie like her steak line. Girls confessed to doing adventurous things like petting snakes and climbing mountains and running half marathons. I practiced in my head for when my turn came again. I planned to say Never Have I Ever stopped reading midway through a book. I knew tons of heathens who did that. I'd probably get them all! I was so ready.

Except I never got another turn. By the time the circle got to Paige again, she and I were the only ones still "in." Everyone else had done everything.

Sorry, Andy, she mouthed at me.

Sorry for what?

"Never have I ever let a boy carry my bag to my cottage the first day of camp."

The girls all "oohed" dramatically.

My last finger went down, and I laid my hand flat on my leg. Why was she trying to make it sound like I flirted with some guy? Was she trying to make me look cool?

She bit her lip and lowered her eyes.

Everyone went silent except Denise. "Who was it?"

"Tyler," I muttered. No way I could hide it or lie about it when dozens of people had seen him help me.

Suzie's face stretched into a strained smile. "Well, wasn't that helpful of him? Good guys here at camp, all of them. Congratulations, Camper Paige. Looks like you won the game you suggested." She produced the gaudiest ribbon I'd ever seen out of her khaki safari vest's many pockets. It was pink and purple with puffy sparkle paint slashed across it that read "#1 Leader."

"Oh, it's so pretty!" Paige pinned it to her tank top and grinned. Suzie smiled back. A real smile, not like the one she gave me. I couldn't believe Paige wanted to win so badly. She was the one who said *not* to tell Suzie about Tyler helping me with my bag because of their history. Now I was in the middle of all their drama, and for what? A "pretty" ribbon?

When Suzie directed us to partner up for the next activity, Paige grabbed my hand. I hesitated and she frowned.

"I said I was sorry," she pleaded.

I sighed and let her guide me to a bottom bunk. Suzie came around and handed all of us a handful of Starburst candies and a paper copy of a key to the statements we had to say as we ate them. I hated Starburst. They tasted like wax.

"Red. Something I love," Paige played along. "I love winning. I'm sorry, Andy. I knew it was kinda bad, but then I saw your face. Please don't hate me."

I grabbed a yellow candy and read from the sheet. *Something that scares you.* "I don't like public speaking." I set the square aside.

"What?" Paige grabbed my arm with exaggerated surprise. "You don't?"

I fought a smile.

"Orange. Something you like about yourself. I like that when I mess up, I make it right. How do I make this right, Andy?"

I sensed a theme. She planned to use every candy to apologize until I forgave her for throwing me under the bus with Suzie. Then why did she do it?

I grabbed another candy. "Red. I love loyal people." Two could play this game.

She pushed out her bottom lip. "I can be loyal."

I raised my eyebrows.

She reached for another red but picked up a yellow one instead. "Something I'm afraid of." She unwrapped the candy slowly without taking her eyes off the wrapper. "I'm scared of saying something stupid and hurting someone. I don't think things through before I talk, and I embarrass myself all the time." She stared at her hands as she folded the wrapper in half. "Please tell me we're okay."

Why did I care what Suzie thought, anyway? It's not like I did anything wrong. I couldn't stay mad at Paige. She was too much like Mom with her can-do attitude, and I didn't have anyone else right now. I sighed and grabbed an orange candy. "I give second chances," I murmured.

She vaulted across the bed and tackled me into the pillows in a huge hug. "You're the best!"

I couldn't hold it in any longer. I laughed.

9

IT'S ALWAYS THE QUIET ONES

After a hundred more activities that involved Suzie lecturing us and a picnic lunch that we had to eat in the cottage because it rained, I was getting cabin fever. When it was finally time to wind down for the night, even Suzie looked frazzled from all the bonding. I grabbed my towel, toiletry bag, and pajamas, then headed to the communal nightmare known as the showers. At least it had stalls, even if the curtains didn't completely close.

I hung my towel on the hook and took my time adjusting the temperature of the water. It needed to be hot enough to wash away my awkwardness, but not so hot that I'd look like a lobster on top of feeling stupid all the time. I kept my flip flops on, even if they wouldn't be enough to combat the probable staph and wart bacteria on the floor.

When I got in, the uneven pressure pelted a weird, sputtering pattern on my shoulders before evening out. After a minute, I twisted the soap-stained handle hotter until the water steamed around me. Like turning up the contrast on an Instagram filter.

I sighed, closing my eyes against the harsh light of the bathroom. Alone at last. I never valued the solitude enough at home. Now, as the white noise of the running water drowned out the voices from the next room, I finally relaxed. Muscle by muscle, my body returned to normal. Today was over. Two down. I did it.

I scrubbed my scalp with my favorite shampoo, letting the grape scent help me feel like myself. Dr. Santos told me to rinse away the scary stuff, to let the drain gobble it up the way it did the soap suds. If there was ever a time to listen to my counselor, it was now.

I imagined the awkward speech floating away, Suzie's pushy voice close behind it. The pity in Dana's eyes after I finished the swimming test could go too, along with Denise's need to call me out in Never Have I Ever. All of it could swirl down the hole in the floor and disappear forever.

What did that leave? Paige hugging me. Tyler giving me his coffee. And Lucas… I shivered as the hot water streamed down my body. Lucas's low, calm voice murmuring "Breathe" after my speech echoed through my head. And what did he say in the cafeteria again? Whatever it was, it had been sexy.

I smoothed conditioner into the ends of my hair and soaped up my body. No way his thoughts were as dirty as mine. I had over a hundred romance novels to fuel my imagination. To imagine him beside me now, helping rinse out my hair, placing a gentle kiss behind my ear…

I shivered again as I turned off the water, grabbed my towel, and dried myself off more roughly than necessary. It was never going to happen. Even if he was interested in me, I wouldn't know what to do. I could read romances every day for the rest of my life and still trip over my words when a guy talked to me.

I slipped on my underwear and pajamas and re-entered the main room.

The girls had settled in, chatting in small groups, writing in journals, or lying down. I made quick work of brushing and braiding my hair, so I didn't have to wait for it to dry. Then I climbed the ladder to my bed and fished my book out from under my pillow.

"Hey," an unfamiliar voice said.

I ignored it. If it wasn't Paige or Suzie, they weren't talking to me.

"Andy, right?"

I peered over the edge of the bed, and a curvy brunette with large brown eyes stared back.

"What are you reading?"

I flashed her the cover of my book. "A romance."

"Like, a romance, or a *romance*?"

I raised my eyebrows. This girl—Emma?—she wanted to know how much spice was in my book. I hadn't gotten to anything like that yet, but I'd read this author before, and my face heated at the thought of anyone opening it up to the middle.

"It's always the quiet ones. Let me know when you're done, yeah? I'd love to borrow it." She flopped onto a bed nearby and pulled up the covers.

I was so surprised; I didn't think to offer her one from my bag. I assumed everyone would make fun of my reading choices, that all these leadership girls would be waiting to pounce on how quiet, how weird I was. But they were all pretty nice so far. I glanced at Paige as she snored softly in the bunk next to me. It was… confusing.

I flipped open my book and began to read.

That night, I dreamt of sword fighting Eric with a gigantic mechanical pencil, the air charged between us as he teased me by parrying all my attacks using a robotic arm. My heavy skirts brushed against my thighs as I lunged for his throat, but he sidestepped with ease.

"Promises, promises," he whispered. I blinked, and it wasn't Eric's faint smile across from me, but Lucas's wide grin.

Tyler watched our match, arms folded, frowning in annoyance.

The next morning, while I sat with Paige at breakfast, I had mixed emotions when Tyler brought me a coffee. He presented it in one of the small foam cups set out for our drinks instead of the large coffee cup he had yesterday, but beggars couldn't be choosers.

"Just so you don't tackle me again," he said as he set it down. To anyone else it would look like he was handing out juice.

Paige's eyebrows disappeared into her hairline, but she didn't say anything.

It didn't stop me from picking up the coffee, careful not to spill a drop. "Thanks," I whispered.

He tapped our cups together gently. "Cheers." Then he walked over and rejoined the rest of the counselors.

Paige opened her mouth to start in on me.

"It's just coffee," I whispered.

Lucas chose that moment to bound into the room, hair slicked back like he'd just taken a shower. My face warmed and my eyes dropped to my half-eaten cereal.

"Heya Campers!" Dana called from the stage.

I didn't know whether to groan or feel relieved.

10

ALL YOU HAVE TO DO IS STAND UP

In no time at all, Suzie dragged us back to the patch of grass outside the Beaver cottage. I tried not to be obvious as I watched Lucas shove his brother and laugh until they disappeared around the next corner. He was so open, so carefree. That even, white smile that he flashed everyone. I never thought I had a type, but between Eric and Lucas… was smiling a type?

When Suzie told us to "Partner up Pardners" in a fake cowgirl accent, Paige chose me right away. I didn't object as she grabbed my arm. It was nice that someone wanted to choose me.

The sun shone through the breaks in the trees as we stood in the wet grass. Most of us wore hoodies in the sharp, morning air. My favorite kind of weather. I breathed it in—it was easier to believe we were near mountains when it felt like this.

"This activity will be short, but it takes a bit of strength and a lot of communication. It might even push you out of your comfort zone a little." Suzie flipped her hair over her shoulder, dropping the cowgirl voice.

Of course, it would push me out of my comfort zone. My zone of comfort was smaller than the iPhone this woman stole from me. What was Eric doing right now? Probably hanging out with his friends on a beach somewhere, pushing prescription sunglasses up the bridge of his nose instead of his hot glasses. And I'd be at home, like always, nose-deep in a world far better than my own. As I looked around at my Beaver roommates, their faces makeup-free and scrubbed-clean, a piece inside me clicked into place. I still wanted to read, but…

"It's pretty simple. All you have to do is stand up," Suzie promised the group.

I tuned in. No way it was that easy.

"Start by sitting on the ground with your back to your partner, then link both your arms with theirs, and use each other's backs as leverage to get up. Simple, right?" Suzie clapped her hands together like she'd given us the best gift ever.

Paige and I eyed each other. I was way shorter than her. Like, way shorter. If she leaned back, she'd fold me in half.

I guess I wasn't the only person worried because Suzie's chipper expression faded. She blew a piece of hair out of her face. "Seriously, Beavers. It's not that bad. Watch."

She grabbed Denise to demonstrate. They counted to three, then pushed from their seated position and with minimal stumbling, stood up.

Well, okay, but Denise was about the same weight and height as her. *Oh, no.* Paige was going to ditch me. It'd be just like school projects all over again. I hated this place.

"You ready?" Paige asked.

"You can't be serious," I said.

She tightened her ponytail. "Why not?"

I stared at her. "How are you going to get up?"

"*Teamwork, Camper Andrea,*" Emma mocked from nearby, then snorted.

We all giggled.

"Or," Paige whispered, "if worse comes to worse, we'll cheat."

I rolled my eyes. There were rule breakers and rule followers, and Paige was a self-defined Convert. I doubted she'd cheat.

We sat down in the dew-drenched grass.

"On three?" I asked.

"Yeah, like one, two, three, and then go instead of going on three."

I nodded, but she didn't say anything. Oh, yeah. She couldn't see me. "Okay."

We linked arms. The last time I linked arms was with Brynn when we went shopping for the eighth-grade formal. I closed my eyes, and it wasn't Paige's deep voice laughing behind me, but Brynn's higher one.

"My feet hurt so bad! When are we going to be done with this?" I whined as I helped Brynn heave the million dresses she just tried on to the reject rack in the dressing room. It was the fourth store we had done this in, and I didn't get it. I had chosen my simple black dress after ten minutes.

"You don't get it, Andy. You have this hourglass thing going on, and I'm super flat. I need a dress that says This girl is skinny, but she's still hot *so Alex asks me to dance."*

She was right. I didn't get it. Alex was… Alex. We watched him pick his nose on the playground in third grade.

"You're totally hot," I said.

"Isn't there anyone you like?" she pestered me for the millionth time.

"Honestly? No." I was only going to the dance because she begged me to, and she knew it.

We exited the store, and she linked her arm with mine. "You're such a weirdo."

"Yep."

She shook her head, her perfect curls falling over her shoulders. "And I love you for it."

Did she? This year felt off. When she went right, I went left. Anxiety gripped my gut, and I held her arm tighter. Maybe if I kept her close enough, the feeling would go away.

It didn't.

Paige's back pressed against mine. "One, two, three!"

We pushed harder against each other's backs and miraculously, were able to get our butts a couple of feet off the ground. I stumbled back a few steps, but Paige's long legs wobbled. She squawked, then we both fell down sideways, laughing.

"Mother effer," she moaned. "That was horrible."

"Yep." I sat back up. "Wanna try it again?"

She turned her head to raise an eyebrow at me.

I gave her a fake, winning smile.

She laughed. "We don't have to."

But under Suzie's hawk eye, we didn't have much choice. We tried another four times, but it was no use. Paige needed more space to stand than me, and it would take a miracle to accomplish it. Finally, we gave up. Suzie flitted about helping other pairs like a hummingbird on speed, so she didn't question us when we gave her a thumbs up.

It wasn't like we were lying. We were happy to be done. Thumbs up.

"Thank ya, Jesus," Paige said when the exercise ended.

Then something happened that I was convinced was a fluke.

"Gather up, Beavers. We've made it to your first free block! Three hours of your time can be spent sharpening your leadership skills. You'll have all kinds of activities to choose from," Suzie promised.

"Activities" was going to be my new swear word.

"From archery to bracelet making, candle dipping, and woodcarving, we love to provide something for every interest. Even helping out in the snack hut."

A few girls laughed.

"Because leadership is *selfless*," she said pointedly, "and every good leader knows that being humble is a necessary steppingstone to success."

Yeah, sure. Like anyone wanted to spend their free time being ordered around. I should've known there'd be a catch to "free time." It was still about activities. I still had to deal with people.

"Horseshoes, basketball, tennis," Suzie continued. "You can even hang out and talk to each other."

Talking was the last thing I wanted to do, but I latched onto "hang out." Could I hang out with a book?

"You name it, we have it. Go have fun!" she chirped.

Finally.

As the rest of the girls dispersed, I blew out a long breath. Paige probably thought I was going to follow her, and for a second I almost considered it, but then I rocked back on my heels. I hated to be a shy girl cliché, but I wanted to read. All of these people seemed to get energy from the activities we did. I got energy from silence. There was precious little of that here.

I whirled toward the cottage, clipping the arm of a guy going the opposite way on the path. Blond hair, kind of muscular. There was no way—but it was. Lucas grinned at me.

"Where's the fire?" he teased.

"Sorry?"

He ran a hand through his hair. His thick, gorgeous hair. "Got somewhere to be?"

"Kinda," I whispered. My eyes flicked toward the safety of the cottage. It was so close. How could his smile make me shy and comfortable at the same time? Those two emotions didn't even go together. I toed the ground.

"Too bad," he said. He folded his arms and leaned back a little, waiting for me to say something.

Why was it too bad? I could feel myself ruining this moment by not being able to say anything.

"Okay… I'm just gonna…" My face burned as I turned and fled to the Beaver cottage, slamming the door behind me.

After a few long minutes, it became obvious my heart rate wasn't going to return to normal, and I couldn't swallow back the bitter taste in my mouth.

I crawled up the ladder to my bed with my eyes closed, thankful none of the other girls were here to witness my panic. He was being nice! He was trying to talk to me! And what did I do? Nothing. Brynn's voice floated into my head.

You never do anything.

Like it mattered. He was super-hot and probably only talked to me out of pity anyway. *But what if he didn't?* I covered my face and groaned.

11

ACCIDENTAL LEADER

I gave myself exactly two minutes to wallow in self-pity. Then I rifled through my bag for the thickest book I could find. The one I was in the middle of wouldn't be enough to distract me. The guy on the cover of this one wore an unbuttoned white shirt. I sighed with relief when he didn't look at all like Lucas. A girl in a barely-there purple dress swooned into his muscular arms. I ignored the fact that she did kind of look like me.

Familiar giggles floated through the open window. Where could I hide long enough to get through more than a chapter? Suzie would no doubt rope me into doing something more social.

I scanned the bunks, but it was useless. The other girls would be here any minute. I sprinted out the back door, garage sale paperback clutched in my hand. Yes! A clump of bushes lined the back of the Beaver cottage. I ducked down and sat between the two fattest ones. Their thick leaves would hide me from anyone who might pass by. I slapped a mosquito off my neck. To hell with going back for bug spray. I was alone.

I leaned back against the logs that made up the wall of the cottage and lost myself in the pages of my novel. Time passed, the voices from other campers fading in and out as the sun played peek-a-boo with the clouds. I readjusted myself into a comfortable slump. The book gave me what books were best at — escape.

"Careful with that, my darling." Reginald pointed to the rucksack over Anita's shoulder, weighted down with all her meager belongings. She'd vowed never to return to a place that caused her so much heartache.

"Why?" she spat. "You think I'm not strong enough?"

Reginald's eyes burned with fire. "I think you're strong enough to move mountains."

Anita flung her bag to the ground and collapsed into Reginald's protective embrace.

His muscles contracted around her as...

I couldn't help the laughter that spilled out of me. I needed this. Teachers made us read novels that they said were good for us, but that wasn't what we needed. Only we knew what our souls craved—mine craved corniness. Guys who were gentle and kind and strong and prideful. Young women who were brash or demure or whatever they wanted to be. The main characters always had friends, and everyone got their happily ever after.

"Camper Andrea? Is that you?" Suzie's red curls peeked through the gap between the bushes.

Crap. Caught. I reached for my pocket to check the time on my phone before I remembered I no longer had it.

"Come along, Camper Andrea. Our next activity is about to start!" Suzie trilled, but there was a bit of an edge to her voice.

Maybe I was imagining things.

I ran back to the cottage and shoved the book under my pillow, then shucked off my sweatshirt and followed the trail of Beaver girls into sunny leadership hell.

It was beginning to feel like a game of Roulette every time a new activity was chosen. Would this be the one to push me off the edge into insanity? When Suzie Sunshine took us out to the middle of the woods, I half expected her to leave us to perform her version of *Lord of the Flies* scenario. Survival of the fittest or whatever.

I slapped a mosquito off my arm. I should've grabbed bug spray before coming back out here.

"All Aboard is about communication."

"Wow, really?" I muttered to myself. Everything was about communication. These people talked like their lives depended on it.

Paige nudged me, covering her mouth to keep laughter from spilling out.

Whoops. I didn't think anyone would hear that. My nerves buzzed. Would the boys join us, or was that a one-time thing? I didn't want to see Lucas again after what a dork I was on the trail. I tried to peek over the other girls. He towered over everyone, so maybe his blond head would stick out and I'd be able to prepare myself mentally.

"What you see before you—"

—is everyone else's back and a bunch of maple trees. Darn my stubby legs. I stretched farther up onto my tiptoes until I almost lost my balance. No boy heads in sight.

"—is a square board suspended by ropes two feet above the ground. Your job is to find a way for every Beaver girl to fit on this board at the same time. You will get five minutes to figure it out."

"That's impossible!" Denise cried. "I've seen cereal boxes bigger than that!"

"What kind of cereal are you eating?" Emma joked.

I chuckled along with the other girls before what Suzie instructed registered. We had to touch each other. Hands all over me, grabbing me—my own personal horror movie. My palms tingled. It was just us girls, but that didn't make it much better.

Suzie started the stopwatch, and the louder girls started arguing right away.

I skirted around the group and eyed the platform we were supposed to stand on. Denise wasn't wrong. It was small. Like, *really* small. We couldn't just try to smoosh together. We'd have to have an actual pattern. A center that would hold. Not all of our feet would fit, either.

"We should all face out and hold hands," Paige suggested.

"That won't work. We wouldn't all fit like that. We'd fall on our faces," Denise said.

"We should all stand on one foot to fit all the feet?" a brunette said.

"What, like storks?" the cheerleader whose name I couldn't remember asked.

"No, we should all sit down on top of each other," Emma deadpanned.

I laughed with a couple other girls as we tried to picture that.

"Remember, you can't hold onto the ropes, and everyone needs at least one foot on the square," Suzie said.

Remember? She never said it in the first place. An idea began to form in my head. I didn't want to say anything in front of the group, but…

"Paige," I hissed.

Paige stopped mid-sentence and turned to me. "Do you have an idea?" she asked with no small amount of surprise.

Well, no. Not now that ten other people were looking at me. I grabbed a stick and sketched it out in the dirt.

Paige frowned as she tried to figure it out, then a slow smile spread over her face. "It's genius!"

The rest of the girls gathered around while Paige explained my plan and delegated who should do what. In no time at all she stood on the platform as we circled her like the rays of a sun, each grabbing each other for balance with her in the middle. Because she was pulled in all directions, she remained centered. And a ton of girls weren't touching me, though I was sandwiched between two of them. We all held our breath as we squished together on the little square.

A smile tugged at my lips when Suzie's stopwatch beeped, and the girls cheered.

"Great job, campers!" Suzie stepped forward from the shade of a nearby tree. "Three minutes, fifty-eight seconds!"

Awesome. Maybe that would be an extra minute and two

seconds I could spend reading instead of participating in an activity equally as stupid.

Suzie waved her stopwatch. "So, let's debrief. Everyone pop a squat."

What a gross way to tell us to sit down. We all formed a lopsided circle on the dirt next to the trail. Why couldn't she let us sit in the grass?

"It's time to nominate an MVP for this activity!" Suzie barked.

"I nominate Paige," one girl said.

"I nominate no one," another girl joked. Then she ducked her head under the manic stare of Suzie.

"I nominate Andy." It wasn't Paige who said this, but Emma. She stared at me, a small smile playing on her lips.

"Okay, okay. One at a time," Suzie said.

The girls discussed how Paige volunteered to be the center, and how she told everyone what to do in a quick and efficient way.

Then Emma spoke up. "I nominated Andy because the whole thing was her idea."

The group fell silent as Paige nodded. "She's right. Andy found the solution. She's the reason we all stopped fighting. We couldn't have done it without her."

Suzie nodded. "So, let's put it to a vote. If you vote for Camper Paige for drawing upon her resources and delegating, raise your hand."

A couple girls raised their hands.

"And if you vote for Camper Andrea, who figured out the solution and stopped the fighting, raise your hand."

More people raised their hands.

"Well, then. Looks like Camper Andrea takes MVP this time!" She pulled out a ghastly pink and brown ribbon from one of the many pockets of her khaki vest and handed it to me. "Congrats." She beamed.

My cheeks flamed as everyone clapped. I wasn't trying to lead. I was trying to get it done.

"Well, go on. Put it on!" Suzie practically fluffed her feathers like a proud mama duck. I could almost see her mentally congratulating herself for getting through to me after all, making me into a real leader.

All eyes zeroed in on me as I pinned the monstrosity to my chest.

Satisfied by my obedience, Suzie launched into a lecture about the importance of listening to everyone, even if they were quiet.

I tuned out as I picked at the hot-glued ribbons of my award. It was actually kind of creative.

As soon as she released us, I jogged away from the group.

Paige caught up to me before I'd gotten too far and clapped me so hard on my back that I had to catch myself from falling face-first into the grass. "MVP, MVP!" she chanted.

"Shut up," I muttered. Why did I have the urge to smile? Maybe it was because Paige was funny, or getting the award was such a joke.

"Admit it, you loved it."

The ribbon took up an ungodly amount of my chest. Two days ago, I would've seen it as a punishment for participation.

I glanced up at Paige's grin, my steps doubling to keep up with her longer strides. She was genuinely happy for me. And Emma was a Victim or at least a very sarcastic Convert. She didn't need to nominate me, but she did. Maybe this camp wasn't completely horrible. Maybe I was happy for me, too.

12

WITH ZERO TRAINING

I didn't have to wait long for the next activity, because during lunch Dana announced in her booming voice that we had been paired up with our partner cottage. "Being a leader in a large, mixed group is a reality of life." She shrugged in an exaggerated way on the cafeteria stage. "Here at Camp Follow the Leader, we want to expose you to every possible challenge!"

It was the only thing she said so far that made any sense. Every group project at school became more difficult when more students were involved. I found it easier to blend in and participate less in large groups, but people argued so much that I usually wanted to curl into a ball and roll away.

"For a fun, quick activity, we're going to see who can make the tallest, most stable human pyramid outside. Find your counselors, then combine with your matching cottage!" Dana motioned to the door like an overexcited flight attendant.

I tromped outside with the rest of the drones, my heart hammering. I hadn't come down from my ribbon high yet. Why did there have to be a co-ed activity? I rubbed my sweaty hands on my jean shorts. Just because we were pairing with a guy cottage didn't mean it was Lucas's.

So, calm down.

It didn't work.

When Paige and I spotted Suzie under the nearest white pine, her freckled face sported a smile so wide I was afraid her head might crack in half. "Beavers!" She waved to us. "Over here!"

Not for the first time, I wondered why we had to be the Beavers? They couldn't have come up with a worse name for a girl cottage.

"Guess what, Beaver sisters?" Suzie clapped her hands with glee. "We're paired with the Hippo cottage!"

Well, that sounds great. I caught Paige's eye and we both smirked. With a name like Hippo, how could any of us resist?

Then a group of gangly guys walked toward us, led by Lucas. Our eyes met for a second, and the air crackled. He cocked his head to the side, and I looked away, biting my lip.

Tyler jogged up behind them. Even though his horrible khaki vest matched Suzie's, he wore it like he was ready to take us on a dangerous safari.

Suzie's smile grew wider; her cheeks puffed out like a freckled chipmunk. The crush she had on him could be seen on Google maps. I should've known if Suzie was this happy, Tyler's cottage would be involved.

"Have fun," he told the guys, then stepped back.

Have fun? That was it?

Suzie opened her mouth like she was going to rant about the type of leadership this took and its importance for blah blah reasons. Tyler arched an eyebrow at her, and she closed it and stepped back into the shade with him.

"Have fun," she said in a tightly controlled voice. When she folded her arms, I assumed it was to keep herself from micromanaging us. Interesting. Maybe this crush of hers wasn't such a bad thing after all.

Most of the guys sank to their knees without being asked so the girls could climb on their backs. Why were we doing this? A human pyramid was a stupid, not-even-a-leadership-thing challenge.

Six-foot Paige beside me eyed the twig-ish boy in front of her, then glanced down at her athletic frame. How could she say no to climbing on this guy without wounding his fragile male ego?

I wanted to laugh, but then it dawned on me: someone expected me to put all my weight on two of these boys and possibly hold other girls up. I squinted against the sun that had decided now was the moment to jump out from behind the clouds like a mortifying spotlight.

Suzie inched toward Tyler on the sidelines, focused on his biceps. With his camo cargo pants, he was like a sexy drill sergeant. In a camp where every girl looked like Leadership Barbie, it was too much.

He didn't seem to notice. He was too busy smirking at Lucas who rolled his eyes.

"I think…" one girl trailed off, blushing a splotchy red. She was at least 5′8″ and on the curvy side. This was the worst activity ever. Like literal torture.

Lucas stood. He brushed back his blond hair with one hand, then looked down at the guys and back to us. He squinted against the sun.

A girl next to me raised her eyebrows and whistled. I had to agree. Where Tyler exuded an untouchable kind of hot, Lucas was like the boy you wished would mow the lawn, his strong arms pushing the mower back and forth over the grass underneath your window. He'd sweat right through his shirt. Then maybe he'd peel it off, and…

"Andy, you okay?" Lucas asked.

"Hmm what?" I blinked.

Lucas wasn't shirtless; he wore a baseball tee. He peered down at me with a concerned expression. "You're breathing really hard."

My face burned. "Oh, um, yes. I'm fi—carry on."

His mouth tilted. Did he know? He couldn't know. Could he? Lucas dragged his gaze back to Paige, who gestured to the guys on the ground.

"Yeah, I see it," he said.

She hadn't even said anything. Leaders found leaders, I guess.

Lucas rubbed his hands together. "Guys, we need a new strategy."

Across the field, another team went for a standing approach and a bunch of guys squatted, pulling girls up to stand on their thighs. When they tried to add a third layer of people, everyone toppled into a groaning heap on the ground. Someone was going to break their neck. I hoped my team wouldn't be that stupid. Was there a flag I could hold instead, like… off to the side? No way Suzie would let me be so lucky.

"Okay, maybe line up by height? Then do it kinda like cheerleaders or whatever?" Lucas said. "Wait, is anyone here a cheerleader? Who can help with this?" He looked at me and I rolled my eyes before I could censor myself. *Seriously?* Like I'd ever be loud enough to be a cheerleader.

A girl named Peyton stepped forward. She was so tiny. I could have thrown her in the air by myself. "Height is good, but also strength."

That put us in a pickle again. None of the guys wanted to admit they weren't strong.

"Dude, that excludes me," one gangly dude said, laughing. He pushed his glasses up over his nose. "I'll move back in line."

Guess I was wrong—the fragile male ego was a myth. Who knew?

We lined up the best we could by height, which put Cheerleader Peyton right at the end, so she'd be the top of the pyramid. Perfect. Except I stood right next to her. What level would that put me on?

A beefy guy named Anders stepped forward and counted us, then looked to the sky as he did the math. "Twenty people is… hmm. It doesn't work out right." He frowned. "We could have more people on the bottom two layers, but it would be shorter. It would give us a stable structure at least."

And I would still have to be close to the top? *No way in hell.* I hated heights so much I could faint right now. This was the most dangerous activity on the face of the planet, and I was *not* getting on top of these people.

My stomach wrenched. I had to say something. *Okay, breathe. You can do this.* "I'm strong," I whispered to the guy next to me even though it wasn't entirely true. Sweat dampened my brow, and we hadn't even done anything yet.

He tapped Lucas's shoulder. "Hey, this girl says she's strong."

"Okay, Andy. Where do you think you'd be good?" Lucas asked.

Where could I go and not ruin this activity?

I tried to inject some confidence into my voice. "End of the second layer." Then I'd have one knee in my back, and I wouldn't be anywhere near as close to the sky. If we fell, everyone would fall on top of me, but maybe, by being on the end, I could roll away? It was the safest I was going to get.

Lucas nodded, and I moved down the line.

"Okay, let's try it," Paige said. She frowned, but thankfully didn't say anything about my chickeny arms as she crouched on the ground. I braced a knee on her back, and mortified, placed my other knee on Lucas. We allowed the remaining campers to crawl up us to make the stupid pyramid.

It was hard to concentrate on balancing when Lucas held half my weight. My eyes kept focusing on where my knee stretched out his baseball tee. I was *on top* of Lucas.

When the last of the campers crawled to the top of the pyramid, my comment about being strong came back to haunt me as my legs began to shake.

"You've got this, Andy," Paige said when it became obvious I was struggling.

"You're strong, remember?" Lucas reminded me from below.

Did I say that? I couldn't remember anything when his voice went all deep and reassuring like that. He could persuade a preacher to sin.

My legs didn't give out. Cheerleader Peyton was right. We all shook a little, but our pyramid was stable. As stable as a bunch of kids piled on top of each other could be.

Dana came by with a measuring tape. Peyton got some guts and put her hands as far as she could in the air, which is what got us second place.

Suzie cleared us to get down, and that's when it all went to crap.

We'd never talked about how to undo this monstrosity. A girl from the third tier stretched one leg down and our whole structure swayed. Then, almost in slow motion, it came down. Screams filled the air and an elbow jabbed into my back as I struggled to get away. With an *oomph,* at least two people collapsed on me. London Bridge came falling down.

Suzie and Tyler ran forward to help us untangle ourselves. *Stupid, idiotic activity that no one had trained for.* What were they thinking? Paige got the air knocked out of her; I bet by me and the other hundreds of pounds that crashed on her.

Lucas rolled out of the mess and pulled me to my feet. I didn't have time to react to the whiplash from how hard he yanked or make anything out of the touch of our hands as we both continued helping people. I had grass stains on my knees, and I'd have a major back bruise tomorrow. One girl massaged her eye. In fact, most people were going to be sore tomorrow.

Once Suzie and Tyler had us all sorted and no one needed a medic, she started in on us. "Leadership isn't just about a goal."

"Wow, we've really leveled up in leadership," I muttered.

Emma nudged my shoulder, and despite my aches and pains, I met her sparkling eyes and smiled.

"It's also about what to do once you've achieved that goal. Sometimes you have to—"

"Give it a rest, Suze," Tyler drawled, staring with amusement at me and Emma.

She shut her mouth. Then she pulled out a pink and blue ribbon and handed it to Lucas with a frown. He took it, looking baffled as the rest of us groaned.

Tyler chuckled. Whether it was at Suzie or Lucas was anyone's guess. "Go get ice. Take a break," he told us.

I could've kissed him.

13

WEAR SOMETHING STURDY

At dinner, Dana announced it would be a good idea to "wear something sturdy" with "real shoes" tonight. No reason why, just a Cheshire cat smile and jaunty wave as she skipped off the stage to join her minions. The ones who were allowed coffee. I narrowed my eyes at Tyler's cup, but it didn't magically float to me the way I wished it would.

Something sturdy. I assumed that meant a horrible wilderness outing, so I copied Paige, who laced up her hiking boots the second we got back to the cottage.

"What's going on?" I asked her as I grabbed a flannel shirt and threw it over my tank top.

She shimmied into jeans, so I hid behind the bunk and stripped off my running shorts to do the same.

"Not sure," she said. "But last year they gave us vague written directions and canoes, and I was too cool to wear my bathing suit. It remains, to this day, one of my life's biggest regrets."

If that was one of her worst regrets, her life was plush. I zipped up my jeans and snapped a hair band around my wrist.

Paige shook a can of bug spray at me—it couldn't hurt. We

stepped outside so the fog wouldn't pollute the cottage and doused each other head to toe.

"Look at the overachievers," a girl from another cottage laughed as she walked by.

My face heated. I couldn't believe it took this long for me to screw up socially. Everyone had been so accepting around here that I'd... well, I'd started to relax.

Paige ignored the girl's comment and eyed their skimpy clothing. "They'll be sorry."

"All campers meet at the archery field!" Dana's voice echoed over the camp minutes later.

Our cottage was the farthest away, so we had to hurry to arrive when everyone else did. When I got there, sweat dampened my flannel, but the weak wind that filtered through the trees at the heart of camp had a little more bite on the open field, so I kept it on.

"Okay, campers! It's do or die time," Dana chirped from atop a chair when we arrived.

How dramatic. No one was going to die.

"You'll be split into groups of twelve and given a map, a flashlight, and a compass."

The sun had begun its descent, and the sky deepened into a brilliant orange. Soon the shadows would lengthen into night. They wanted us to do an activity in the dark? A nervous murmur spread through the crowd as people whispered to each other.

"When you get to the rendezvous point, a campfire with s'mores will be waiting for you!"

Most of the whispers stopped as people perked up. For s'mores? Really? Now if they offered us coffee, that would be another story.

"What if we don't make it to the ray-voo point?" one guy yelled.

"Rendezvous," Dana corrected. "You'll make it."

Uh, okay, Ms. Non-Answer. Some of these people would stand in the middle of the woods arguing until they froze to death. Emma especially. I did a quick sweep of the people near me, but her brown hair didn't stick out anywhere. Too many campers.

"I wonder how they're deciding the teams," Paige murmured.

Even as she voiced her concern, counselors around us sectioned people off in random order by counting and handing over what looked like plastic freezer bags of stuff. A counselor with short purple hair gestured to both of us.

"Eleven, twelve," she said in a nasal voice as she slapped green stickers on our shirts. "You're the green team. Here's your stuff." She shoved a bag at Paige. "Have fun!"

I looked around at the rest of our group. Three girls and nine guys. The other girl with us wore short shorts and a crop top. Not exactly the outdoorsy sort.

"Okay, so..." Paige pulled a map out of the bag.

"Let me." A dark-skinned guy with a crewcut sprang forward. "I'm a scout."

"You're in Boy Scouts?" the Crop Top Girl teased. "Aren't you a little old for that?"

He gave her a withering look. "You obviously don't know what Scouts is like. Do you want s'mores, or do you want to get lost in the woods?"

She popped her gum.

"I can read a compass," another guy said. "I think."

"I can read one too," Paige threw out. "But you can have it if you want."

"No, you take it. I wasn't that confident." The dude grinned at her.

In fact, many of them had a smile for Paige. She wasn't the kind of girl who needed makeup or heels. She could kick half their butts and she knew it. That kind of confidence needed to be bottled.

Paige grabbed the compass, and the boy scout guy kept the map. One of the guys took the flashlight, and I prepared myself for all kinds of forest-at-night horrors. Ticks. Poison Ivy. *Were there bats?* Please, don't let there be bats.

We dove into the forest, our feet crunching over dead leaves and twigs. Twice, a guy grabbed my arm and pulled me back onto the path, and I murmured a thank you. It was weird that he touched me, but I didn't complain since he might've just saved me from a bear or something. The shadows in the woods leeched the light from the path as the sun disappeared behind the trees.

The guys couldn't stop talking about the s'mores. Interesting. I'd never spent much time around boys. I guessed the food-motivated stereotype was correct.

"I know, right?" Paige giggled to the boy scout after he whispered something in her ear. "I could eat like a thousand."

He laughed.

Okay, maybe everyone wanted the food.

A couple of people fell behind in the dark as the forest faded to fuzzy shapes in the dimming light. The watery beam of the flashlight flickered in the hand of one of the front leaders. Would it be enough?

The night pressed in around me, the low voices of my group and the crickets in the grass joining together into an eerie white noise. Mosquitos buzzed in my ear, but the "sturdy" clothes and bug spray I wore did their job for now. Maybe this wouldn't be that horrible—I didn't have to get up in front of anyone.

"Come on, we've only walked for like, ten minutes," a guy's voice rose out of the forest behind me. A feminine huff responded. Guess Crop Top Girl was living up to her vibe.

The leaves rustled, then were silent.

"Hello?" the guy said. "It's probably another group. Maybe we can join together." He didn't sound too confident about that.

No one answered. Just another rustle of branches and this time a deep growl.

"Oh my god, it's a bear!" Crop Top Girl screeched.

I sped up. If bears lived this close to camp, the leaders would never let us be out here alone. Right?

"Seriously, if you don't hurry up, I'm leaving you," he snapped.

The girl made a pathetic choking sound.

I slowed my pace. This wasn't right. It was just like…

I shook my head. No. He was helping her. He was just annoyed.

"I'm out." The guy charged past, swearing under his breath about helpless chicks.

"Wait! Don't leave me here. Rob!"

The rustling in the leaves grew louder.

I turned back and moved toward her voice. Rob was a real winner.

"Rob!" the girl cried again. "There's something—" Her bloodcurdling scream echoed in the darkness.

I ran forward blindly, no rational thought in my head but to get to the girl. When a shadow rushed toward me, I forced every single bit of my body weight forward and tackled the shape to the ground.

"Ahh! What are you *doing*?"

Crap. Guess I'd tackled Crop Top Girl.

"Sorry!" I cried. I jumped to my feet and tried to help her up.

Deep laughter surrounded us, and a flashlight clicked on.

Thank God, other campers. But wait, what happened to the growling and the… I folded my arms. They tried to scare her on purpose. Those jerks!

The wide smile of a boy I'd never seen before appeared above the beam of another flashlight. *"Oh my god, it's a bear!"* he mimicked in an exaggerated scared falsetto. "That was epic!" He high fived the guy beside him.

My eyes darted between each of the guys in the group as I scooted the Crop Top Girl behind me. She didn't appear as concerned anymore, but she didn't understand. There were too many of them. They were—

A blond head surged forward.

Lucas?

My mouth dropped open in shock as my eyes met his.

"I'm going to kill you!" The girl bounced around me to smack the chest of the guy in front.

My hands shook as they curled into fists. "It's not funny," I said, my voice low.

The guys ignored me, their eyes drifting over Crop Top Girl's curves, the goosebumps on her skin evident in the flashlight's beam.

Except Lucas. He looked straight at me. "Andy, is that you?"

"It's not funny," I said again, louder, my heart in my throat. I blinked, and I wasn't standing in the middle of the forest in a group-sanctioned activity. I was at Sarah Jacob's party after the dance freshman year, and this time it was Brynn behind me.

• • •

"Come on, it was hilarious," a guy said as he fist-bumped another. "She squawked like a chicken when she fell in."

Brynn's breath caught behind me as she shivered in her dress and high heels, now soaking wet after being bodychecked into the pool.

But it wasn't funny. And I didn't know what to do. I wanted to push them *into the pool, but I'd never do something like that.*

"We'll get you a towel, drama queen," one of the guys said with a wink.

"Thank you," she said quietly. Brynn was being quiet. *All because this douche-canoe offered her a towel after being the biggest jerk ever?*

"Let's go," I said.

She glanced at me, then swiped under her eyes where her mascara was running.

"I have a change of clothes in my car from practice, Brynn. I'm sorry. They're just being stupid." Alex toed the ground.

"Seriously, let's go." I didn't trust any of them. So what if they were drinking? That made it worse. It wasn't funny to dunk anyone in a pool at night. She was fully clothed, for Pete's sake. Alex might be trying to be nice, but Brynn didn't need to continue to hang out around these people.

"Thanks, Alex," she said, skirting around me. "It's no big deal," she whispered as she passed.

But it was. It was a huge deal.

"I'm leaving," I whispered.

"Yeah, that's alright," one of the guys said. "You're bringing down the party anyway."

I tried to catch Brynn's eye, tried to plead with her to come with me. We were only three blocks from my house. We could walk back together.

"If you're tired, you can go, Andy. Don't wait up, though." She smiled as one of the guys tossed her a used pool towel from the deck.

And now it was happening again.

"Andy?" Lucas turned and shoved the guy still laughing. "Shut up. Are you okay?" he asked me again.

Crop Top Girl was flirting with the ringleader of their prank at this point, but I'd seen her wipe away the tear on her cheek not two seconds ago while she pretended to look back at me. This was complete and utter bullshit. What the hell was wrong with people?

My nails pressed into my palms as I shivered in anger. "You're not funny. It's not okay to scare people. You guys are assholes."

"Shit, you scared her," one of the guys said.

But I wasn't listening. Lucas's eyes never left mine as his cheeks got ruddier even in the pale glow of the flashlight. Good. Let him be embarrassed or mad. Let them all feel something. Why did I think he was cool, that he was different? Maybe this wasn't his fault, but he didn't stop them. That was almost as bad.

His eyes widened, but I shook my head. No, he didn't get a free pass. How did he not see how mean this was?

"I'm sorry," the guy said to Crop Top Girl. "She's right, that wasn't cool."

Maybe he meant it. Maybe he didn't. I didn't really care.

"Andy…" Lucas reached for me.

I yanked my hand out of the way as a dark energy thrummed through me. How *dare* he try to touch me? No one was allowed to touch me right now. Maybe not ever.

"You coming?" I called over my shoulder to the girl, knowing she wouldn't. She was just like Brynn. I marched into the darkness anyway. Maybe my rage could light the way.

"Wait, Jen! I'm sorry!" a male voice called out.

Flip flops scuffled behind me before the girl tugged on my plaid. "You didn't have to do that," she said, breathless.

"Are you okay?" I whispered. My voice had dropped back to my normal register, and now my body shook as the adrenaline faded.

Jen paused, and then… "No. But you still didn't have to help me."

I nodded, though she couldn't see it in the dark. Now we had a new problem. The trail had disappeared into the pitch black of darkness, and we didn't have a flashlight, a map, a compass, or a group. I might've just screwed us both.

14

I KNOW WHAT YOU DID

Jen shivered. "Do you know where we are?"

No. I had no idea. I searched for the moon through the tops of the trees, but I couldn't see through the cloud cover. Not one star cast any light on the world below.

What were our options? We could fumble along the path until we stumbled into another group or got completely lost in the forest, we could head back and try to find the guys who just acted like total idiots, or… or nothing. That was it.

I closed my eyes. Going back to the guys was not an option. They were jerks. But that was the only thing that made any—wait.

The faint scent of campfire filtered through the trees. What had Dana said we were doing again? S'mores? S'mores required marshmallows, and marshmallows needed fire. I closed my eyes for a second as relief flooded my body. We were on the right path.

"We've got this," I told Jen. Could I follow my nose to safety?

"I hate nature," she grumbled back. "And I can't even see you. How are we going to walk together?" The whine in her voice was unmistakable, but I knew it came from fear. She'd taken a chance by following me instead of staying with the jerkoffs, and now I was failing her.

But it didn't have to be that way.

I pulled my plaid shirt off. The cool air raised the hair on my arms, but I didn't care. She might be a brat, but I knew what it was like to be out of my comfort zone.

I felt into the darkness until my hand ran into her shoulder. She shivered, but that wasn't why I took my flannel off. We could be cold together.

"I'm Andy," I said. And waited.

"Jen," she finally said.

"I was thinking maybe we could both hang onto my plaid and walk together." I didn't see the point in telling her how screwed we were if my nose steered us wrong, but if I wasn't mistaken... we couldn't be that far from the end of the trail.

Silence. Then: "Fine." A note of gratitude tinged her voice. "I can help you," she said with more confidence.

We shuffled forward, both of us holding a fistful of my plaid for the next ten minutes.

Jen huffed. "We're never going to fi—" She ran smack dab into the back of someone solid.

I screamed.

Jen screamed.

"Finally!" the annoyed guy said. "Stop screeching and let's go."

Jen shoved him. "Try not to be such a—"

"It's okay." Relief flooded through me. We did it. We made it back to the group.

The scuffle of shoes and more rustling filtered around the perimeter, and a wavering beam of light illuminated us.

"You okay, Andy?" Worry colored Paige's voice. "We were just about to go back for you guys."

I didn't want to embarrass Jen, so I didn't say anything. None of this was her fault. Now, at least if we were lost, we'd all be lost together.

"Your precious snowflake friend is fine. Let's go. I don't want to do this anymore," Jen snarled.

I suppressed a sigh.

Time stretched in the complete darkness. No artificial light from phones lit the way or helped us with GPS. The flashlight had to be split between the map and the compass as sticks crunched under our shoes and leaves brushed our shoulders. I kept expecting to run into other groups, but I guess they must've had different maps. Either that, or we weren't following ours right.

The minutes dragged on until we broke into a clearing dotted with fires being stoked by counselors.

"Green team!" The purple-haired counselor called us over. "We almost sent out a search and rescue!" she joked.

I scanned our surroundings. The other teams crouched near their fires. We were last.

Thankfully, she had a few bags of marshmallows and other s'more supplies to soften the blow. The guys dug in like rabid wolves.

Jen let go of my plaid to hug herself. I offered it to her silently. She shook her head and went to sit on the stump closest to the flames. Her eyes were puffy, her eye makeup smudged.

"Andy!" Paige said. "Are you okay? I was so into figuring out the compass I didn't even stay with you! I suck." She kicked a rock.

I could sense Jen's watery eyes on me.

"I'm good. Sorry I'm slow," I said.

Paige shrugged, and we went to get s'mores together. Jen stared into the fire.

Funnily enough, we'd been directed in a large circle around the camp. We were back on the far side of the archery field.

I took a seat, leaving some space on either side of me. I didn't feel like a s'more, but everyone else devoured them. Most of the guys were sloppy about it; crumbs flew as they recounted the hike through the woods in ridiculous detail and talked about all the activities going on at camp.

Paige and Jen chatted with each other and the purple-haired counselor. Paige's hands moved in dramatic circles as she spoke.

I closed my eyes and basked in the warmth of the fire, the smell of smoke. My bug spray had worked. I'd dressed right. I had kept up, even if no one knew it. And maybe I couldn't stand up for Brynn the way I wanted to, the way a real friend would've freshman year, but I did tonight for Jen. This night wasn't the worst thing to ever happen to me.

After about half an hour, the counselors called it quits and dumped buckets of water over the campfires, the sizzles echoing across the open field. Just like that, darkness covered us again, and all we had were the flashlights we'd been given earlier to get back to the cottages. Jen, Paige, and I met up with the girls we knew from Beaver cottage while the boys branched off to find a guy with a light.

"I know what you did," Paige said after Jen slipped into the cottage next to ours.

"What are you talking about?"

"She told me you helped her."

Interesting. Jen didn't seem the type to spill so easily. The counselor must've pulled it out of her.

"So? People help me all the time."

Paige remained quiet for a second. "I don't think you give yourself enough credit, Andy."

I shrugged.

We stripped down in the cottage and put on pajamas. The other girls trickled in, and the cottage filled with the semi-quiet breathing of sleeping teenagers.

Lying in the dark, it wasn't Lucas's embarrassed face that flashed behind my eyelids before I went to sleep, or even Brynn's panicked one from freshman year, but Jen's. I pictured the way she'd looked as she stared at me across the flickering flames of the campfire, like she saw something in me other people didn't.

I don't think you give yourself enough credit, Andy.

15

WORK THROUGH THE KNOTS

I was about to pull my book out from under my pillow during free time the next day when Paige talked me into braiding bracelets. It didn't take much convincing, since she'd been so nice to me last night.

I followed her, but she kept sneaking glances at me and frowning.

"What?" I finally said. "You're weirding me out."

"Nothing," she said with an innocent smile as we pushed through the door of a cottage with a sign above the door that read "Bracelet Hut."

"Uh huh." Whatever it was, I wasn't dragging it out of her.

A cute college girl with intricately braided hair looked up from sorting threads when we entered. "Bracelets?"

Paige nodded, and the girl bounced over to us.

"You're my first customers today!" She sat us down at a long table in the center of the room and had us select our thread colors and braiding style.

My first reaction was to shy away from so much personal attention, but Paige soaked it up like she was sunbathing in the girl's conversation. Emma and one other girl from the Squirrel team dragged themselves through the door and the tutorial started.

The college girl showed us how to do intricate weaving step-by-step, over and over again, patiently answering everyone's questions. I wasn't horrible at it.

The girl from the Squirrel team struggled a little while Emma preferred to drink from her water bottle and watch the rest of us instead.

Paige kept tangling her fingers in the string, and she spent more time getting knots out than doing the craft. She pasted a smile on for ten minutes, but her patience wore thin. She closed her eyes. "Why is this so hard?"

I'd never seen Paige be anything less than perfect, and it fascinated me the way she tried to control her emotions. What would she do if she lost it? Cry? Stomp away from the activity? No, that wouldn't be leadership-y. I was tempted to see what it looked like when her confidence ran out, but that wasn't nice either. I may not have friends back home, but I knew how I'd want to be treated.

"Here." I set up her same colors on another hook. "It's right over center, left over center, right over..." I showed her the sequence with exaggerated movements.

I carefully gave her the strings, so she had them in the correct fingers. After reciting the directions to her for four or five rounds, she had it.

"How are you so good at this?" she sulked.

I don't know why she was surprised. It was on brand for me to be good at a silent activity. "My dad takes me fishing," I murmured.

"Fishing?" Paige made a face. "What does that have to do with anything?" She handed me her mess of a bracelet again.

"Because untangling fishing line was half my childhood." If I could figure out a line, I could figure out a string. Same thing, different textures.

"Why not just cut the line when it tangles? It's cheap enough, right?"

I detangled her bracelet and handed her back her strings, pushing down my frustration. "Right."

Except that's not how Dad and I fished. *You have to work through the knots,* he'd say in his gentle voice. *It's important to work through things, Andy.* Did he and mom think I quit trying at school? That because I didn't bother with friends, I had cut the line?

Paige and I worked in silence for a while. She managed two bracelets in the next hour. I had about ten of varying styles and difficulty, but that didn't matter.

Paige beamed with pride as she tossed me one. "Friendship bracelets!" It was like a switch had been flipped, and she radiated joy. It made me happy, too. So did the fact that she handed me my favorite color.

"I love cherry red," I murmured.

"Really?" She seemed surprised.

"You'd look good in cherry red," Emma said from her corner. She'd given up on the more complex knots and had braided her strings together.

I gave her a tentative smile.

She glanced at me. "Lipstick, specifically. I can already tell it would rock with your skin tone. Have you tried it?"

Have I tried red lipstick? I snorted. "Uh, no."

She shrugged and took another sip of her water. "We could do a makeover if you want, and you can try it. I have tons of stuff with me."

I looked at her sooty eyeliner and immaculate dark purple nails. I was tempted. But then I thought of Brynn. It didn't matter how much make up I wore. I'd never be like her. I'd never fit in with that crowd, so what was the point of looking like I wanted to? I shook my head.

"What do you want to do next?" Paige asked me as she gathered bits of cut off string to throw away.

Read. I always wanted to read.

"I heard about last night from Jen," Emma said. She fiddled with the label on her water bottle.

"Yeah, Andy helped her when she got lost." Paige beamed at me again.

"Not exactly how I heard it," Emma said.

I raised my eyebrows. I wouldn't reveal anything Jen didn't want shared. It was her embarrassing moment.

"I heard you told Lucas to suck it when the boys tried to scare Jen in the woods."

I shrugged. I mean, that wasn't exactly what happened, but… I frowned. I still couldn't believe Lucas was a part of that stupidity. I mean, I got that guys could be peer pressured too, but seriously —*what was he thinking?* My crush on him had cooled.

"Whoa, really?" Paige's eyes widened as she looked to me for confirmation. "I thought you liked him."

My shoulders were going to fall off from shrugging this much. To my relief, the college girl chose that moment to swoop in and compliment our bracelets. Emma sat back in her chair and studied me as I cleaned my area. It didn't look like she planned to join Paige and me on whatever jaunt Paige had planned next.

"Great job, Andy," the instructor said in a quiet voice as I turned to leave. "You managed to calm Paige down, and she was able to do the braids herself. You know…" She bit her lip. "That's the kind of leadership that not everyone appreciates."

"Uh, thanks," I said. Paige would've figured out the bracelets eventually. I just sped it up.

"MVP, MVP," Paige chanted as I pocketed the bracelets I'd made. They'd make good bookmarks if nothing else.

"You're ridiculous."

She held out her wrist for me to fasten her bracelet, then grabbed mine so she could do the same for me. Then we set off in search of another "free" time activity.

When we broke through the trees into the center of camp, white pieces of fluff floated like snow, coating the picnic tables, and swirling around our heads. It was a direct contrast to the sharp greens around us. Drifting in tiny wind currents, it landed softly on our shoulders and hair like warm snow. I picked a little off my shirt and examined it. What *was* this stuff? It was like dandelion fluff, but not.

I couldn't help it. I giggled. Only here, a place already so alien to me, would the earth open up and produce fake snow.

Paige rotated in a slow circle, palms up. I mimicked her. We twirled and laughed as it landed on our hair and shirts and arms. We spun faster and faster, the white of the fluff blending into the clear blue sky like tiny moving clouds. I closed my eyes.

Then I hit something hard. And warm.

"Whoa, there." *Lucas.* He held my shoulders until the world stopped shifting, and I stepped away. He picked a large piece out of my hair.

I couldn't hide my smile. "What is it?"

He raised his eyebrows. "Cottonwood. It comes from the trees." He pointed to the imposing circle of trees around us.

"It's cool."

His mouth turned up into a half smile. "You're cool."

"What?"

He shrugged, then shoved his hands in his pockets. Today his shorts were such a bleached-out khaki they almost looked white. They showcased his tan legs and arms, so different from my pale skin.

I struggled for something to say. "I, um—"

"Can I—"

I stopped and motioned for him to go ahead.

"Can I talk to you for a second?"

We both looked to Paige, who threw her hands up. She turned to go, then whirled back around last second and pointed at his chest. "Be good."

He smiled grimly.

We both watched her stomp off. Man, she really didn't like him. Note to self: ask about that as soon as possible.

I hugged myself. Without her, my confidence slipped away.

"So about last night," he started.

I pressed my lips together. If he expected an apology, he could shove it up his—

"I'm sorry. I really am, Andy. I knew it was stupid, but I went along with it anyway. None of the guys knew how scared she'd get, and that's not an excuse." He ran a hand through his hair and flicked away a tuft of cottonwood that came off on his hand.

"Why are you telling me this?" I whispered at the ground.

"Because I care what you think." He matched my volume. "And it was a dick move."

I flinched at the swear word, even though swearing didn't bother me. "I'm not the one you guys should be apologizing to."

"I know. I already talked to Jen this morning, and so did Trent. It got out of hand and like… I want you to know, that's not my…" He groaned, frustrated. "I'm not like that, I swear."

"Why do you care what I think?"

Lucas stared at me wide-eyed. "You can't be serious."

But I was. He shouldn't have to explain himself to me, so why was he? Was it because he didn't want to get in trouble with his brother? Was it because everyone needed to see him as the golden boy? Was it because he—

"Hey, Luke!" A basketball whirled toward us.

Lucas caught it effortlessly.

"We need a fourth!" a redheaded kid said. He jerked his head to the basketball court as he jogged past. "You coming?"

Lucas didn't answer for a long moment, his eyes still glued to me.

I raised my eyebrows. What was he waiting for?

"See you later, Andy?" Lucas said as he jogged backwards to the court. With his hair peppered with cotton, he looked like a hot Jack Frost. This guy was too much.

Dana's voice boomed through the speaker, and for once, I was relieved to make my way to the cottage for another leadership experience. At least I'd be able to talk to Paige about whatever the heck had just happened.

Except Suzie had us each sit on our own beds for the next half hour to complete stupid worksheets. I thought I was done with school for the summer. One of them had a box drawn on it and we were supposed to write everything in the box that we liked to keep to ourselves and everything outside the box that we were okay with everyone knowing. What did that have to do with leadership?

"Camper Andrea, would you like to share?" she asked when most everyone was done.

I still couldn't get a read on her. Was this whole act fake, or was she really like this? And why did she always pick on me?

"Uh…" *Great.* Now I sounded brain-dead.

"Just read out what you have written in your boxes."

I hadn't written anything, and even if I had, if I shared what was in the box, wouldn't that make it out of the box now?

"Pass."

Suzie's eyes narrowed. She handed out another worksheet.

As soon as she turned her back, a paper airplane sailed onto my bed. I looked over at Paige, who smiled and motioned for me to open it.

The lack of phones here reduced us to passing notes like elementary school kids.

I unfolded the paper, careful to still appear busy with the new worksheet Suzie gave me in case she decided to hover again. Paige hadn't filled hers out at all. Instead, in the box she wrote:

What happened with Luke????

Why did everyone keep calling him Luke when he introduced himself as Lucas? Whatever. Unimportant. I scribbled back my answer quickly.

He said sorry.

Her reply came back in an instant, this time bouncing off my face in the form of a wadded-up paper ball instead of a refolded paper plane.

And???

So many question marks.

He went to play basketball.

She rolled her eyes at me when she read it. I threw my hands out in question. What did she want me to say?

Did he flirt with you?!

He said he cared what I thought. That wasn't flirting, though.

I don't think so.

The look of relief on her face was almost comical. I had to ask.

Why don't you like him?

She stared at the paper for a second. At this point, we were writing on the back.

"How are those worksheets, coming, girls?" Suzie asked.

We both gave her thumbs up. She couldn't see they were blank from where she stood on the ground. This time when the paper came back, my heart jumped into my throat as I unfolded it to read what Paige wrote.

I just know what he's like.

Okay, and what was he like? That was the thing about camps that people went to their whole lives, I guess. Everyone here knew each other well. I started to respond, but Suzie's hand slipped over the edge of the bed, and she grabbed my blank worksheet.

"Oh, did you need more time?" she asked, her forehead scrunched in concern.

I nodded, my face glowing red hot.

Paige shook with laughter behind Suzie's frizzy red hair.

I chucked the wadded-up worksheet at her as soon as Suzie moved on to someone else.

"*Sorry,*" she mouthed.

I rolled my eyes and got to work creating my own personal "Ladder of Success." If Suzie thought this would change me into a complete extrovert, it must be true.

16

THE BOY SCOUT

"Do you remember that guy?" Paige asked the next morning as we wandered through the wet grass on our way back from the cafeteria.

Ten days. Ten days and I'd drown myself in coffee. I might even drink a Red Eye.

"What guy?" Literally everyone flirted with her—it was exhausting. She'd nodded to a boy who passed us ten seconds ago, and he forgot how to walk. The guy actually tripped over his feet to talk to her.

She huffed. "The one from the hike. Obviously."

"Obviously." The one who offered to do the compass thing? The one who left Jen in the woods? No, they weren't alpha enough for her.

"The boy scout," I remembered. Yeah, they'd be a good pair.

"Marshall." She kicked the path and a cloud of dirt and cotton puffed up. "When we were working together, I don't know. There was something there, you know?"

"Mhmm." My alpha theory held up to this new piece of information.

"Do you think he'd go for someone like me?" Paige bit her thumbnail.

He'd be so lucky.

"Yeah, I think you have a shot." I gave her a wry smile.

"I'm serious, Andy. He's so cute and nice and responsible. Did you know he volunteers to walk dogs for shelters? He only lives one town over from me." She stopped dead in her tracks. A shirts and skins basketball game had broken out next to the flagpole. Marshall was playing. How convenient.

I had to admit he did the skins team proud. Passion was always attractive, and this guy's concentration as he threw the ball into an old basket above the cracked cement of the makeshift court was unbreakable. His abs didn't hurt his case, either.

"So go say hi."

"Will you go with me?" she whispered.

If having a silent weirdo next to her would help, I could do that much. "Sure."

She floated to the sidelines. As if the universe knew she had a thing for Marshall, the game ended.

He dumped part of his water bottle over his head, which okay, it was hot out but that was cheesy. When he spied Paige, a grin spread over his face. "Hi, Navigator!"

"Hey," Paige whispered. She hadn't been as shy on our hike from hell.

He raised his eyebrows. "Hey."

"This is, um. This is Andy," she stammered like I hadn't also been on the hike with them.

"Hi." He set down his water bottle.

Paige giggled. She *actually* giggled. This was painful. I had to help.

"Paige is on the volleyball team at home," I offered. It was an athletic thing. And he was doing an athletic thing.

"Oh, yeah?" He turned to her.

"Yeah." She didn't meet his eyes.

"I bet your serve is awesome."

That did it. When she lifted her chin, her face transformed from shy into the Amazon warrior she totally was.

He tilted his head in silent challenge, fighting a smile.

The real Paige emerged. "Play tetherball with me and find out." It was the closest we had to volleyball here.

"Game on," he said. They jogged off without so much as a glance at me.

"Thanks, Andy," I said to myself. "No problem, Paige. Oh no, you guys go on without me." I grinned.

"Talking to yourself?"

I jumped about a foot in the air as Lucas emerged from God knows where. He wore a white tank top and long shorts with white tennis shoes. Not everyone could pull off a look that casual, but he looked… Fine, he looked really good. His hair was wet like he'd just taken a shower or gone swimming.

He picked up the abandoned basketball and dribbled it.

"I'm not talking to myself." How did this guy seem to catch me in every embarrassing moment possible?

Lucas ignored my lie and offered me the ball. "Wanna play?"

17

HORSE

I'd never played a game of basketball in my life, let alone tried to make a basket while a guy I didn't know how I felt about tried to get the ball from me. I started to back away.

"Okay, not basketball. Horse?" he asked, hopeful.

I don't know how long I stood there, biting my lip. Long enough for it to be beyond awkward, but Lucas never wavered. He just waited.

The rules of Horse were easy enough for even me to follow. Maybe I overreacted in the woods. It wasn't his idea to scare Jen, and he was sorry for it now. And he was so, so patient while inviting me to do a thing. I should do the thing.

"Scared of losing?" Lucas teased when I still didn't reply.

I snorted. He was talking to the wrong girl. I didn't have a competitive bone in my body. "Okay," I relented. "One game."

He took two steps, bent his knees, shot, and *whoosh*, the ball went through the hoop in about a second flat. Because, of course, it did.

I shook my head, then put my feet in the same spot and lined myself up with the basket. Then I bent my knees and let the ball go. It travelled about three feet straight up and came back down, bouncing in front of us.

Lucas's lips twitched. "Looks like that's an H."

I stuck out my tongue. He didn't have to rub it in.

"Ooh, she has claws," he said. He positioned himself a few feet farther away and shot again. The ball hit the backboard and bounced off.

I bounded over to the grass to retrieve it. Did I have a chance in hell of winning? Probably not. Was thinking about it easier than absorbing the fact that this tall, hot guy wanted to spend time with me? Sure was. It was my turn, and I had a plan. I stood right under the net.

Lucas frowned.

Then I squatted and used a granny throw to get the ball up through the net and back down, making a perfect basket without ever hitting the rim. Let him try to do that.

He whistled. "That's a weird one."

I smirked.

He arched an eyebrow. Then he positioned himself under the net.

I tried to smother my laugh as he bent into the granny throw position.

He wasn't even close to getting it up through the net. When it came back down, he had to duck as it bounced off the bottom of the rim. A fit of giggles burst out of me. Even his failures were epic.

"Oh, you think that's funny, do you?" He ran after me, and I sprinted behind the nearest bench, unable to control my laughter.

"H?" I said innocently.

"Uh huh." He scowled, but it was the kind of scowl where he was fighting hard not to smile.

"And it's my turn," I reminded him.

For a second, I thought he might chase me around the bench. He didn't. But I wanted him to. I could outrun him. Or maybe I'd let him catch me.

Wait, what? Why would I want that? That was so not me. Was this what a real crush felt like? I hadn't felt the same way about Eric. My nerves turned me into a walking disaster around him. Lucas was... well, he made me nervous, too, but right now it felt easy between us. I liked that.

It didn't matter; no one found true love at summer camp. Movies made it seem romantic, but that was stupid since in the end everyone goes home and that's that. Dr. Santos's voice echoed in my head. *Is that why you feel safe? Because nothing can happen?*

Lucas grabbed the basketball from the grass and dribbled it. When he was a couple feet away, he held it out to me with one hand. I reached for it, but he began bouncing it again, out of my reach.

I folded my arms, rocking back onto one hip. *What a showoff.*

"Only for you, Camper Andrea," he mocked.

Crap. Did I say that out loud? "I'm sorry, I..."

He chuckled and pressed the basketball into my hands in a way that was like a promise. A promise of what, I had no idea.

I wobbled as I lined up my shot from another weird angle close to the basket. I missed and Lucas took his turn, nailing it from across the court. He knew I was terrible at long shots, and he was exploiting it, but his warm, confident smile was so hot I didn't care.

My turn again. We played for a while, both of us pretty even since I wasn't good at long shots and his short ones were crap. I caught him smiling at me more than once, and it made my stomach go all floppy, which was so lame. It was even lamer that the silence between us as we played was the most comfortable I'd felt since getting to camp.

Ridiculous.

Is it though? A tiny voice inside me asked. All my romance novels started this way, with this exact tension. The heroine often didn't like the hero at first, but she *was* aware of him. I couldn't be more aware of Lucas if he were the literal sun.

"That's E, Andy. Looks like I win," Lucas's voice rumbled next to my ear. "You know what that means."

We hadn't bet anything, so no, I didn't. I held my breath as I spun to face him. If this were one of my books, he'd kiss me now.

He folded his arms. "You have to do six pushups."

I almost collapsed in a fit of laughter. What the hell?

"Those are the rules," he said without a trace of humor.

"In what world?" I wheezed. "Where'd you come up with six?"

"I don't know. When Tyler and I play it's ten, but you're a girl, so…" He winked.

I chucked the basketball at his head, and he dodged. "Hey!"

I walked over to the grass and got down on my hands and knees.

"Andy, I was just kidding. You don't have to." He started toward me.

"Rules are rules." I had zero upper body strength, but I'd be damned if I didn't force ten pushups out of my weak body. By the time I finished, my arms wobbled like spaghetti.

Dana's cheery voice floated over to us from the ancient camp speakers. "Time for food! Nourishment! Eat all the things!" she joked.

He helped me to my feet as a breeze kicked up, plastering our shirts against our skin. I shivered, and we turned to walk to the cafeteria.

Playing with Lucas released the icky feeling I'd had since my encounter with him in the forest. He was pretty… everything. Pretty normal. Pretty cool. Pretty nice. Pretty hot.

"Thanks for the game, Andy." He glanced back at the abandoned basketball court.

"Uh, you, too." *You, too?* Kill me now.

His biceps strained as he tucked the basketball under his arm while we walked. "You're kinda kickass, ya know? Like you're quiet, but not a pushover. I like that. I didn't think you'd hang with me after…"

"If Jen's okay, I'm okay," I said firmly, realizing it was true. We really were fine, Lucas and me.

He blew out a breath. "Thank God. You're kinda intimidating."

My mouth dropped open. Had he looked in the mirror? Did he need a vocabulary lesson on what the word intimidating meant?

Before I could come up with anything to say, he sprinted away to catch up with a group of guys.

What was he thinking, saying that kind of stuff to me? I shuffled along toward the cafeteria and smiled at a couple of girls who were staring at me across the path. Lucas was the reason these people saw me. I was anything but kickass. I waved at the girls and scuttled in the direction of the cafeteria. For food. Nourishment. To eat all the things.

But I didn't want to go there. Everything would get awkward with Lucas if I ran into him again, and what if Paige was with Marshall? I didn't want to think about sitting next to him too… It was overwhelming. Everything here was overwhelming.

I walked the perimeter of the camp until I got to the snack hut.

Paige sat next to Marshall as they chowed down on ice cream cones. His dark head bent down to whisper in her ear, and she batted him away, blushing. All it took for them to click was a map and a compass.

I was happy with my books, with silence and calm. Normally.

Right now, I wished I was more like Paige, more like the rest of the people here. How easy it would be to flirt and be carefree about it, to make friends like it was the most natural thing in the world. I could finish that conversation with Lucas, be as badass as he thought I was. But it was useless. I couldn't get a personality transplant. For the first time in a long time, I wished something would click for me.

18

BROTHERS

I skipped the cafeteria. Playing Horse with Lucas messed with my head, and I didn't know what to say to him if I saw him there. I was already tripping over everything I said to him. So, I dug into my pocket for my unused spending money and grabbed a couple granola bars and an ice cream sandwich from the snack hut, steering clear of Paige and Marshall so they could have their moment. Could I survive on granola bars and ice cream the rest of camp? It was worth pondering.

I needed silence—needed to think. To read. At home, everyone was content to leave me alone, but not here. It was so overwhelming, and I needed it to stop, just for a second. When I got to the cottage, I shoved the too-sweet snacks down my throat and grabbed my book. Holding it to my chest, I realized I only had two options. Hide in a bathroom stall or risk getting pulled into another activity. *Bathroom stall, here I come.*

Ten minutes later, Paige called my name from the bunks and my heart skipped a guilty beat, but then it was silent again. After a couple more minutes of breathing in the stink of hairspray and mildew, I crept out of the bathroom. A couple of girls had set up a chess board on one rickety table in the cottage.

"Paige was looking for you," the blonde one said without glancing at me.

"Thanks." I climbed into my bunk and pulled my sleeping bag over my head, then snapped on my flashlight. Everything about it said, "leave me alone."

I struggled to concentrate with the groans and cheers of the two girls playing their game. Even with no one around, they made a big show of it. When someone yelled "Check mate!" I bet it echoed in the boys' cottages on the other side of camp.

"Andy, there you are!" Paige's voice rang out in the cottage again. She whipped the sleeping bag off my head like it didn't matter that I was obviously not available. "Let's go shoot some arrows!"

I flashed her the cover of my book. "What's Marshall doing?" I asked, hopeful she'd take the hint.

"Oh, he's coming with us. I'm going to beat him into the ground. He's gonna wish he was never born," she said with a savage glint in her eye. I was happy for her strange, competitive flirtation she had with Marshall, but "third wheel" didn't register with this girl.

The chess girls began to pick up their pieces. I knew I should've stayed in the bathroom. Paige was confident I could do archery. Lucas thought I was brave. None of these people saw me clearly at all. I wasn't this outgoing, participation-award-getting girl. I was a book girl.

But Paige didn't let up. "So?"

"I'm good here." I patted my bed. Did she think I was lonely? That was nice. Unnecessary, but nice.

"Come on, Andy. It won't be the same if you're not there."

No amount of puppy dog eyes would make me choose to pick up a weapon, even a bow and arrow. I knew how that would go down with the state of my nerves today.

She jutted out a pouty lip.

It didn't work. Much.

Maybe I could convince her I had other plans besides reading alone in the cottage so she wouldn't think I needed company. "I can't. I'm… going running in a minute." I'm going running? I didn't want to run.

Paige frowned. "Really? I didn't know you ran."

Yep. Because I didn't. Not anymore.

"Oh, yeah. I took a break since I'm here, but you know… I miss it." It was insane how the lies tumbled from my lips with no effort. Was I a sociopath?

Her eyes narrowed. "Where are you running?"

I had no intention of getting myself lost in the woods. "The uh… beach."

"The beach." She folded her arms.

"Yep."

Paige arched a well-shaped eyebrow. "Want us to come with you?"

God, no.

"I don't run with people."

She nodded slowly. "Okay. I'll see you later, then."

I smiled. "See ya." Great. Now I had to go running or feel guilty all day about lying.

As soon as she left, I deflated. I hadn't run since track freshman year. Brynn hated it, but I loved it. Another thing we didn't line up on when we went to high school. I dropped the sport, hoping that was why we weren't doing as much together, but it didn't end up mattering. I could've joined again. I didn't. It never crossed my mind to do anything without Brynn.

I laced up my tennis shoes extra tight the way I used to, and a wave of doubt swept through me. What if I wasn't any good anymore?

I trudged to the beach like I was on my way to a funeral. If I didn't do this now, Paige would find out, and I'd be in trouble. Why did I lie? Reading was a great pastime! I should've stuck to that. But I also didn't want to make Paige feel like I didn't like her.

Brynn's face flashed before me. *"You're shutting me out. You're shutting everyone out. I want to do things. Why don't you ever want to do the things I want to do?"*

As I rounded the corner of the path, I sighed—a new problem presented itself. The beach wasn't very large. How did I not remember that? No wonder Paige looked at me strangely.

Another thing I wasn't counting on; people were swimming. I sighed again. I'd just steer clear of them by running farther back on the beach, near the tree line. I tightened my ponytail. It was now or never. Maybe one sprint across would be good enough for Paige to not call me out.

I set off at a medium pace, trying not to kick sand on anyone's towel. Every time I stepped down, I sank into about six million inches of sand. Running? I couldn't even walk in this crap.

After ten seconds, sweat dripped down my brow, and my thighs were chafed from rubbing together. I couldn't stop, though. I couldn't fail at yet another thing. I refused. I turned my head toward the trees. A well-worn path would be much better if I could make it there.

I pivoted and jogged up to one of the trailheads, just beyond the beach. If I went right, it would loop me around the camp and take me back to the cottage. Well, close enough. So what if I was out of breath and out of shape compared to how I used to be? I was good at this once. I could be good at it again. Earbuds and a running mix would make this more pleasant, but I'd have to do without.

"Hey, Loudmouth." Tyler jogged up to me, looking all kinds of… Tyler.

Why was he able to jog across the sand and I wasn't? Unfair.

"You going for a… run?"

How kind. No one could call what I'd done a run. "Yeah." I was beyond mortified. He was so put-together, and I was so…

"That's cool."

I nodded and tried not to let on that this conversation seemed awkward and out of nowhere. He may as well have had a sign taped to his forehead that read *I am checking on you.* The only thing that could make this worse was—

"Andy!" Lucas's voice rang out.

I closed my eyes. *Hey God, this isn't funny.*

"You jog?" He shook the water from his hair as Tyler looked on, looking immaculate as always. Despite the similarities in their facial features, everything about them was different. Where Tyler was well-groomed and calm, Lucas was messy and loud and free-spirited.

Why were they even here right now? How could I have gained both of their attentions during the run from hell? Ugh, and I couldn't even catch my breath to appreciate the scenery they'd created for me.

"Yes," I huffed. "I like to run." They needed to leave so I could finish it.

Lucas and Tyler stared at each other over my head. Lucas's eyes narrowed and he jerked his head to the side.

Tyler frowned.

I couldn't care what the heck that meant. If I didn't run, I'd be forced to stand here in the blazing sun while my literal soul dripped out of my body and evaporated. I'd pass out and embarrass myself even more than I already had.

I'd run the Himalayas before I let that happen. After I emptied my shoes of all the stupid sand weighing me down.

"Catch ya later, Loudmouth." Tyler jogged off.

I narrowed my eyes at his back. Stupid, fit, running guy. He just had to rub it in.

"So, what's the story?" Lucas asked as I pulled off my tennis shoes and dumped out the sand.

"Why does there have to be a story?" I slipped one back on, not able to meet his eyes. My skin prickled, but I wasn't sure if it was the unrelenting sun or the beginning of a panic attack.

"Uh, you just ran through the worst part of the beach with a crazy look on your face?"

Wait, the worst part?

"What other part would I run through?" I hopped as I put my other shoe on.

He tried to hide his smile and failed. "Most people run near the water to avoid knee-deep sand."

Well, that made horrible sense. I couldn't do anything right this summer. "Guess I like a challenge."

He chuckled. "No, you don't."

He was right, I didn't. "Get out of my head," I said, too tired to argue.

"Whatever you say, *Loudmouth.*"

"Yep. Whatever I say." My filter malfunctioned whenever he was around. "I mean…" *Crap.* He was being nice to me, and I was acting like a total brat.

"You going to run the outside trail?"

Wherever that was. "Yeah." I bit my lip. I didn't want him to offer to come with me. I'd say yes, but he literally stole my breath away, and—

"Okay. See you at the caf, unless you're planning on skipping out on me again?"

He noticed. I ducked my head. "Sure."

Lucas stumbled backwards toward the beach. "Promise?"

"Promise," I mumbled, turning away. I would not check out his bare chest or the way his board shorts hugged his hips right now. I couldn't run from this awkward moment fast enough. Kicking my knees up, I found solid ground under a canopy of trees. The path to the right was well-worn, and campers streamed down it to get to the beach I just came from.

But the path to the left… I turned onto the quieter path. As I ran, I tried to regulate my breathing, straighten my back, all the things I'd learned freshman year in track, but my body hadn't done any running since then, and the air that I managed to suck in came out as hot as lava. My side ached after only a minute or two. I must've gassed myself out on the beach.

So slow down.

I calmed my pace as sunlight broke through the trees onto the path in front of me. I could walk back to the cottage.

But I didn't.

When I got back to camp, sweat soaked my shirt and a grin tugged at my lips. It had taken five minutes of torturous running for me to get my pacing back, but I had. Counting my breaths as I forced myself forward cleared out my brain of everything I couldn't solve. All that remained was breathing. All that existed was survival. That's why I used to like running. Not because I was good at it. I liked how it made my brain settle, made it quiet.

Brynn always laughed when I told her that. *"You're already too quiet," she'd say.*

Some people couldn't understand. I slipped into the shower and washed my hair and body, trying to kill the rest of "free" time. Reading wasn't in the cards for me here, and the only way I might get any silence, any alone time was to live in the bathroom.

If I'd stayed home, if Dad had taken pity on me, I could be on my third or fourth novel by now. I'd have a tan from reading outside. I'd be comfortable.

Lonely.

No, comfortable. There'd be no Suzie, no Dana, no boys on the beach.

And no Paige. No Lucas.

I rinsed my loofah and watched the purple suds chase each other down the drain. Lucas thought I was intimidating. More like intimidated. I couldn't catch my breath, couldn't even stop to think, since every moment here came with a side of conversation and participation.

"You okay in there?"

Oh my God! I can't even take a shower!

"Fine, sorry." I twisted the knobs with extra force. Once I dried off and threw on some clothes, I pulled aside the curtain to Emma touching up her eyeliner.

"Did you need the shower?"

"Me? No, but dinner is in a minute. Thought you might be hungry."

As if on cue, Dana's voice echoed outside. "Grub! Come eat, campers!"

"Want me to help you do your make up?" Emma held out her eyeliner.

I shook my head. It was camp. I hadn't worn any since Mom abandoned me here. I didn't even know if she packed me any.

Once I was halfway to the cafeteria I realized that I should've waited for Emma and invited her to sit with me. It would've been polite. *Ugh.* I was so bad at this social crap.

A cloud passed over the sun, granting me with momentary shade as I pushed through the cafeteria doors. The day wasn't over yet, and I was already exhausted. I never should've gone running.

I stepped into the cafeteria line and selected a pre-wrapped burger, then scooped a huge pile of half-frozen fruit salad onto my plate. Skipping lunch for junk food had made me extra hungry for something real and colorful.

When I got out of line, I couldn't find Paige anywhere. I'd gotten so used to following her around that I didn't consider the possibility that I'd be standing here like the dork of the world with no one to sit with. She must still be at the archery field with Marshall.

I set my tray down at an empty table and tried not to squirm. It was easier to pretend I wasn't a loser with a phone in my hand to look busy. I picked at a frostbitten blueberry, my appetite gone as the tables around me filled up.

It looked like I could be lonely anywhere.

After another five minutes of feeling like a complete dope, I picked up my burger. Lunch would go by faster if I ate and left.

I shoved the burger in my mouth, taking the biggest bite I could.

"Whoa, hungry much?" Lucas flung his tray down across from mine. "See, this is what happens when you skip meals," he teased.

I choked down the food and followed it with a large gulp of water. "What are you doing?" I hissed.

Lucas stopped mid-bite. "Eating?" he said with a full mouth. "What am I supposed to be doing?"

Eating with *me*, though? We hadn't done that since the first day when I gave the speech of stupidity.

I took another sip of water and grimaced at the fact it wasn't coffee. The withdrawal was real. "Why can't campers have coffee?"

He chuckled. "Do you need a coffee, Andy?"

"Only every minute of my life," I muttered.

He stopped eating and leaned his chin against his fist, staring at me. "And this coffee would make you calmer, less sarcastic?"

I nodded as I forked a chunk of pineapple into my mouth.

"Then I don't think you should have any."

I glanced at him in shock.

He just smirked. "I like this Andy."

I rolled my eyes.

He laughed, and I stared at the way his Adam's apple bobbed up and down in his throat. Even his neck was masculine. Then his hand slid across the table, tentative at first, until it rested right beside mine. An invitation. He wanted me to hold his hand, in front of all these people?

Their conversations bubbled up around us, but no one paid any attention, which okay, was ideal, but they *could*. My heart slammed into my ribs again, again, again. I couldn't touch him. Wouldn't. It would mean something, and I didn't, I couldn't…

"I have to go," I whispered.

"Okay." He retracted his hand.

I pulled my tray off the table and returned it at the first station, pushing through the doors into the air, into the oxygen. The breeze was now cool, but people congregated everywhere. They walked in and out of the cafeteria, laughed with each other near the snack shack, huddled in groups talking about God knows what. Why were there so many people everywhere?

My feet barely touched the ground as I sprinted back to the cottage, weaving between conversations and laughter. I needed to get to home base, to safety. To silence.

But as soon as I opened the cottage door, Suzie the Social swept me into the circle of girls she seated on the floor. It turned out to be a session of us sitting knee to knee, spilling our guts. Did this camp even have a schedule? I never got one. Free time was never at the same time, and except for the nighttime hike from hell, it seemed like Dana would make an announcement for us to do something as a cure for her boredom.

Like now. This wasn't even a game. Suzie called it "Secrets," but I know she totally made it up. It was just talking. I got to know more than I ever wanted to about everyone's lives. Who they dated. Their frenemies. Their weird families. Their pets. Peyton cried as she told us about multiple hamsters who died in hilarious ways. One was named Goliath. He got attacked by a malfunctioning Roomba vacuum.

My brain hadn't recovered enough from everything with Lucas to make talking in front of a group any easier. I blew it, and I actually freaking liked him. How hard would it have been to hold his hand when that was so clearly what he wanted me to do?

And now I was failing again. Every time it was my turn to say something, my brain seized up and I couldn't think. I could give my favorite color or the fact that I didn't have any pets, but anything past a one-word answer? I couldn't remember. All I could taste was copper, and I practically blacked out every time Suzie prodded me.

After a while, she got it, but she frowned every time I whispered "pass." I couldn't rally for her. I just couldn't, and I wasn't exactly sorry. Who were these people that they got to know things about me? I didn't ask for that.

So what if Paige clucked over me like a concerned mother hen and Emma deflected Suzie every opportunity she got? I couldn't even be grateful. It was like I'd swallowed gravel. Everything was too bright, too loud, too much.

Lights out was a relief.

I laid on my mattress for at least five minutes counting. Inhaling. Exhaling. Finally, the vise around my lungs disappeared, and I could breathe again.

"How was running?" Paige whispered to me from her bunk. "I saw you talking to Luke."

I didn't want to think about Lucas, how he'd walked backwards to keep me in his line of sight or how my stomach clenched when he talked to me. I rolled over. "Did he run with you?"

She wasn't going to let this go. I sighed. "No."

"Were you sad?" she said through a yawn.

To be alone? "No."

"Do you think..." she trailed off. I waited for her to finish her question, but she didn't. The sounds of soft breathing around me blended into a white noise.

"Paige?"

She must've fallen asleep. She sure was interested in Lucas and me. Maybe she wanted me to be as happy as she was with Marshall. Or not. Her earlier comments about being careful with him still haunted me. I should ask her about it in the morning.

But I forgot.

At the crack of dawn, Suzie instructed us to wear stretchy clothing, because we were combining with the Hippo guys again.

Her eyes sparkled when she told us, like she was sure she'd given us this huge gift, but we all knew the truth. I considered telling her about Tyler's engagement but stopped myself. It wasn't my secret to share. Tyler had his reasons for keeping it to himself.

So, we trudged through the camp, and Suzie herded us into a single-file line on a narrow path in the woods. How many trails did this camp have? As terrible as my beach run had been, I was glad I hadn't attempted one of these. Roots and branches snagged at our feet and clothing. It was an injury waiting to happen.

I slapped mosquito after mosquito off my neck, my legs, my arms. I should just wear bug spray twenty-four seven. Suzie never told us what we were doing until we were neck deep in leadership. Maybe it was her way of forcing us to be prepared for anything, but it sucked.

A clearing appeared ahead, and we spread ourselves into it. The boys followed closely behind us. I was too short even on tiptoes to figure out the activity, but Suzie's shrill voice carried over the crowd. She tried to be nice about quieting the group, but her words took on a borderline-psycho edge when no one listened the first time.

Lucas sidled up beside me and Paige.

My heart jumped into my throat, and I fought to swallow it back down to where it belonged.

I pretended to scratch my neck as an excuse to glance at him. His T-shirt today was a medium grey that stretched over his shoulders but hung slack where his waist dipped in. I knew how smooth his chest was, how his hips jutted out into that sexy V. Faded jeans hugged his thighs this morning, ending in combat boots on his feet. Guys like him could wear the simplest things and make them look high quality. Was he aware of how hot that was?

My eyes skimmed over the tousled waves of his hair. Had he fallen out of bed like that, or did he stand in front of the mirror, styling it into a way that made all the girls go crazy?

His gaze caught mine and my heart stopped. Lucas bit his lip, trying to contain his laughter. I could've died. So caught. So mortified.

I returned my attention to the front of the group. While I'd been checking out Lucas, everyone else had been paying attention to Suzie. I tuned in for the last part of her speech.

"... lucky that here at camp, we just happen to have a forty-foot opportunity!" People around me cheered. Then the crowd shifted, and a huge wooden structure peeked from behind the trees.

Forty feet? The rock-climbing tower had to be twice that height. A gigantic, square looking peg thrust into the ground with ropes for scaling different courses lining the outside of it. Helmets lay scattered near it on the ground.

"Oh *hell*, no," I said before I could stop myself.

Paige doubled over with laughter next to me, and Lucas tried and failed to hide a smile. I didn't care. There was no freakin' way this woman could get me to—

"This is a double-leadership challenge. You'll have the rope leader guiding the crew on the ground, and the brave climber up top. Everyone will get a chance to be both by the time this challenge is over!" Suzie yelled that last part, and the Beavers and Hippos around me cheered in response.

Wait, we had to hold each other's ropes? Nope, no way. Teenagers couldn't handle this alone. Why weren't there adults doing that? And I was on a team of girls! Wait, that was sexist. But I mean, come on. I wasn't letting them heave me up that wall, and I had zero confidence in my climbing skills. I couldn't even climb into my top bunk without vertigo.

"Who wants to go first?" Suzie asked. Hands shot into the air right and left, but her beady little eyes had found their prey. "Camper Andrea, what about you?"

19

FORTY FEET OF HELL NO

Over twenty pairs of eyes zeroed in on me.

I shook my head. "It's Andy."

"Come on, be brave," Suzie encouraged. "Trust us to have your back."

Um, no. What the heck? Did she hate me for saying two words to Tyler? Did she think pushing me would make me snap into that leader role that she knew I so desperately wanted to avoid? But everyone was looking at me.

If I did it, then at least it would be over. Waiting for my turn while my stomach churned would be worse, right? "Okay." Like climbing a wall had anything to do with leadership.

Her face lit up like a Christmas tree. "Way to step up!"

I grabbed a helmet and the girls cheered. How many people had worn this? Did they spray for lice, or like, wash it at all?

Emma turned to me; her face pulled into a sarcastic expression. *"Be brave, Camper Andrea,"* she mocked.

I gave her a nervous smile, then clicked the helmet strap under my chin. Emma wouldn't let me fall, right?

"Let's go," a girl complained.

Emma walked to the rope where everyone else in our group who didn't have to climb the darn wall yet waited to receive instructions on how not to let go and drop me. She gave me an over-the-top, cheesy thumbs up before tuning in.

That inspired a lot of confidence.

I edged closer to the wooden structure. The nearer my feet shuffled, the taller it stretched. What if the rope broke? There was no telling how often this thing got checked for stability. I was willing to bet never.

A black bird careened overhead, flapping its wings. It settled on the ledge of the squared-off top. *Just perfect.* With my luck, I'd get pooped on, too.

Tyler crossed over to me, holding the black straps of a harness.

"You're a climbing instructor?" I whispered in horror.

"As much as anyone is." He winked.

I glared at him. That was so not funny right now.

He got right to business, showing me where to step and where to pull up on the straps. His hands moved fast and sure as he tightened the loopy buckles on my legs, brushing against my midriff before he fixed the bigger strap.

My face blazed. He might be much older than me, but I wasn't immune. A handsome guy's hands were on me. I might die of embarrassment before I even had a chance to fall off the climbing wall.

Then he uttered two words that removed everything but fear from my brain. "You ready?"

No, I would never be ready.

But the rope was attached, and my "teammates" held it, waiting to support me.

I placed my tennis shoe on the first rock and reached up. My butt would be on full display as I climbed, framed in by the harness. *Just great.*

"Come on, Camper Andrea, pave the way!" Suzie's happiness grated on me. For the first time in maybe ever, I was tempted to flip someone off. But of course, I didn't. This wasn't like Jen in the woods. The only person suffering here was me.

"She likes to be called Andy," Paige's voice corrected behind me, as if I hadn't been doing it since I arrived here.

"Go, Andy! You've got this!" Emma cheered me on.

My hands shook. "I don't—"

"Camper Andrea, it's time to lead by example!" Suzie chirped.

"Suze, dial it back," Tyler mumbled. "Okay?" he called to me.

What else could I do?

I left the safety of the ground behind and began to crawl up the wall like a dorky lizard. Right foot, left hand. Left foot, right hand. Stretch, grab. Push off. It was like a puzzle—a dance—each step and pull like fitting another piece into place. Before long, the tingling in my arms faded away. I was doing it! I had to be at least three quarters of the way up. I looked back to the team holding my rope to smile at them, show them I was okay.

What a stupid idea.

I wasn't three quarters of the way up. I was less than half. It didn't matter. The ground shifted beneath me, and I gripped the narrow pieces that held me in place. *Oh my God, oh my God, oh my God.*

"Andy? Andy, are you okay? You're almost there." I could barely hear Paige's voice over the roar of my heart thudding in my ears.

I was *not* almost there. Try almost dead! I was going to fall, and it didn't matter that a bunch of them held the rope. They were teenagers! They wouldn't be able to hold me, and I was going to die! Why did I ever agree to this? They pushed and pushed and called it encouragement. I didn't work that way! I didn't thrive under pressure like they did, and now everyone—*oh, God.* My chest started to seize.

Stop, stop, stop! Breathe. I needed to climb the rest of the way up and then I'd be okay. I craned my neck to find the top ledge. No way. It was so far up there. My arms and legs tingled. This position made my hips ache.

"Camper Andrea, it's okay. Being a leader is about pushing through fear. I know you can do this!" *Freakin' Suzie.* I didn't want her stupid advice right now.

"Andy, just climb back down or let go," Tyler said in a calm but firm voice.

Climb down. Why didn't I think of that? I felt with my toe along the wall for the next rock down, but it was too far. My heart slammed against my ribs and the tingling came back full force, snaking from my fingers up through my arms and into my body. I couldn't get to the rock below me without letting one of my hands go. My fingers dripped sweat.

I was going to lose my grip.

I squeezed my eyes closed, and a tear leaked out and down my cheek. They *knew* I was scared. They made me do it anyway. What kinds of jerks made someone do something they didn't want to? I opened my eyes and stared at the wooden wall because I couldn't stare anywhere else, and I laughed. This was so horrible! Terrible to the point of hilarity.

My shoulders shook and that was all it took for me to lose my grip and fall. Scrambling for purchase, I came up empty and screeched. This was where I died. Broken neck from peer pressure—they could write it on my tombstone. I thought my life would flash before my eyes, but all I saw was the backs of my own eyelids. I plunged down, the whizz of the rope through the carabiners a horrible reminder that teenagers should never be in charge of each other's safety. Then, with a painful jerk, the harness caught me. Slowly, the team lowered me to the ground.

Okay, so maybe I wouldn't die from a fall. Embarrassment would kill me instead.

Nervous laughter erupted from my mouth. Tyler gave me a weird look as he unbuckled me from the harness. It was all so painful it was comical. Suzie and the rest of the girls surged forward, but Tyler blocked their way with one muscular arm.

"Give her some air," he commanded.

Paige peeked around him. *Are you okay?* she mouthed.

I couldn't stop laughing, even as my chest tightened further. I didn't even recognize the harsh, desperate wheezing that escaped my mouth. Tears streamed down my face. I threw my hands up in a helpless gesture, then collapsed on the ground. *Stop it,* I commanded myself, but I couldn't. The tingling hurt now, blending into the pain radiating from my heart.

"Andy, you okay?" Paige asked again, louder this time.

"Of course, she's not okay. Look at her!" Emma cried. "You all pushed her too hard!"

"Me? You were the one—"

I couldn't hear the rest as my fingers pushed into the dirt under the grass. Black spots danced in front of my eyes. *Don't pass out.*

More feet gathered in front of me, surrounding me.

No. Please don't look at me. Don't... But, of course, they all did. If I didn't need my arms to keep my face off the ground, I'd use them to curl up into a ball and die right now.

And it was so *funny.* My throat protested as the manic laughter scraped through it. I couldn't breathe, couldn't—

"Luke, no." Tyler's sharp voice broke into my peals of laughter.

"Shut up." Lucas scooted toward me on his hands and knees, getting his jeans dirty. He caught my eyes, and I stared back, helpless, chortling on the ground. I didn't want this circle of shame. *Stop it,* I commanded myself again, but it didn't work. I wanted to ask him to help me, but I couldn't get enough air. This was *not* happening.

Lucas inched toward me in slow motion, the leaves leaving speckled shadows on his gray shirt. His bright blue eyes met mine, never breaking contact, like I was a wild animal.

And like an animal, I watched him. Wheezing. *Help me. Hide me.*

He nodded like I'd spoken aloud. And maybe I did, I don't know.

When he was within range, he pulled me against him in one quick movement and hugged me tight.

Too shocked to fight it, I froze. His warm chest pressed against mine, my tears seeping into the shoulder of his T-shirt. He smelled good, like soap. I had to focus on my breathing to be able to get any air at all through his bear hug. It distracted me, and my brain shut off as I breathed in and out, in and out. Eventually, my body relaxed one muscle at a time. My laughter became soft crying. Lucas loosened his grip. I leaned against him, my body still seeking solace, until what had happened came crashing down on me.

I pulled my face out of the crook of his neck, and he stared down at me, more serious than I'd ever seen him. "Okay?"

No. Hell no. All around me, people murmured. Paige and Emma whispered to each other. Tyler's jaw flexed as he glared at Lucas. Suzie's hands rested on her hips, annoyed.

I pushed away from Lucas and scrambled to my feet. I didn't even thank him. As fast as my shaking legs would carry me, I stumbled into an awkward run.

Oh my actual God.

20

THE BAD IDEA

The inside of my purple sleeping bag might be a million degrees, but it was safe. It was so tempting to stay here in my purple cocoon of shame and admit defeat. Instead, my embarrassment morphed into rage, and I reached for my phone before remembering Suzie still had it. I swung my head over the edge of the bunk, but the bucket was nowhere in sight. You know what? Fine. We were allowed to use one phone. One I hadn't allowed myself to go near before now because I didn't want to grovel to Mom. But this wasn't desperation. This was rage.

My hands balled into fists as I marched over to the phone shack and dialed her number.

She picked up after three rings. "Hello?" Background chatter and laughter filtered through the earpiece, but I didn't care. It was probably another one of those stupid benefits that made her feel like a "great person."

"Mom?"

"Andy! Hi, honey! Hang on. I have to get somewhere quiet so I can hear you."

Rustling crackled in my ear, and then, "Okay, sweetheart. How's camp?"

"Horrible. I want to come home."

A pause. "I… I don't think that's a good idea," she said in a quiet, very un-Mom voice.

My hand tightened on the phone. How could I make her see reason? "I don't belong here. This place is for people…"

People like her. It was why she sent me. But she needed to understand.

"It's for people who aren't me." *Please get this,* I wanted to say and didn't. *Please accept me. Please love me for who I am, not who you want me to be. I can't stay here.*

"But Andy, it *could* be you," she said, completely oblivious. "You don't understand how much potential you have, honey."

Why did adults always do that? Say something and tack a nonsense "honey" or "sweetheart" or "darling" to the end of it, like what they were saying wasn't harsh? It was as bad as texting someone "lol" every ten seconds, even though nothing was funny. And my mom? She was the queen of this.

"What's so wrong with being me, Mom? Do you hate who I am this much?" I couldn't stay after what had happened.

"Andrea Jane, I never said such a thing."

She didn't have to say it. I wasn't enough. She knew it, and I knew it.

"But that's what you're saying by sending me away, by keeping me here." For the first time since middle school, I was on the verge of yelling at my mom. "You don't like who I am, so you're trying to make me into…" And then it came to me. "Into you! Not everyone wants to lead, Mom. Some people just want to be left the hell alone!"

Despite her shocked silence on the other side of the phone, I could sense her still on the line—this was new for both of us. She wanted me to be rebellious? Well, wish granted. She'd pushed me over the edge. I hoped she was happy. I don't know why I bothered calling. She wasn't going to pick me up.

I hung up, the clang of plastic against metal way more satisfying than tapping a button on a screen.

Who else could I call? Dad would team up with Mom like he always did. I didn't have any friends whose parents would come get me. No people with cars that knew me well enough. The camp would never go for it anyway, though I was sure Suzie and everyone on both teams at the wall today wouldn't have blinked an eye at me leaving.

Out of options, I turned on my heel and with long strides started back to the cottage. I would pack my things and find some way to get to a bus stop. It would be less obvious, and I could get away with it. I wouldn't go home after my conversation with Mom, but I'd figure it out. I didn't care if I had to walk for miles. I was not staying when the goal of the camp was to embarrass me to actual death.

"Andy." Paige's voice called from behind me. "Andy, wait."

I didn't stop.

"Andy—" A hand circled my wrist and I ground to a halt, unwilling to pull her along like a kite behind me.

"It's going to be okay. Really."

I gritted my teeth. "No, it isn't."

"Did you call your parents? Is that why you're coming out of the phone shack?"

I closed my eyes, a tear leaking out. "Yeah."

"Are they coming to get you?" *Even Paige wanted me gone.*

"No. She won't."

"Andy, I'm sor—"

"I don't want to be here, Paige. Look at me." I pointed to my chest. "I'm not going to make it another eight days. I'm not leadership material. I don't want to be forced to be someone I'm not."

That was at the heart of it. Mom preached self-acceptance, and this whole camp was about seizing the day, but I *had* accepted myself. I'd seized my books. Just because people couldn't understand it didn't make me wrong.

"Andy, I'm going to say this with a lot of love, okay? I hope you're still my friend when I do." She folded her arms. "I don't think it's about leadership. You're really scared of something."

"Yeah, heights." *Duh.*

"And?"

"And nothing." *Ugh,* she was just as bad. I didn't need another therapist.

"Okay," she said slowly. "Well, rock climbing doesn't really make or break you as a leader, ya know?"

No kidding.

"Do you want a hug?"

I remembered the hot squeeze of Lucas's arms and my face flamed. I shook my head.

"You can talk to me, you know."

"Sure." But I didn't have any huge revelation I wanted to share. No dark secret that I needed to somehow get over. What was it with people here? Just because I had a panic attack, it didn't mean I was broken. Everyone had phobias.

Not wanting to talk on and on wasn't a damn disease. Maybe I enjoyed listening more than throwing in my opinion every two seconds. Maybe I liked to think before I shoved my foot in my mouth. I wanted to go home!

I deflated. Getting to a bus stop wouldn't help me. I couldn't go home when Mom would just drive me right back here to "finish what I started" like she always told me to do.

Dana's voice chirped over the camp-wide speakers. It was time for the horses to head to the troughs. As one, Paige and I walked toward the dining commons. It's not like I had any other choice.

"So, after you ran off…" she started.

Nope. Not going there. "I don't want to talk about it."

"Yeah, it sucked. But Luke… I've never seen him like that. You know Tyler yelled at him after you left? Luke yelled right back. It was a real brotherly moment."

My feet slowed. I didn't want Lucas to get in trouble for helping me. I could still feel the hot pressure of his shoulder against my face like a brand. The way he smelled like soap and sunshine. "Why were they yelling?"

"Oh, it was a whole thing. Tyler was all, *You could've made it worse,* and Luke was like, *Well, none of you were doing anything*. Then Luke went off on him and Suzie for forcing you to do it when you were scared. How that's not leadership and stuff."

I couldn't help myself. "What did Tyler say to that?" It's not like he forced me to climb the wall. He was part of it, but...

"You mean Suzie."

"Suzie?"

"Yeah. I can't believe you missed it. She started crying and apologizing. Tyler had to drag her off before she completely lost it."

I winced. Suzie Sunshine wasn't my favorite, but I wouldn't wish drama on anyone. I was so good at avoiding it normally, but now all of it centered around me. Nausea roiled in the pit of my stomach. How could I go to lunch and face any of these people when I'd caused such a scene?

"I wonder how he knew to hug you like that?" Paige said.

"I don't know."

She frowned. "Did it make you feel better?"

I slowed as the building came in sight. "I don't want to go in there," I whispered.

"Did it make you feel better?" she asked with more urgency.

"Yeah," I said. "It did."

Without another word, she pushed through the door. The noise washed over us. Other campers laughing, eating. That hot dog and baked bean smell. I liked baked beans.

"I'll run interference," she promised.

I nodded weakly and followed in her wake as we got our hot dogs, beans, and a roll each. As we exited the line, Emma's dark brown hair caught my eyes as she set down her food at a long table. Before I could obsess over how that wasn't the invitation it seemed like, I slid my tray next to hers.

After everything that happened today, it was scary to sit down next to someone new. But her yelling at everyone next to the wall echoed in my mind. *You all pushed her too hard!* I wanted to be friends with this girl. The girl who did for me what I tried to do for Brynn. For Jen.

She squinted at me for a moment. "So you're scared of heights, huh?"

"Ya think?" Paige said as she slid in next to her. I noted the defensiveness in her tone.

Emma scooted her peas to the side of her plate. "It was kind of crappy for Suzie to make you do it." She paused. "To make you do it first, anyway."

Paige's shoulders relaxed.

No kidding. I glanced over to the counselor table. Suzie sat next to Tyler, poking at her food as she spoke to him. He'd pushed up his sunglasses for once, his face scrunched in concern as he said something back.

I tried to hang on to my righteous anger at what had happened, but it felt wrong. Suzie's light had been put out because of me. I sighed. I didn't want that, no matter how annoying she got.

Then Lucas sat down next to me.

I could've cried in frustration. I didn't want any pity. Especially from him.

He set a cup of coffee next to my tray.

I supposed he could stay for a bit, then. How was everyone getting coffee? Did Tyler sneak it to him? I breathed in that beautiful coffee bean smell.

"You gonna eat that?" he pointed to my roll.

I shook my head. Coffee was the only thing that could make me better right now. I wanted to bathe in it. "Is this for me?" I asked, not caring what his answer was. It had entered my radius, so it was mine now.

He raised his eyebrows. "I don't drink coffee."

I closed my eyes as the bitter black liquid traveled down my throat.

He fished the roll from my plate. "They only gave me two. Can you believe that? I'm still growing."

I opened my eyes. Could it really be this easy? Was he going to ignore what happened?

"I'm going to go for a walk later, you know, after whatever the next things is." He grinned, waiting.

I nodded.

Paige and Emma remained quiet, suddenly very interested in their food.

Lucas swept his hair back from his forehead and caught my eye when my fork was halfway to my mouth. "So, you wanna go?"

"Uh…" Yep. That's all I had. I was the "uh" girl.

His cheeks colored a pale shade of pink. "You don't have to. It's okay."

Wait. Was *he* nervous? It was the first time he'd asked me to do something in front of anyone else. Was that a milestone or something?

I bit my lip, exhausted. I didn't want to be here, but he wasn't making it awkward. He acted like he hadn't squeezed the panic out of me an hour ago. This guy had saved me, and he did it so effortlessly that I was equal parts impressed and awed by him. Never mind that I owed him big time.

My heart slammed into my ribs so hard it might escape and run to the cottage the way I wanted to. The correct answer was yes. I had to say yes. If I didn't, I'd be the worst person ever. *Ow. God, my chest still hurts.* My body was getting whiplash from this day. "Okay."

"Right," he said with an emphasized T. "Sorry I made this weird." He swung a leg over the bench of the table to leave.

I placed my hand on his arm, then immediately pulled it back. He never said I could touch him. I couldn't look at him now as I muttered, "No, I mean, sure, I'll go." I wanted to. His calm happiness was a salve to the burn of this camp, and I…

He smiled that megawatt smile. "Yeah?"

I nodded one too many times.

He beamed at me again. "Sweet."

He traded small talk with Paige and Emma for a few minutes, but I couldn't join in. Blood roared in my ears. He wanted to hang out with me. This was a date, not us walking together because we needed to go the same way. And he'd asked *me*. Not some string bikini-wearing, uber-confident, leadership-material type of girl. Me.

He excused himself with a casual salute, grinning as he rejoined the Hippo table. I wanted some of that confidence, the ability to excuse myself without apologizing or phrasing it as a question.

The table around me went quiet. Paige and Emma continued to stare at me.

"I—" Emma began, but she cut off when Tyler and Suzie sat down beside her. Weren't they eating on the other side of the cafeteria?

Their appearance wasn't enough to silence Emma for long. "This is a bad idea," she hissed. All eyes zeroed in on her, then me.

"What's a bad idea?" Tyler said.

21

BECOMING BRYNN

I tried to catch Emma's eye. *Don't,* I wanted to plead with her. I didn't need her telling Tyler about me and Lucas when it might cause friction between the two brothers.

She didn't get the memo.

"Andy," Emma pointed her purple-tipped finger at me, "has a date with your player brother. What do you think about that?"

Tyler's smile faltered, and he shoveled a forkful of salad into his mouth.

"It's always the quiet ones," Suzie joked, sipping a bottle of water.

Yeah, she didn't get to talk to me. Pretty much ever again.

"What are you guys going to do?" she continued. "The schedule doesn't allow for much."

Suzie and her darn schedule. This was none of her business. It was none of anyone's business what I did or didn't do with Lucas.

"Excuse me," I murmured, rising from the table.

"It's a bad idea," Emma tried to argue again. "Paige, tell her it's a bad idea."

Paige winced. "I don't know, Andy. I just don't know."

I shrugged like it didn't matter, even though it did, and deposited my tray on top of the trash can on my way out the door. But a light touch on my shoulder stopped me outside the cafeteria.

Suzie's face was pale under her freckles as she opened and closed her mouth once before speaking. "I owe you an apology, Camper Andrea. At the wall challenge—"

"It's fine," I ground out. I really didn't want to hear it. We both knew she was only apologizing because of Tyler.

"It's not okay. I guess I just…" She stared back at the cafeteria door. "Next time will you tell me if you're scared?"

She couldn't be serious. I tried. She never listened. I didn't want to have a heart to heart so she could feel like a good person again or face Tyler, *who had a fiancée*. I nodded once.

"Maybe we take it easy the rest of the day, yeah?" She smiled tentatively.

I sighed. I couldn't stay mad at someone so… Suzie. "Sounds good."

"Awesome. And… I am sorry, Andrea."

I waved her off, even though I didn't know what "taking it easy" the rest of the day meant to someone with her kind of energy.

It turned out I didn't have long to wait. Ten minutes into reading my novel, the girls filtered out of the cottage, pulled into an activity. No one came to get me or hustled me along. In fact, Emma gave me a pitying look as she capped her mascara and headed out.

Suzie really meant it? She was leaving me alone for the rest of the day?

Awesome.

I shifted in my sleeping bag. I didn't want to think about the wall, about Suzie, about… Lucas. It could all wait. Wasn't this what I wanted all along? For people to leave me alone so I could read? I turned the page of my book.

But I couldn't concentrate. The girls' screeches floated through the window. I didn't want to be a part of whatever was going on, even if they were excited screams instead of scared ones. I turned another page. Why did I feel so left out, then?

I leaned toward the window. My roommates gathered on the side of the hill next to the cottages throwing water balloons as the boys circled around the back of their group.

I almost called out a warning, but I would've been too late. A big, fat, orange blob exploded all over the back of Paige's head, and she cried out, clutching her sopping hair. Did she know Marshall threw it?

She motioned to Emma like a third base coach.

I grinned. *Oh, she knew.*

Seconds later, two big red balloons smashed into his face. As he blinked away the water, Paige and Emma high-fived in front of him. Then he grabbed a massive blue balloon, and both the girls screamed, rejoining the rest of the Beavers. Safety in numbers, I guess.

I sat back. A weird tingle spread through my body. Shame. Embarrassment. I should've been out there.

When the Beavers filed back into the cottage, most of them dripping and moaning, Paige checked on me first. "How ya doin', Champ?"

Emma punched Paige on the arm. "She's fine."

"Did you get some rest?" Paige tried again.

My heart warmed. They weren't excluding me. They were trying to help. I nodded.

"What are you going to wear on your date with Luke?" Paige asked.

I set my book down. "Um. I don't know." I should've thought about that. Should've been planning my outfit this whole time. Normal girls would. My stomach clenched. I was already bad at this, and I hadn't even seen him yet!

Emma rummaged in her bag and pulled out a clean towel, scrunching her hair dry.

Paige nudged her.

Emma rolled her eyes. "Do you want me to help you with your makeup?"

"That's okay," I whispered. She was being so nice, but my chest hitched. I should know how to do my own makeup. It would look weird if I didn't. And more importantly, if I put on makeup, it would be like a neon billboard that screamed I LIKE YOU! If he knew I liked him, he could hurt me. I didn't know if I wanted to let anyone have that power.

"Well, have fun then," Emma said as they both headed for the showers.

That was weird. I expected them to grill me, for all the fuss they made back at the cafeteria. I released the fists I'd been clenching in anticipation. Why did everything with girls come back to guys, anyway? Paige and Emma were acting super weird about Lucas—that's what triggered my fallout with Brynn, too.

Stupid boys.

Why did it always have to be a big thing? I wanted Brynn to be my friend, but she chose Alex. It was never the same after that night. She talked to me less and less, and never invited me to another party with her because she said it wasn't my thing. We were too different.

I dragged her down.

I'd loved that she was my only friend, but Brynn? She shone like the sun when she was absorbed into the popular crowd. She had tons of friends who cared about the same things she did. She didn't need me anymore.

And now Paige and Emma had a problem with Lucas, which made it that much worse. Was I turning into Brynn? What time was it anyway? I looked at the clock hanging on the wall. *Oh, crap.* Did I miss dinner, too? Now I was hungry *and* nervous! Should I go casual, like I didn't care that we were doing this? My jean shorts and black tank might work, but I had a dressier white top somewhere. Should I wear my flip flops, or would they ruin the look? Would Lucas even care?

My heart raced, and I squeezed my pillow tight. I'd never been on a date. No one ever singled me out like this. I liked Lucas, but... I swallowed. Why couldn't I enjoy this moment? A boy wanted to spend time with me, get to know me, and *oh God,* what if he tried to kiss me?

I reached one hand to touch my lips. Did I even bring lip gloss? Would a boy want to taste a glossy cherry or was that gross? My toothpaste wouldn't hold out for more than an hour, and I couldn't chew a piece of gum because I'd forget to spit it out. It would be in my mouth while he was kissing me, and he'd be so disgusted and...

With shaky legs, I climbed down the ladder and rifled through the clothes in my bag. Black wouldn't be as hard to wash out if I puked, so that solved that. And nestled among the emergency tampons was my tiny makeup bag. Mom had packed it for me, after all.

I headed to the bathroom and changed in one of the stalls, then took the bag to a dingy mirror. My eyes were my best feature, so I'd start there. Maybe if I didn't think about why I was putting on makeup I could do this. My hand trembled as I tried to apply eyeliner, and after three attempts, I gave up. Sweat beaded my brow and upper lip, and it wasn't even that hot. I stared at myself in the mirror, and a scared, pale girl stared back.

Why was I doing this to myself? I'd been through enough today. If I went now, I'd probably cry and run away. No one wanted to date someone like that. Lucas made a mistake. I bet he only asked me on a walk to talk about the wall. To make sure I was okay. I acted like this was a date, but to him it was just... I wiped off the runny makeup and climbed into my bed mortified. I wouldn't be anyone's pity date. He said I was a badass earlier. Now he knew for sure I wasn't.

Once I secured my sleeping bag around my shoulders, I grabbed one of the many books shoved between the thin mattress and the wood of the bunk. Gerald was about to ask Sophia to the dance, and like me, her nerves rebelled. She'd still go though, and they'd dance and talk and kiss. I held the book tightly. But she had the whole first half of the book to get used to how much Gerald liked her.

Standing Lucas up was horrible, but this wasn't my fault. He gave me no warning. I wasn't going to let anyone pressure me. Not Suzie with her rah-rah camp crap, and not Lucas, even if he did like me and I might... no. If it didn't feel right, it wasn't, and that was that. I lost myself in the pages of the predictable plot, and when the sun had set and the natural light streaming through the windows gave way to shadows, I dog-eared the page and set it down. By the time my eyes fluttered shut, I was calm.

The next morning, I was ready to face the world again.

I'd fallen asleep dressed in last night's outfit, so I went with it. Tank tops were wrinkle resistant for the most part, and casual was how I needed to look after being the biggest jerk ever. Most of the girls were still sleeping when I slipped on my sunglasses out of habit, dimming the too-bright world.

I shut the door behind me and found Lucas leaning against the porch rail when I turned around. What little appetite I had dried up as panic pulsed through my veins. He was mad. He was annoyed. He deserved better. He was...

I finally looked at his face. He was... unreadable? I opened my mouth to apologize but no sound came out. He had probably moved on to another girl in my cabin, and that's why he was here. I wouldn't blame him if he did.

I gave him a helpless shrug, then skirted around him, trying to get out of his way.

He fell into step beside me and kept to my slower pace though his long legs could've gone twice as fast. Did that mean he was here for me? I should say sorry. Right now.

"You didn't show up last night," he murmured as we rounded a corner. He sounded different. Quiet.

Birds cheeped their early-morning songs from the dew-covered trees, oblivious to the way my chest tightened.

"I'm not... I couldn't." I couldn't be that girl, the one who was super carefree and okay with all the prying eyes at his cottage and mine. Any person we passed by would talk about us, and I couldn't handle that attention. I didn't even know why he bothered with me.

He blew out a breath and squinted at the clouds hiding the sun above us. "Yesterday was hard for you. Maybe it wasn't the best time."

I shook my head. He wasn't wrong, but it wouldn't have mattered. "That's not it."

"Okay. Then why did you say yes?"

He had every right to ask that. I was in the wrong here. But I couldn't say that out loud, because then I would have to admit that I was scared, and I wasn't. Not of *him*. Not really. Just... I couldn't explain. I adjusted my sunglasses, reassuring myself he couldn't see my eyes.

"You felt pressured," he guessed.

How did he know that? And how did he know what I needed at the wall? It made me like him all over again. And now I'd ruined it. I nodded.

He winced. "I'm sorry."

Some of the tension in my shoulders eased. "Me too."

"Should I just…" He ran a hand through his already-messy hair. "Do you want me to leave you alone?" The vulnerability in his voice killed me. He'd gone out of his way to be so nice to me, told me I was cool, teased me into talking to him, and shooting hoops with him. And then I let him down.

"No," I whispered. And I meant it. I wasn't caving from pressure this time. As awkward as this conversation was, I needed it. I needed him to understand, and the fact that he wanted to get me… a lump formed in my throat.

A smile tugged at his lips. "So, we're okay?"

"Yes."

Lucas caught my hand just as we reached the door of the cafeteria. "I'm not giving up on you, Andy." He twirled me around.

I stumbled out of the spin, giggling. "I don't want you to."

22

ALL TIED UP IN KNOTS

In a not-so-drastic turn of events, we ended up outside the cafeteria doing yet another bonding activity with the Hippo cottage thirty minutes later.

"Okay, everyone get in a circle, facing in," Tyler directed.

Of course, it would be a circle. Everything here was a circle. Leadership was all about being good at circles.

We shuffled into a crappy oval.

"Hmm. Twenty might be too many. We should split in half," Suzie said to Tyler, her lips an inch from brushing his ear.

He didn't so much as blink. "Sure, Suze. Half of you get in a new circle," he called out.

I moved with some others to get into a new circle, and Suzie bustled around until there were ten in each. The Hippo guys made up most of my circle, and the other consisted of mostly girls. I tried not to be self-conscious about it or that Lucas was stationed right across from me.

"Okay." Tyler cleared his throat and moved away from where Suzie had parked herself, which was basically in his pocket. "Everyone reach your right arm toward the center and grab someone else's hand. None of you are allowed to grab the hand of the person right next to you."

My skin burned as I pressed my palms against the denim of my ripped shorts, willing my hands not to sweat so much. Then I reached out and a red-headed guy clasped my fingers with his pale, freckled hand. *This isn't awkward at all.*

"Now, everyone needs to reach their left arm in and grab someone else's hand. Again, make sure it isn't the person right next to you."

We all fumbled forward to reach for someone else. Lucas's hand found mine first. Our eyes met and his face stretched into a blinding smile. Warmth bloomed in my chest. I couldn't even duck my head because my body was pushed so far forward.

"Okay, now the fun part!" Suzie chirped. "Without letting go of the hands you are holding, you have to work together to untangle the human knot. The goal is to end up in a perfect circle again!"

Tyler's more practical instructions continued. "You can go over or under each other's arms, or through legs if needed, as long as you don't break the chain in the process. You can't let go of someone's hand and then hold it again. It's about problem-solving, communication, and leadership. You know the drill."

Suzie's face pinched at his last comment, but her smile remained pasted on her face. "Since we have two groups, we should see who can get this done first. Whichever team wins gets thirty extra minutes of free time tonight before lights out." Her eyes strayed to Tyler as she said this, but he'd moved toward our group to referee.

"Okay, go!" he called.

Lucas tugged me forward. I gave him a small smile and he flashed me a big grin.

I can't believe I'm holding his hand.

It was a good hand, too. Dry, warm, slightly callused from outdoor activities or maybe a sport. Right now, he had to hold my hand, but that smile meant something. He wanted to even if he didn't have to do this activity with me. If there wasn't a knot of arms between us, we'd be holding hands for real.

The other group got loud fast as they talked over each other, trying to figure out a strategy for getting themselves untangled. Not us. Our group focused on Lucas. He towered above most of the group and had the closest thing to a bird's eye view out of anyone.

"Okay, guys." He stretched his neck up to get a better picture of our interlocked hands. "Jeremy, go under Rachel and Chaz's arms and you should be able to untangle a little more." How did he know everyone's name? We hadn't been at camp that long.

"Okay, now—" He pulled me along with him as he troubleshooted for other people, always calm. Always on top of it. If someone disagreed with him, they figured it out together. About half the time, he deferred with a shrug.

Tyler stood, a silent sentry at the side of our game, sunglasses slipping down the bridge of his nose. What did he think of his brother taking charge? I tried to catch his eye, but his head turned to a pair of hands that threatened to separate at any second.

Not a moment later, Lucas teased the two campers. "Aiden, come on, man. Katie can't be that hard to hold onto. We're going to beat them."

"Dude, I have to pee," Aiden complained.

"Five minutes, yeah? You can make it five minutes," Lucas said.

"Fine," Aiden said through gritted teeth. Either he had to go really bad, or he had a problem with Katie, who turned away with a scowl.

The fighting in the other circle escalated as Emma got into it with some guy. Tyler's eyebrows rose, but Suzie stepped in. The yelling didn't stop, though. She appeared to make things worse instead of better. Our own circle was mostly unknotted.

"Andy?" Lucas pointed to where I needed to go over his arm in order to undo a problem he'd created by moving another person. He bent down and so did the others near me so that I could step over.

This put his face to close to my chest. My breath hitched. He had to see the problem. Any second now, he'd recalculate. Either that, or I'd fall on him. I stayed rooted to the spot, waiting.

"Come on, Andy. You've got this."

I gritted my teeth and resolved to move as quick as possible. If we brushed each other, it wouldn't be for long—no big deal.

I should have known better.

No sooner did I jump over his arm with one of my sneakered feet, then the next followed suit. I tripped and started to let go of his hand. I was going to ruin this for the whole team!

But just as quickly, he tightened his grip and pulled me forward, catching me with his knee. Our hands sandwiched between us, and his face—*oh, God.* His face was squished right between my boobs.

I panicked, but he was already righting me. "All good," he said as we all straightened, but his ears had colored a bright red.

Kill. Me. Now.

A minute later, our team figured out its circle, while the other group remained hopelessly tangled. We let go of each other's sweaty hands, Aiden ran off to pee, and *finally* the game ended.

"Great job, everyone. It's pretty clear who the reward goes to." Tyler smiled.

"Just remember..." Suzie's curls were frizzy from running her hands through them as she negotiated with the losing circle. "Even if you don't win, it's a learning experience. You're figuring out how to work with people. If it's easy, great, but it won't always be that way."

Her eyes narrowed the tiniest bit at Lucas. Did she think he had an unfair advantage, having Tyler for a brother? They were both that kind of level-headed leader, the one you couldn't help but respect.

Lucas shrugged and threw me a sheepish smile that I didn't know how to translate.

When we broke up for a break and leisure time, I lengthened my stride to catch up to Emma. She stalked away from the losing team, an enormous aqua and pink ribbon pinned to her chest.

I laughed. Hadn't she just been screeching at the top of her lungs?

She jumped when she heard me, then glanced down at her chest. "Oh. I made *progress.*"

I smirked.

"Shut up."

My grin widened.

"Saw you with your group," she said.

"Yeah?" She saw me, or she saw that I boobed Lucas? How was I ever going to live down the embarrassment?

"Yeah, that was painful." She kicked a rock on the path back to the cottage.

"Right?" I glanced over my shoulder for Lucas; he'd be avoiding me like the plague now.

She huffed. "I'm not talking about the challenge."

I frowned and waited for her to explain as a breeze lifted the leaves of the trees around us in a gentle sway.

"I thought you weren't interested in Lucas. You stood him up."

I thought she'd say something about it at breakfast, but she never did. I guess it was time to own up. "Yeah, I… panicked."

"You panicked."

I nodded.

"Look, Andy. I like you, so I feel like I should tell you that Luke? He's not what someone like you needs." She slowed her pace.

"Someone like me?" I shortened my stride to match hers.

"Yeah. You're so… you know. And Luke…"

"Wow, thanks." I couldn't keep the snark out of my voice this time.

"You know what, fine," she snapped. "It was hard to watch, okay? And we all saw it."

My mouth dropped open in shock. "I—I'm sorry." *Why do I feel the need to apologize?* I wasn't all over him. If anything, it was the opposite. She couldn't see how awkward I was? It was super obvious to everyone else.

"Just—never mind." She stomped off.

This time I didn't try to keep up with her. Was this what it was like to have girlfriends? Constant drama? It was giving me heart palpitations.

And worse, was she right about me and Lucas? Maybe I *should* back off. Even as I had the thought, I knew I wouldn't.

I'm not giving up on you, Andy. And I didn't want him to.

Paige ran to catch up with Emma, but I stayed back. They could eat without me.

The wind kicked up, and goosebumps spread up and down my

arms. I'd go get a sweatshirt and maybe by then they'd be off somewhere else.

They whispered to each other, no doubt about me. Paige glanced back, worry in her eyes. *Yep, totally about me.* Relief washed over me when the path widened and split into two, so it wasn't obvious I wanted to get away from them.

If I'd been wearing a sweatshirt when we played the game, I wouldn't be half as embarrassed when Lucas's head ended up between my boobs. Emma thought I was throwing myself at him? I wanted to throw myself off a cliff.

I'd forgotten I got extra "me" time because our group won the challenge until Paige reminded me in the cottage.

"So, I guess you're going to hang out with Luke, huh?" she said nonchalantly.

I wasn't fooled. "It wasn't my first thought." Not until she said something. Now sweat broke out over my forehead. Would he want to see me? Or was he too embarrassed, too? What if he waited for me somewhere? It was all too much.

Standing in crowds of people and having to participate physically, mentally, and verbally had taken a toll on me. Each time I got a moment, I was bombarded by a lesson meant to teach me how to not be me.

This Emma drama wasn't helping anything. She didn't want to tell me what was going on, but she still yelled at me? I needed an escape.

I wanted Lucas to like me, but this wasn't going to be a summer of transformation. Despite what Mom wanted, I wouldn't return home tan, happy, and outgoing. And despite what Paige and Emma thought, I wasn't here to have some grand summer romance with the hottest guy at camp, even if he was the most patient, perfect… no.

Ugh, I need a book.

23

HEY, LOUDMOUTH

Since I started camp, I'd had trouble centering on any one book, but I knew what would fix that. I pulled my favorite novel from the side pocket of my bag and headed toward a sturdy-looking tree on the edge of camp that faced the woods. If I sat somewhere different each time I did this, there was less chance someone would find me, right? I angled myself so I'd be invisible to anyone walking down the path.

The rough bark of the tree scratched my back through my thin tank top, and the damp soaked through my shorts. I didn't care. I flipped to the place in my book where I'd folded over the page and lost myself in the familiar words that transported me to Medieval times. People were confusing. Books weren't.

Their lives were hard back then. No dentists with degrees, no doctors who washed their hands, no electricity or running water. And yet, I craved that simplicity. High-born girls were allowed to read for hours on end. They wore modest clothing without being called a prude. Being bashful was seen as attractive. Elizabeth pretended to be a boy for half the book, but Marek always knew she was a girl because he was that observant and attentive.

Observant. Attentive. Two qualities that described Lucas. Was that why I was so attracted to him? Because he was like a romance novel hero? Before now, I assumed guys like that didn't exist. Well, not in high school, anyway.

But hadn't I always wanted to be like the main characters in my romance novels? Pursued like I was something valuable?

When Lucas' warm blue eyes flashed my way, I was exactly the right amount of nervous, the right amount of excited. And when we talked, it felt comfortable, familiar. Just like with Paige and Emma.

Paige and Emma.

I liked them. I liked Paige's self-confidence, the way she listened to people with all of her being, appreciated them for who they were. And Emma—she was intense in the best way; perceptive. Now they were being weird, and it had something to do with Lucas.

The first guy I ever liked had to be the problem between the only two girls who wanted to hang out with me since Brynn. Was it wrong to be selfish for once? Couldn't I have everything? Friends and a guy who liked me?

I lifted my eyes to where birds chattered in the Cottonwood branches above. The wind ruffled my sweatshirt, but it didn't chill me. The ground beneath where I sat was warm because my butt had gotten used to being damp.

The smell of pine and cut grass and that faint scent that made me think of sunshine enveloped me. It felt right, the semi-silence of nature. I opened my book again.

Marek was about to tell Elizabeth about the hidden fortune of his grandfather when a shadow fell over me. Startled, I looked up.

It was Tyler.

He stood there a moment, his ever-present sunglasses betraying zero emotion. He could be mad, amused, or anything in between.

Time moved strangely when I read. Sometimes a scene could last seconds and feel like years if it was described in detail. Today, the sun had gone from bright yellow to a muted gold.

I'd definitely missed an activity involving a circle by now. Probably multiple leadership speeches. I sat frozen over the pages of my novel, waiting for Tyler to haul me up by the arm and return me to Suzie's cheery wrath.

But he didn't. He sat down next to me, our shoulders close but not touching. He leaned back against the tree. "Hey, Loudmouth."

Here we go. I folded over a page and closed my book, pressing the well-worn copy to my chest. A few chapters from the end, I hoped to finish it with a flashlight tonight.

"Had enough teambuilding for today?" he asked.

I resisted the urge to laugh at his sarcasm. But my face betrayed me, the corners of my mouth lifting.

He turned to me. "I get it." Then he pushed his sunglasses up onto his head. I shifted a few inches away from him. It was awkward being this close to an attractive older guy. My body vibrated with a strange awareness, even though he wasn't the brother that made me weak. Lucas always looked like he was on the verge of laughing, but Tyler was the picture of calm. How could identical eyes say such different things?

I expected him to talk to me, to try to get me to do something leadershippy. It was this camp's M.O. after all. If he asked me to join the others, I would because of the laid-back way he approached me. I valued that.

He didn't push me, though. We sat in silence for a long time, him with his eyes closed, resting against the tree. So I did the same. It would have been better had I been truly alone, but I needed this. I didn't want to talk to anyone—I wanted quiet.

"Tyler, where did you go? I finished the activity, and I thought that maybe we could—" Suzie's voice cut off.

I opened my eyes.

She looked from Tyler to me a few times, confusion replacing her usual glee. Her eyes lingered on where his sunglasses rested on top of his head. I smiled when I spied the tan line that stretched across his face from them. *Not perfect, after all.*

"Camper Andrea." Her lips stretched into a fake smile. "We missed you at the Co-Op Challenge."

I nodded. "Sorry," I said, sounding anything but.

"Are you okay?" She eyed my book with disdain.

"Yes. I am now."

Her lips pursed as she glanced back at Tyler. It took me a second, but then I got it. She thought I meant that he made me feel better. *Crap.*

I opened my mouth to explain, but Tyler had gotten to his feet. "Thanks, Andy." He glanced down at me. "I needed that." He turned to Suzie. "I'll see you at the meeting in a minute?" Without waiting for her answer, he turned and left, lifting two fingers in the air in a casual wave.

Suzie's eyes followed him as he entered the Hippo cottage.

"Next time, Camper Andrea," she said, her features tight, "you should let someone know where you're going. Then we wouldn't worry so much." Her wild hair frizzed from her head, and her freckles blended into her sunburn. The way she narrowed her eyes struck fear into me. Perhaps Tyler had come to me on his own without talking to her.

"Okay," I said meekly. How could I survive this woman another seven and a half days?

She nodded once and stalked off to our cottage. Well, I couldn't go there, now. I guess I had to sit here under the tree until she left for whatever counselor meeting she had with Tyler.

What a pity.

I opened my book and settled back against the tree.

24

SUZIE SUNSHINE

The next morning, a coffee waited in my normal spot at the cafeteria table. I raised my eyebrows, but Paige, Emma, and Marshall ignored my pointed glance at my cup, talking a mile a minute about a sporting whatever. I didn't push it or participate in their conversation, because I had no idea where I stood with them at this point, and my brain cells hadn't resigned themselves to participating in life yet today. Whoever gave me liquid happiness this morning must have an inside track to my brain.

I did a silent cheers to them in my head.

Fortunately, we weren't starting the day with anything physical. Before long, Suzie and Tyler led us to a firepit, where everyone sat in a large—*gasp*—circle. Marshall and Paige and Emma sat on one side, Lucas on the other. I told him I didn't want him to give up on me, but my action right now could speak louder than words. I could do this. I grabbed one of the clipboards Suzie handed out and perched next to him.

Lucas scooted closer. "In a good mood this morning because of your coffee?"

I nudged his shoulder. I knew it was him! "If you tell me there's a coffee maker in your cottage, I'll riot," I whispered back.

He snorted behind his clipboard.

Suzie stood. "The purpose of this exercise is to figure out which items would be the most useful if you are deserted on an island, and rank them one to fifteen, one being vital and fifteen nonessential."

I looked down at the paper clipped to my board. Why did it matter how important each of the items were if we had all the items? The water jug would be important. So would a mirror because it could signal planes or whatever. I doubted any navigational equipment would prove useful, since we were, by definition, stranded. I paused over an interesting one: twenty feet of opaque, plastic sheeting. I chewed on the inside of my cheek, then marked it as important.

I completed the page before most everyone else; they labored over it like the world depended on them ranking crap on a worksheet. Emma beat me, though. She flashed me a wicked smile as she showed me her clipboard—she'd scrawled a number one on every line. She jumped up and scooted in on my other side.

My breath froze in my lungs before I forced myself to exhale. She wanted to sit with me after she yelled at me about Lucas? Did I miss something?

"What?" she said. "Marshall and Paige are coupley and gross. Look at them."

I did. They were both filling out their clipboards, sneaking glances at each other and hiding their answers like one might cheat off the other. Good grief, she was right.

"What a lame activity," Emma complained under her breath. "A good leader is prepared with *all* the supplies. You know what this list is missing? The same thing as this camp: a phone. I swear, this is how horror movies start."

I nodded in solidarity, though honestly, I hadn't been missing mine the last day or so. Books beat phones, anyway. I scanned the rest of the circle. A couple of people scribbled answers on their clipboards and others frowned like they were trying to crack the code. I risked a smile at a skinny camper across the circle from me. He pushed up his glasses, sighing. Could I be witnessing my first Victim?

Bored, I drew stars in the margins of my paper until people stopped scratching in their answers, and the room fell quiet.

Tyler stood. "The next part of this is to try to come to an agreement as a group on the numbers. Don't be afraid to speak up and voice your opinion. The great thing about this is that everyone will have a unique perspective on the items." He sat and gestured to the group.

A beat of silence passed.

Lucas spoke first. He projected his voice to the whole group. "The plastic is basically useless. What would I even do with it? I could try to catch a fish, but I have the net, so why would I need plastic? It would stop the water, too." He moved his hands as he spoke, the muscles in his forearms accented by his Henley shirt. *God, he's beautiful.*

He had exceptional speaking skills—maybe that was the reason everyone nodded along, even when what he said made little sense.

"Let's take a vote," Tyler said. "All those who think the sheeting should be lower on our needs list?"

Most everyone raised their hands.

"Camper Andrea," Suzie said. "You didn't raise your hand. Why don't you tell us, real big and loud, why you think the sheet of plastic is important?"

I swallowed. I hated public speaking, and she knew it. Why was she doing this?

She gestured to the group.

Fine. "It has multiple uses."

"Like what?" Lucas leaned toward me, his expression interested. He squared his shoulders, a clear indication he'd argue for his side.

Didn't he know I didn't want to talk? I rolled my eyes.

His mouth twitched as he fought a smile, the challenge written all over his face.

I narrowed my eyes. "Like waterproofing a shelter. Catching the rain for drinking water. Making a poncho. Wrapping it around a cut to keep it from getting dirt in it. I don't know, it's useful." Right now, it might be useful to smother myself, so I didn't have to continue talking.

Lucas opened his mouth to object, but then closed it and frowned. I had him. And he knew it. I smirked.

Just because I was quiet didn't mean I was stupid. Just because I didn't object to everyone's shenanigans didn't mean I was okay with them. And just because I didn't join in with everything didn't mean I was a snob. This entire camp didn't understand the definition of introverted.

Emma started a slow clap next to me, but I elbowed her, and she fell silent, though her shoulders shook from suppressed laughter.

Tyler laughed too, breaking the tension. "She's got you there, Luke. Did Andy change anyone else's mind?" Most hands went up. "Okay then. Let's put it in our top five." He pulled the clipboard from Suzie, whose knee was practically glued to his, and made a mark before handing it back to her.

From then on, whenever Suzie looked like she might call on me, Tyler would change the subject or call on another person before she could say my name. He was kind of obvious about it, but I appreciated the effort.

I did take a little satisfaction in the fact that when the "answers" were revealed, the plastic sheeting made the top five, but it was a short-lived victory.

As we stood and stretched our legs after the activity, Suzie weaved through the other campers and motioned for me to follow her down the path. Was she going to congratulate me on my sudden participation? A girl could hope. We stepped a few yards into the woods before she turned to me.

"Camper Andrea," Suzie started. "I know it's easy to like Tyler because he's a nice guy, but..."

My face blazed with heat. Was she seriously hinting that I *liked* Tyler?

She shook her head like she'd thought better of what she'd been about to say. "It's hard to show your leadership skills if you don't speak up a little more. How do you feel about making that your goal this summer?" She gave me a winning smile.

I wasn't fooled. So what if Tyler was a nice guy? Was he not allowed to be nice to anyone but her? I wasn't even his age! I wasn't trying to steal her crush.

She planted her hands on her hips and waited for an answer I didn't have.

Ah, screw it. I didn't have to stand here and take this. No other camper had talked about their "goal" this summer, so I didn't have to make one, either.

I walked away. She called after me, and I burst into a run. What could I have said to change her mind, anyway? I didn't want Tyler, and she obviously did. How could he be so oblivious? He needed to tell her he was engaged. I didn't know why he didn't tell everyone. Did he want all this attention?

I stopped running. She wasn't chasing me.

Tyler wanting attention didn't fit; our personalities were more similar than anyone else here, and that kind of spotlight was a nightmare to both of us. Is that why Suzie was mad? I shuddered. I didn't want to get in the middle of it, and Suzie shouldn't try to put me there. I'd already found myself in the middle of things I didn't want to be.

From out of nowhere, Lucas slung an arm around my shoulder. "My brother likes you."

When he said stupid crap like that, I couldn't register all the parts of him that touched me. First Suzie, and now Lucas was grilling me about Tyler. I didn't like him. He didn't like me. Why couldn't a girl and a guy be friends without people making stupid assumptions? I pulled away.

"Hey, wait." His arm tightened around me.

I pushed against him, and he released me.

"Sorry. I just meant that he thinks you're interesting, for a camper. I can relate, though for me…"

A couple of girls jogged past us on the trail, laughing. Lucas paused until they were out of earshot again. "Just don't be in that camp. He's taken, remember?" A sad note entered his voice. Poor guy. He must be compared to Tyler all the time.

"We're all in the same camp, silly."

It took him a minute to register what I said, but when he did, he threw his head back and laughed as we walked to lunch. I loved that about him, how his eyes crinkled shut with complete confidence that the world would wait for him. He used his whole body for every emotion. There was something freeing in that. Something special. We were so opposite.

As soon as we parted ways, I sought out Emma. She'd been quiet during the list activity, and we'd both been ignoring her blowup after the human knot thing. I didn't know what her issue with Lucas was, but I wanted to make sure she wasn't still mad at me. So, of course, when I got back to the cottage, I couldn't find her.

"Let's go to the lake! We went to all that trouble of taking that test and we never go!" Paige whined as soon as I entered.

I folded my arms. She watched my water test from hell. Did it have to be swimming?

"Please, Andy."

I didn't know why she needed me there, but I scrounged around for my bathing suit in my bag anyway. Maybe Emma would pop up on the way there.

"Yes!" she squealed when my blue one piece emerged. "This is going to be so fun! Just wait."

Even though I tried to draw it out, her excitement had us changing at lightning speed. I wrapped my Little Mermaid towel around my hips and slipped on my flip flops instead of my tennis shoes. Paige wore yet another skimpy bikini—this time black.

"I'm too tall for most one pieces," she confessed as our flip flops slapped against the hard dirt path to the lake. "And tankinis look weird on my body."

I eyed her long torso. That made sense. I felt bad for judging her earlier.

When we broke through the trees, the swimming scene assaulted us from every angle. Girls laid on colorful towels while guys flirted with them. A bunch of people swam in the shallow water behind the rope, and a few guys tried to push each other off the floating dock. The huge slip 'n slide cascaded down a hill with a line a mile long.

My gaze caught on the screaming girl rocketing down the plastic into shallow water.

I expected Paige to lay out her towel and join the girls baking in the sun. I could do that. Close my eyes and enjoy the warmth. It sounded like heaven.

She didn't.

Paige ditched her shoes and threw down her towel, then walked toward the water lapping at the crunchy sand. I followed, even though it was the last thing I wanted to do. The most I could hope was that we'd stay in the shallow end and talk.

"Come on, Andy!" She dove under the rope.

A chill swept through me that had nothing to do with the cold temperature of the water. "I'm coming."

She didn't hear me, of course. Halfway to the floating dock, her long arms ate up the distance with powerful strokes.

Don't be a wuss.

I ducked under the rope.

25

I LIKE A CHALLENGE

Channeling my inner Ariel lasted about ten seconds before I slowed, and the cold, murky water lapped at my mouth and nose. Swimming was hard work. By the time I got to the dock, I was dying to get my hands on the ladder. I wasn't the only one.

Lucas's wet head surfaced next to me as I treaded water, waiting in line. "Hey."

Was he following me? The greenish water lapped at my face. "Hey," I puffed. Only one more person in front of me and I could hang on to something.

"You okay?"

"I'm fine." I'd rather die than ask him for help. The ladder opened up and I grabbed it, heaving myself out of the water and onto the dock fast, so Lucas didn't have a face full of my butt for more than a split second.

The red dock bobbed back and forth with the weight of the other swimmers, but I could handle that better than I could handle swimming where I couldn't touch the bottom. I plopped on the end closest to the beach and swung my legs over the side. I'd search for Paige when I wasn't gasping for air.

Lucas followed. He shook his hair out like a dog, spraying me.

"Hey!" I laughed.

He gave me a wolfish grin. "You're already wet." The sun glinted off his bright smile, and I blinked.

I had finally caught my breath, and he had to steal it away again like that.

Lucas leaned back on his arms and smirked at something behind me.

I followed his line of sight. Paige and Marshall circled each other and laughed on the other side of the dock, trying to push each other into the water. *So that's why she wanted to come out here.*

The way they shoved each other, their hands lingering on each other's bodies, made it feel like maybe I shouldn't be watching. She found ways to touch his chest, and he brushed against her thighs countless times as she squealed and ducked out of the way.

Nervousness swirled inside me as I watched Lucas out of the corner of my eye. Today his shorts were white, and they rode low on his hips; muscles flexed in his arms as he shifted beside me.

I wanted to run my fingers through the damp hair that framed his cheekbones. But when he looked up, I hugged my knees, shyness stealing any words I might've said.

He scooted closer to me, oblivious to the direction my thoughts had taken. "Who do you think is going to win?"

Huh? Oh, Paige and Marshall. I turned my attention to them. Marshall had strength on his side, but Paige stood taller. She stretched to reach him but clawed the air which produced a laugh of genuine delight from him. "Oh, Paige definitely," I said even though anyone could see Marshall planned to dump her off the dock.

"I don't know," Lucas sing-songed.

Seconds later, Paige squawked, and they both tumbled into the water. Lucas and I laughed.

"If it were us, I'd win," Lucas said.

I rolled my eyes. "Probably."

He sprang to his feet. "Wanna see?"

I narrowed my eyes. "Don't you dare."

"I like a challenge."

Before I could do anything, he threw me over his shoulder like I weighed nothing. *Holy hell, how is he this strong?*

"Put me down!" I shrieked. I beat my fists against his back. If he threw me in the water, I would drown. I should've worn the stupid lifejacket like I promised. "I'm not kidding!"

"Okay, okay." He squatted and put me back on my feet.

My heart hammered so hard it flooded my ears and no words came through.

He squinted at me with concern, then raised his hands in front of him, palms out like he did at the wall.

I wasn't having it. We wouldn't be in a situation where I was panicking if he didn't act like such a jerk in the first place.

He ran a hand through his hair. "Look, Andy, I'm sor—"

I didn't even think—I pushed him in the lake. I caught him so off-guard that he yelped before landing with a splat on his side.

I sank to my knees and peered over the edge. *Oh no. Why did I do that?*

"Yeah, Andy! You show 'em!" Paige yelled from the water.

Lucas surfaced, sputtering. His hair was plastered to his head, and he finally looked less than perfect for once. I was the worst person ever. A giggle escaped me.

Lucas turned to me, effortlessly treading water. "She's not even sorry!" he teased.

I threw my hands in the air and kept laughing.

He swam around to the side of the dock to climb the ladder, but I knew what came next. He'd want to throw me in to get back at me. I couldn't let that happen. I'd rather suck at swimming on my own terms. When he'd climbed halfway up the ladder, I slid over the edge of the dock and sank into the water.

"Coward!" he called, but I was already doggy paddling for the beach.

"Yep!" I yelled back. My voice rippled over the water, louder than I intended. Something about trying not to drown in front of a cute, athletic guy must've gotten to me.

When I reached the shore, he'd already passed me and was

waiting with my stupid Disney towel. He wrapped it around my shoulders like I was a toddler. I frowned. I wasn't helpless.

I shrugged it off and laid it on the sand about twenty yards away from the nearest group of campers. I was half in the grass, but I didn't care.

When I stretched out, I closed my eyes against the bright sky and wiggled my body to make an Andy-shaped indent in the sand. The goosebumps that peppered my skin disappeared as the beads of water that clung to me sacrificed themselves to the sun.

Lucas flopped down next to me, not even caring that he didn't have a towel or that sand clung to every inch of his skin. "You yelled at me."

If my eyes weren't closed, I would've rolled them. "I yelled *to* you." There was a difference.

"I liked it." Of course, he did. Such a weirdo.

I tried to concentrate on the warmth seeping into my skin and the slight breeze that dried my exhausted arms.

"You're always surprising me."

Really? Huh. Maybe I wasn't exactly consistent from his point of view. I hung out with an athletic Amazon, ticked off Suzie, freaked out over heights and water, pushed him in the lake, and yelled at him. None of it tracked with the withdrawn bookworm I was. This whole place threw me off balance.

"Are you asleep?" he stage-whispered.

Should I pretend to be? I shook my head slowly.

He scooted closer to me until his arm pressed against mine. "Is this okay?"

I nodded. I didn't care who saw us here together. The heat radiating through Lucas's arm into mine was worth it. The way he shifted his head to lean on my shoulder was worth it. I could die happy right now.

And it wasn't like my books. I didn't compare him in my head to some hero sweeping me off my feet. He was a nice guy I liked, and I wanted to be in this moment where I didn't feel pressured to say or do anything significant. I could just be me.

I didn't know how long we laid on the outskirts of the beach basking in the sun, not talking, but our free time came to an end. Dana's voice blared through the speaker, and we all gathered our things and headed to lunch.

At one point, Lucas looked like he wanted to say something, but he shook his head and kept walking. I bit back a smile, remembering how his body had splashed into the lake earlier. *It's not funny!* It was totally funny.

We separated to get dressed, and when I got back to the cafeteria, I had to wait for a million years in line. Once I reached the front, I was pleasantly surprised by the sub-making station. Now, this I could get into. I piled the veggies high and put on way too much cheese, grabbing some sour cream and cheddar chips on the way to my seat. I'd taken a huge bite before Lucas slid into the seat in front of me.

I froze for a second before I resumed chewing. I hated being so close to people, even my parents. When I had to practice my handshakes in Careers class and got paired with a guy, my heart threatened to flatline. But this wasn't like that. Lucas had been covering for me since I got here. And I'd never forget that moment at the wall as long as I lived. We had a connection.

A comfortable silence descended as we ate together.

It was only when we got up to leave that I realized Paige and Emma never sat with us. They must've been busy.

26

IT WASN'T A RACE

"Okay, campers!" Suzie screeched the second we got back to the cottage.

It was like doomsday every time she used that phrase because right after it, she'd announce the next stupid activity and expect everyone to be excited about it.

"It's time for the next awesome leadership activity! I know you've been enjoying them so far, but you're *really* going to like this one." She gave an exaggerated wink. *Wait. That meant…*

"We're going to do this with our male counterparts, Beavers, so pair on up so we can get started."

Pair? I looked to Paige helplessly, but she was already out the door. I sighed and followed her to where the Hippo cottage stood outside waiting for us. How did they get here so fast? Even more alarming was how fast everyone broke off into pairs. My hands tingled as Marshall sidled up next to Paige. I craned my neck and looked for Emma.

"Good thing I've forgiven you," Lucas said as he walked toward me. "Or this might be awkward."

I rolled my eyes. Like it was so hard to get pushed off a dock when you had the skills of a gold medal swimmer. I raised my eyebrows, but he didn't say any more. Unlike me, he focused his attention on the instructions Tyler gave the group.

"...so choose who the person with the blindfold will be and who will give directions. We'll start once you've got it sorted out."

I peeked between Lucas and Paige and held back a groan when the course came into view. A grove of trees spanned the area in front of us, and pieces of red tape were strung between their wide trunks like trip wires. Stumps littered the ground. I'd seen this before on reality television. Minefield. One of us would have to be all yelly and tell the other one to go right or left or whatever to get through an obstacle course.

"What do you want to be?" Lucas asked like I had a choice. I couldn't yell for crap, so it looked like I'd have to trust him not to kill me.

"Blindfolded."

He frowned. "What?"

I snatched the red bandana from his hand with a scowl. I wasn't talking *that* quietly.

"Oh, okay." He smiled. "Don't worry. I'll be with you every step of the way."

No, he wouldn't. He'd be yelling at me every step of the way.

"Now remember," Suzie chirped as I struggled to tie the bandana around my eyes. "You can be next to your partner, but don't touch them unless they look like they're about to fall. This is a trust exercise. It's also an exercise in giving clear, concise directions. Learn how to be the kind of leader who knows how to follow. Don't peek!" She giggled.

Lucas brushed my hands away when the bandana came undone and tied it snugly around my eyes. He pushed the folds into layers until it blacked out everything.

"Good?" he asked.

If good meant helpless, then yes. I should've chosen to be his voice if partners could walk with each other the whole way—too late now.

I nodded.

"Okay partners," Tyler shouted, "the goal is to get them around —that—and back to your starting positions. It isn't a race. It's about finishing. Good luck! And go!"

"Okay, walk ten steps forward and then stop." Lucas's hot breath on my neck made my heartbeat triple. This was such a bad idea. A very sexy, very bad idea.

I stumbled forward ten steps.

"Okay fine, more like twelve."

I shuffled forward another two.

"Quarter turn to your left and walk fi—six steps."

I pivoted and with a little more confidence picked through the grass another six steps. I hadn't fallen over yet. A girl to my right squealed and there was a crash in the underbrush. That wasn't concerning at all.

"Don't worry." Lucas's breath tickled my ear. "I won't let you fall, Andy." Goosebumps broke out over my arms, and he hadn't even touched me. How pathetic.

"Get on your knees."

"What?" I squawked.

"You need to crawl under the tape," he explained.

"Oh." No doubt my face matched the stupid bandana. I got on my hands and knees in the wet grass and waited for his next direction.

"Crawl forward until I tell you to stop."

This time a guy cursed somewhere in front of us.

"Camper Andrew! Language!" Suzie admonished.

"I stubbed my fu—my toe!" he called back.

My shoulders shook with laughter as I inched forward over the moss and sticks.

"Okay stop. Now get on your belly."

"This is ridiculous," I muttered.

"You're going to have to army crawl for the next part."

Did he take me down the worst possible path or what? I didn't hear anyone else thrashing around on the ground.

"Trust me," Lucas said when I didn't move.

Okay then, Mr. Cranky Pants. I army crawled, the tape above me grazing my sweatshirt as I passed through.

"Okay, now stand up."

I did. My jeans and front felt wet and dirty.

"Now it's going to sound weird—"

This whole thing was weird.

"—but you're going to want to walk in a spiral. Here, let me…"

And then he was right over my shoulder again, muttering sexy little rights and lefts and forwards and stops in my ear. With my timid steps, it took us forever to get through the obstacle course, but Lucas's voice stayed level, and he never got upset or impatient.

I couldn't say as much for Paige and Marshall. Her sharp voice pierced the air. "No! Your other left! You don't know right from left?"

"I'm trying!" he yelled back.

The low tones of Tyler mediating almost pushed me over the edge, but I managed to tone myself down to just a giggle.

"Think that's funny, do ya?" Lucas laughed too.

I nodded. "Don't tell Paige."

"I won't."

Once we stopped spiraling, I expected the whole thing to be over, but nope. Torture didn't have time limits.

"Okay, now raise your right foot," Lucas said. "We're going to take four big steps, and I want you to do it sideways."

Shakily, I did as he asked, listening for the voices of everyone else as they tried to figure it out, but I heard nothing. Shouldn't we all kind of be on top of each other?

I stepped over four times.

"Reach out your left hand."

I reached out my right and it met the solid wall of his chest. Shocked, I yanked my hand back. "Oh! I'm so—" In my embarrassment, I lost my balance and pitched forward. I braced myself for impact, but it didn't come.

Like at the climbing wall, Lucas's strong arms hugged me tight. He pulled me back up. "I told you I wouldn't let you get hurt," he murmured.

I nodded. Was I breathing? I might not be breathing.

He steadied me before letting go. "You should fall more often, Andy."

My heart rate skyrocketed. Okay, he was definitely flirting with me! "What now?"

After a pause, he said, "Reach out your left hand."

I did as he asked, and my fingers scraped against the rough bark of a tree.

Lucas pulled my bandana from my eyes, and the sun momentarily blinded me. An imposing red X marked the tree as the end. Did we win? I looked back at the course in disbelief. Several different colored paths lay behind us. Blue, green, yellow, orange, pink, and red. The blue looked the easiest, but also the longest. The red was the shortest, but it was treacherous—the one Lucas had chosen.

"And we have a winner!" Suzie proclaimed. She sprang forward and pinned another giant monstrosity to Lucas's chest, this time pink and black.

"I thought you said this wasn't a race!" a girl complained.

"Why'd you do the most difficult course?" Suzie asked Lucas.

"Because I knew she trusted me." Lucas stared at me. "Right, Andy?"

Oh, boy. I was such a goner. "Right."

Tyler cleared his throat.

Lucas broke eye contact with me. "Let's watch the rest of them suffer."

I followed him to the side of a grassy hill; we sat down and watched the others as they yelled at each other. No one was angrier than Emma, who screamed from the easiest course. "You jerk, I just ran into a tree!"

"Well, you didn't really do what I—"

She pointed to the tree. "Finish that sentence. I dare you."

"Okay, go right."

"For how long? Do I just go right until I fall off the face of the planet?"

It was immature and horrible of me, but I burst out laughing.

Lucas did too, wrapping one arm around my shoulder as he pointed to a guy and girl sitting on the stumps. The guy had taken off his white shirt and was waving it around with a stick.

"Leaders don't give up, Camper Noah!" Suzie called.

"This one does!" he yelled back.

Lucas's arm sat heavy on my shoulders, but I didn't brush it off. The goosebumps from earlier returned, even though his heat seeped through our clothes, melding us together with a force stronger than the sun.

"If I ask you to hang out with me, are you going to stand me up again?" he whispered, a thread of uncertainty in his voice. I picked up a piece of grass and twirled it between my fingers. Without my phone, I had nothing to hide behind. His arm went slack, and I shrugged out from under it while I considered his question. Guilt over standing him up still plagued me, but this time he gave me an out when he asked. He wasn't trying to pressure me, and he didn't push me to say anything. He just waited.

I could appreciate that. Lucas was the kind of person to dive headfirst into everything. I liked to dip my toe in the water, get used to the temperature before floating. I admired his ability to adapt to my style. He'd backed way off, been so respectful, and now… now it was easy to like him back.

"I won't stand you up." I wanted to be brave enough to deserve someone like Lucas.

"I'll take what I can get," he said. "And just so you don't change your mind, we're doing it now. Like right now. Let's go play horseshoes. It'll be like Horse, only this time you'll have an advantage."

"Yeah?"

"Yep. I've never played horseshoes."

I had with my dad many times. I wasn't terrible.

Suzie and Tyler struggled to break up a fight below us in the obstacle course—Emma reached for the throat of her partner while he held her off with one beefy arm. As soon as Tyler had it handled, Suzie's frazzled voice rose above everyone else's. "That was… thank you all for doing your best."

Tyler laughed from where he blocked his camper from Emma's angry scowl. "That's it for tonight. Good work, everyone."

The campers fled like rats from a sinking ship. Before long, Lucas and I sat alone on the hill, his wide blue eyes watching me like there was nothing else he'd rather do.

27

HERE WE GO

Deodorant.

I couldn't hang out with Lucas without at least fixing my hair, changing my dirty wet clothes, and putting more deodorant on. "Give me ten minutes?"

"Sounds good. I'll get us some water."

I wanted to skip all the way to the cottage, which was ridiculous. I wasn't a skipper. I even rolled my eyes during that requirement in elementary gym class. So, I walked faster than normal instead.

But as soon as I got to the cottage, Emma and Paige descended like vultures. I braced myself for all the questions. Did I like Lucas? Were we going out? Had we kissed?

It wasn't about that.

"Andy, there's an egg relay in five minutes. I love egg relays! You have to be on our team. Come on!" I'd never seen Emma more excited. That was a switch. In the last activity, she'd been about to maim a dude.

Could I do both? Throw some eggs and run over to Lucas after? No. I wouldn't put myself through that kind of stress. I was too nervous already. Leading a double life, even for an hour, would exhaust me past the point of caring about the rest of camp.

"Next time? I'm… doing something else." I didn't want to tell them about Lucas yet. They acted odd around him anyway. Was it jealousy? Distrust? Unless they cared to tell me, it shouldn't be my problem.

"Something else? Or *someone* else?" Emma asked.

"Ew, don't say that kind of stuff." Paige shoved her.

Too late. My body had turned a shade of rather-be-dead red.

"I'm going to the horseshoe pits." I should invite them along to be nice, but I didn't want to. I wanted to be with Lucas… alone.

They exchanged a look. "Okay, we'll uh, ask Marshall," Paige said.

I smiled at her gratefully. "Cool. I know you like him. You'll get to talk to him more."

From the look on Emma's face, I'd said the wrong thing. "See ya, Andy," she said, her tone barely civil.

"See ya." Did everything tick this girl off?

I grabbed a teal tank top from my bag and retreated to the bathroom. Once I'd changed and washed my face, I looked in the mirror and sighed. My hair stuck out everywhere. I couldn't even force it into a ponytail. It frizzed out at the ends so much that a brush would make it worse. I twisted it up and snapped the hairband in place. A messy bun beat looking like I'd grabbed a telephone wire. Before I left the room, I remembered deodorant and applied some.

I tried to see myself the way a guy would. The sun had left my cheeks a rosy pink; My thin arms hung limp against my sides. I glanced down at my complete lack of chest and wide hips. I wasn't even attracted to myself.

Stop it, I could hear my mother saying. *You're a beautiful girl inside and out. The sooner you realize that, the sooner everyone will see it shining out of you.* It was such a Mom thing to say. Maybe she was right. Maybe she was wrong. Whatever she was, I grabbed my sunglasses on the way out. Life was safer when people couldn't see my eyes.

To my relief, when I returned to the main room, Paige and Emma were gone. It might've been fun to do the egg thing, but they asked me after Lucas did. I couldn't stand him up twice. I didn't want to.

This whole camp stapled on a smile and pretended to be excited about every little thing, but Lucas wasn't like that. Even with his bigger-than-life personality, he still seemed calm. He excelled at reading people. He adapted as soon as he figured me out. So that meant he was either hyper-focused on converting me to the ways of their leadership cult, a psychopath, or maybe... just maybe, he liked me.

And I shouldn't care about that when Mom forced me to come here. I should be focused on trying to go home, but I wasn't. Just because I was doing something she wanted me to didn't mean she was right.

Maybe I liked him back.

It was that maybe that made me walk faster on the way to the horseshoe pits, that made me return his wide smile when I crested the hill. If he was a psycho, I was a goner. I was already in too deep.

"Saved us a spot," he said as he handed me two red horseshoes.

I looked down at the other four empty pits. "My hero," I deadpanned. I couldn't stop smiling. He was like glitter in a first-grade classroom. His enthusiasm got all over me.

"So there's a sign over there. Pretty basic rules." He pointed to a wooden post with a laminated list of rules and a small chalkboard to keep score. "Prepare to be crushed."

Unlikely. "Oh, please."

"Ooh, she trash talks. Well, prepare to be amazed." He rolled up the sleeves of his Henley, and I tried hard not to stare at his forearms, but it was a losing battle. Before this moment, I didn't know a guy rolling up his sleeves was even a thing I could be attracted to.

His first throw was too high, but the horseshoe rolled close to the post.

He stuck his tongue out at me.

I laughed.

His second throw was too low and hard, and he missed by a mile. The horseshoe rolled almost all the way up the hill behind the post.

"Go ahead," he said in a gallant voice. *Uh huh.* If he'd been a real gentleman, he would've let me go first.

I took my stance, pointing the ends of the horseshoe in front of me instead of holding one of the arms the way he did. I took a couple practice swings, then let the horseshoe fly. As it left my fingertips, I could already tell it wouldn't be my best throw, but I was still warming up.

It turned end over end too many times, hitting the ground in front of the sand and rolling up close to the post.

He groaned. "Here we go."

I lined up my next shot. This time when the horseshoe left my grip, I could feel it was going to be a ringer. It turned in the air once and perfectly circled the post without ever nicking it. My throws weren't powerful like some players, but accuracy was the name of the game, not muscle. That's why I was good at it.

I smirked.

Lucas whistled. "I have a feeling that by the end of the day we'll be even."

I snorted. He wasn't even going to touch me in this. Horseshoes took more finesse than putting a ball in a net.

We collected our horseshoes, and I marked my score on the chalkboard behind us. Then we reset for another round. The sun shone down with just the right amount of warmth and the breeze tugged at my shirt. For a second, everything was perfect. I was in my element in horseshoes, and somehow flirting with a boy I liked. I smiled.

Then, just for fun, right as the horseshoe left his hand, I leaned over and stage-whispered, "Don't screw up."

His throw went wild and ended up at the pit nearest ours. "What the heck?" He turned to me with narrowed eyes. "You can't do that."

"Do what?" Secretly, I was happy that one sentence from me could bring the uber-confident Lucas to total distraction.

Now he knew how I always felt around him.

I played nice on his second throw, and he ended up tinging the post. Beginner's luck. It wasn't like it was a ringer.

He pumped his fist into the air. "Yes!"

My mouth twitched. He was so… I couldn't find the word. Passionate? Funny? Kind?

I set up for my throw, but his breath tickled the back of my neck just as I was about to release the horseshoe. I flinched.

"Who's distracting who now?" he taunted.

Shivers skittered down my spine, and the horseshoe dropped several feet short of the post.

He didn't move away, and neither did I. It was like the blindfold challenge, only different. He didn't need to be this close. He wasn't telling me what to do. It was almost like he was waiting for me to freak out or something. But I stayed put. I wanted to.

"Andy," he choked out. His hands were rough against my arms as they slid down to my hands. I dropped the other horseshoe and our fingers intertwined. He laid his head on my shoulder.

It was an interesting position to be in. His body almost but not quite pressing against mine. No pressure to kiss. Maybe to hug. It was so intimate, almost protective. Like a knight from one of my books saying goodbye to his lady before a big battle. I wasn't immune to how this felt. Who could be?

I closed my eyes and reveled in the fact that a few weeks ago, I was afraid to shut my locker too loudly. Now I didn't care that the horseshoe had fallen on a guy's foot because he was holding me in a way I never knew I needed. The faint scent of his woodsy soap filled my nose, and I let go, let myself exist without the self-consciousness that plagued me since birth.

"Lucas?"

"Yeah?"

"This won't stop me from kicking your butt."

He laughed and it rumbled through both of us before he released me. "Do your worst."

I did. When we left the horseshoe pit, he hung his head. "I should've made you play Horse again. Now I look like a wimp."

"Ah yes. The wimps who overthrow horseshoes. I've heard of those."

"Shut up."

"Make me." I laughed.

He arched an eyebrow. "You're different."

"I'm not."

Of course, I was. This was nerve-wracking and easy at the same time. I was different because he was different to me than any guy had ever been. Guys I grew up with saw all my struggles, all my awkward moments. Who'd want to date the girl who peed her pants rather than tell her kindergarten teacher she had to go? Or the girl who tried to monitor how much other kids ate so she could eat the same amount during lunch? No one. That was completely neurotic.

After we said goodbye, I floated back to my cottage in a cloud of confidence. Lucas did that to me. When I pushed through the door, a horrible yet hilarious sight greeted me. Paige and Emma were covered in egg and yelling at each other.

"You didn't have to throw it at me!" Paige screeched. She tried to pull the yoke out of her hair with one of those crappy brown paper towels that lived in every public restroom.

"You ruined my favorite top!" Emma glared at her, her chest sopping wet.

"Why would you wear your best shirt to an egg competition?" Paige yelled. She had a point.

"I didn't think you'd trip into me and send the egg flying. How do you even do that? It's a relay, for God's sake."

"It wasn't my fault. Marshall was messing around with—"

Then they saw me and clammed up. I walked to the bathroom and came back out with more soap-covered paper towels. They didn't take them from my hands. I set them down on the single table in the corner.

"This never would've happened if Andy was there," Emma said to Paige like I wasn't even in the room.

Paige crossed her arms. "Stop it."

"You know what's happening, and you don't say anything!"

Paige gave her a look, but what it meant, I had no idea.

"Ookay then. I'm sorry I already had plans." I mean, I wasn't really sorry, but it felt like the right thing to say.

Paige threw the soiled paper towel into the trash and grabbed one of the new ones I'd brought. "It isn't your fault. We know how—"

Emma stepped on her foot.

"We know how camp romances can be."

"You guys are being weird."

"I know," Emma said. "Just forget it." She pulled her shirt off and wadded it into a ball. She left and the sound of water running drifted out of the bathroom. When she came back, she shrugged. "It will probably soak out."

For a long moment, none of us spoke. Silence was my go-to, but both Paige and Emma looked uncomfortable. I should do something, ask them to play chess or whatever. Except I didn't know how to play chess, so maybe not that. I bent down and pulled out some of my books. "Wanna read?"

Paige looked at Emma. Emma looked at Paige.

"We're good," they said in unison.

Whatever. They could suit themselves. I climbed into my bunk and pulled the bookmark out of my favorite book. The sun was sinking fast, and orange light spilled through the slats of the dusty windows.

I heard them leave, and when they called goodbye, I waved without looking up. Then I snuggled into my sleeping bag. The guy in the book had morphed. He no longer had long, dark hair and tanned skin. Now every time I imagined him kissing the heroine, I saw blue eyes and felt a swimmer's toned body beneath her fingertips.

It didn't bother me half as much as it should have.

Something heavy sat on my nose. I opened my eyes. I fell asleep with my book on my face.

It wasn't the first time this had happened, so I couldn't be that surprised. Had anyone noticed?

As soon as I peered over the edge of the bed, Emma exploded in laughter. "Oh my God, I wish I still had my phone. It was totally gram-worthy. There was a naked lady on your head, Andy!"

"She's not naked." I flipped the cover over to make sure. Okay, fine, her dress was dangerously close to a wardrobe malfunction. So what?

"Grumpy, aren't you?" Paige teased. "Get up so we can grab dinner. I'm starving."

I groaned. My eyelids might as well have been filled with sand. Naps were kind of the devil. Food would make this better. I needed a muffin or something. Except Lucas would be at the cafeteria. My heart pounded twelve decibels louder. How could I be excited and want to puke at the same time?

What I needed more than ever was a cup of coffee. A caramel macchiato. A cappuccino. Heck, I'd even drink it black.

Emma pulled on a baseball tee while Paige ran to the bathroom. Then we all walked to the cafeteria together.

"So how was hanging out with Lucas?" Emma said. She appeared interested, but I heard a bite in her voice I couldn't figure out.

I ignored it. "Good. We played horseshoes. It was no big deal."

"Everything with Lucas is a big deal. Like, all caps BIG DEAL."

I shrugged. They didn't need to know every detail.

"Do you like him?" Emma pestered.

"I don't know," I lied.

Paige and Emma stared at each other above my head. That was the problem with hanging out with giants.

"Let's eat," Paige said. We entered the cafeteria, and the noise of a hundred "leaders" talking over each other drowned out my thoughts.

Coffee would make it easier to figure out Paige and Emma's cryptic comments and to think about Lucas. I needed the clarity it provided. No coffee arrived for me, though. I couldn't handle that. It was either Lucas or Tyler getting it for me, and I didn't want to be ungrateful, but they couldn't cut me off like this. I could deal with being nervous or happy or whatever if it came with coffee.

"I don't know how you guys do it," I muttered.

Emma swallowed a mouthful of food. "Do what?"

"Exist without coffee." I stabbed my salad with my plastic fork. "I can't live like this."

"You have an addiction."

I glared at her.

She rolled her eyes. "It's not like you don't know where the coffee is."

My eyes drifted to the unmarked door that had to be the staff lounge.

"How much do you want some?" she teased.

"I'd kill for it." No joke.

She took a sip of her water. "Then go get some."

Paige frowned. "I don't..."

"Come on. She's not going to get in trouble. It'd be like kicking a puppy." She rolled her eyes.

I couldn't even be offended because that's how everyone here saw me: a Victim. Quiet wasn't allowed here. Shy was a swearword. Who gave a crap about any of that if I could get some coffee? Desperate times called for desperate measures. Coffee measures.

I pushed up from the table.

28

THE GREAT COFFEE CAPER

Paige reached out a hand like she wanted to yank me back down. "Don't do it," she said. "You'll get in trouble."

So what? What would happen if I got in trouble? I'd get kicked out? I'd been trying to go home since this started. The only thing keeping me here besides a lack of transportation was…

"Don't do what?" a voice behind me said. *Lucas.*

Emma and Paige fell silent as he slid his tray next to mine on the table. I couldn't deal with their weirdness without coffee. I scanned Lucas's hands. No coffee. That settled it.

I strode over to the staff lounge door, trying to look nonchalant, like I belonged. Then I slipped in.

Inside, six metal folding chairs surrounded a beat-up circular table. The counter boasted a deep sink and wonder of all wonders, a coffee machine. It was a monstrous metal thing with a wicker basket perched next to it, full of packets of tea, hot cocoa, and the gross instant stuff. No Keurig cups or espresso settings here, but who cared? Not me. Three inches of coffee remained in the pot and a bunch of disposable cups sat next to the machine.

I skirted around the table and poured myself a coffee in record time. As I snapped the lid on, the door opened again.

I had nowhere to go, nowhere to hide in this sad excuse for a staff lounge. I stood there like a deer in headlights as one of the counselors I'd never met before walked in and sat down.

She nodded to me, then closed her eyes, pinching the bridge of her nose. She didn't even care I was here. Maybe she thought I was fetching coffee for one of the other staff members. How lucky was that? I snuck around the other side of the table to the door. Victory swept through me as I pushed it open. I'd done it. I'd gotten away with stealing twelve cents worth of coffee!

Then Suzie emerged from the shadows like a lion in a predator documentary. "Hi, Camper Andrea!"

I yelped and my coffee went flying. It splattered all over the floor in a big brown puddle. I didn't even have the presence of mind to be embarrassed. *My coffee.*

"Where did this come from?" Suzie cried.

I stared down at the splatter. "It's coffee."

"From the counselor's lounge?" she asked.

"Yeah." I should've taken a sip before opening the door. Who cared if someone else was in the lounge? That girl didn't give a flying rat's butt what I did.

"I think it would be a good idea for you to obey the rules and go sit with your friends."

I looked up. Suzie's face twitched, her smile cranked up to eleven. Did she use a bite splint at night to keep her from cracking her teeth? My mom had one of those. She said it was from years of fake smiling at her job. Suzie was totally a fake smiler.

"There wasn't a sign," I whispered. I grabbed some of those stupid brown paper towels from the bathroom and rushed back before someone could trip in my wasted coffee. I had the cup in the trash and the mess cleaned up in less than a minute. Then I rejoined Paige and Emma and Lucas at the table.

"That went... well," Paige tried.

Emma lost it. She laughed so hard that the next table looked over.

"Are you okay?" Paige asked me once Emma got ahold of herself.

"No," I said. "She spilled my coffee."

That sent Emma over the edge again, but I hadn't meant it to be funny. Two tables over, Tyler raised his eyebrows at Emma's loud-as-heck laughter, then looked straight at me. I rolled my eyes, and he winked as Suzie slung a leg over the bench in front of him. Did he know what I was up to the whole time?

I rummaged in my pockets, pulling out the packets of instant coffee I'd managed to snag. Four wouldn't be enough to last me the rest of camp, but it would have to do for now.

Lucas chuckled. "You little thief."

"So?" I grumbled as I emptied the package into my cup of water.

He slipped me a folded, lined paper and retreated to his table of Hippo boys. My face warmed, and I shoved it into the back pocket of my shorts before anyone else could see.

It may as well have burned a hole into my butt the whole meal. I couldn't concentrate on what anyone said. I could feel his stare across the cafeteria as I winced through my not-so-instant coffee.

When I couldn't take it anymore, I excused myself to go to the bathroom. The paper was warm and fragile in my hands, and it almost ripped when I unfolded it.

His handwriting was jagged, but readable. I expected something like *Do you like me? Circle Yes or No*. Or a long letter with lots of corny lines. But this wasn't a movie.

Canoes. 8pm.

Eight? That was right before curfew. We just hung out at horseshoes, but he wanted to see me again? Why did it make me ten times more nervous than earlier?

Because it's a date. A real one.

I shivered, even though the soggy air of the camp bathroom was anything but cold. When I rejoined the girls, my eyes fastened themselves to his table without my permission.

He raised his eyebrows in silent question.

I nodded slowly.

He smiled, then dug back into his food. How could anyone eat as much as he did?

"Earth to Andy!" Paige joked. "You okay?"

I stirred my instant coffee with one of the red mini-straws from the hot chocolate station. "Yeah, why?"

"Paige and I were going over to Cornhole to hang out and kick some major butt. You wanna come?" Emma asked. For the second time she'd invited me to do something today. I couldn't say no.

"Sure."

As soon as we finished our meal, Emma, Paige, and I tromped over to the field where the wooden boards and bean bags waited. *Good.* I could hang out and distract myself from the fact Lucas plus moonlight would equal disaster.

Due to the popularity of the game, we had to wait in line for forever. Paige talked about Marshall's back muscles or something, but my brain kept disconnecting from the conversation. *8pm. 8pm. 8pm.* I never needed a watch before because I used my phone. The only clocks here were in the buildings, so I couldn't even obsess over each minute that ticked closer to Lucas.

"Andy?" Paige held bean bags out to me. "We can play together and kick Emma's butt. Looks like one game is all we're getting anyway," she grumbled. More people had filed behind us.

"Bring it," Emma said and widened her stance, like she could run defense on us lobbing bean bags at a board with a cut out hole.

"Okay then." I threw the first bag. It reminded me of horseshoes, but lighter. The bag hit the board and stayed. It didn't go in the hole, but…

"That's points!" Paige squealed.

"One point," Emma corrected.

Paige stuck out her tongue.

Emma went next and she got one in the hole on the first try. She pretended to dust off her shoulders and I laughed. Paige got two on the board, and on it went. All three of us were so up and down that it became clear we were evenly matched. When we got to our third tie, the people behind us started to get antsy.

"Dude, there's like, not that much free time left, and I wanna play!" a girl said.

"Oh, cry me a river. I've been here for forty minutes!" the guy behind us whined.

"Shut up!" Emma yelled. "I've got this," she whispered like her entire life hinged on the last bean bag of the game. She weighed it in her hand, narrowing her eyes at the slanted brown board.

"Come on!" the forty-minute guy complained.

Emma ignored him and let the bag fly. It wasn't hard to predict its descent. It was all over.

Emma knew it, too. Her smile stretched wide. The bag hit the board and slid an inch, then collapsed into the darkness of the center of the board. It was in the cornhole.

"No!" Paige cried. She sank to her knees and raised both hands in the air. "Whyyy?"

"Get up, Drama Queen." Emma smirked as she reached down for Paige's hand.

We all laughed. It was enough to distract me for the next hour, before 8pm came back to haunt me. 8pm, when Lucas wanted to meet me in a romantic spot. 8pm, and I couldn't get out of it if I ever wanted him to talk to me again. I told him I wouldn't stand him up.

My whole body rested on the hands of the old analog clock that ticked in the cottage when we returned at seven.

The girls went to play tetherball around 7:30. I begged off since it was a two-person game. They left me in the cottage without much fuss. I waited a minute until they disappeared from sight, then ripped my clothes off to change into the sexiest outfit Mom packed—a form-fitting tank and my shortest shorts. If I was being honest, I didn't own a single sexy item in my whole wardrobe.

I rushed to the communal bathroom and pulled a brush through my hair. A slight crimp lingered where my ponytail holder had been. Maybe it would disappear if I kept running my hands through it.

I hesitated before putting make up on, my hand tapping the mascara tube on the corner of the sink. If I put it on, that meant I wanted to impress him. Oh, who was I kidding? I twisted open the darn thing and opened my eyes wide to apply it.

Ten minutes later I walked down to the waterfront and tried to look like I didn't care where I was going. I was early. Wasn't the rule to never be early? It showed desperation. Too late now, though. Dusk had settled into the sky, and it would be dark in less than half an hour. We could get in trouble for being late for lights out, but right now, I just didn't care, because it was Lucas.

When my feet hit the sand of the beach my stomach clenched. It was empty. Hadn't he said to meet him near the canoes? I hugged myself. That's what I got for getting to places early. I sat down on the beach. A breeze kicked up over the lake and the sand rose to bite at my ankles.

I pulled my knees in, not from the cold but out of habit. Look small, be small. Be safe. I rested my chin on my knees and stared at the dark water lapping at the dock.

"Hey." Lucas sat down beside me. "I wasn't sure you'd come."

29

JUST A VIBE

I pushed my hair behind my ears. "Why not?"

"Are you kidding?"

"Um, no?" I pushed my toes into the sand.

He chuckled.

"What?"

He held up his hands in surrender. "Nothing."

We sat in silence for a few minutes, staring at the lake. It rippled with the breeze as the sand around us shifted. White pines towered behind us, their shadows lengthening in the gathering dark.

"I love it down here," he whispered. "It's so calm."

I grinned. I'd been thinking the exact same thing.

"She smiles!" he said. "My mission is going well."

My grin grew wider. Of course, I remembered every comment he made, but the fact he remembered his promise meant something.

He turned to face me, his legs crossed. I mirrored his position. "Play a game with me, Andy."

The sky burned orange now, light splashing against the side of his face. Anticipation pulsed through me. I would've done just about anything with him at that moment. I nodded.

He bounced in his seat. Leaders were so pumped about the

games this place made us do. Lucas had Volunteer written all over him. "I ask a question and you have to answer it honestly. Then you get to ask one."

Okay, easy enough. It forced me keep my hands to myself. The temptation to lean over and smooth his hair that never quite looked brushed, consumed me. Would he'd be cool with that? I didn't want to assume anything. I'd never caught the attention of a guy, friend or otherwise. "Will you start?"

"Of course, and I'll be nice… this time," he said with a wink. "What's your favorite color?"

"Red."

"Really?" His eyebrows shot up.

I cocked my head to the side. "Really."

"But red is so…"

"Bold. Brave. Everything I'm not, right?" I picked out a stone from the sand. A black one.

"I wasn't going to say that."

I dropped the stone. "Well, that's why I like it." I turned and looked through the trees to the camp. The cottonwood had finished shedding.

"That's… interesting."

I returned my attention to Lucas. "Is that good or bad?"

"Interesting is always a good thing," he murmured.

My face warmed. "It's my turn."

"Open book over here." He grinned.

I could only think of to ask one thing in the moment, and it would ruin it.

"What's your relationship with your brother like?" They didn't talk much, even though Tyler was Lucas's counselor. Was that awkward? I didn't have any siblings, so I didn't know.

"Ouch," he said. "You really do want my brother, don't you?" His voice was light, but the muscles around his mouth tightened.

"No. Just curious since you're in the same cottage. You don't have to answer." I guessed some topics remained off limits, even to the stupid game. Why did I have to ask something that made him uncomfortable?

He expelled a gust of air through his teeth. "I'll answer." In the sand, he traced a slow spiral with his finger. "Tyler and I are cool most of the time, but I look like him. We're good at the same sports." He blew out a breath. "It would be great to be my own person, but I'm not going to do different stuff just to prove I'm not him."

He hadn't said anything monumental. Nothing I should have been able to relate to as an only child. When he spoke, I found him so compelling. I didn't know anyone else like that.

"You're not the same."

"Yeah, he's gentler. Not so in-your-face. He doesn't need to be loud because people already see him. Kinda like you."

He was wrong. People didn't see me. Lucas was the only one who noticed me. And just because Tyler and I were both quiet didn't mean I liked him.

"It's no big deal though." He laughed bitterly.

He didn't see himself clearly at all. "For what it's worth, I like you better."

Lucas snorted and stared at the sky.

I stared at the darkening clouds too, and it gave me enough courage to tell him the truth. "Being near Tyler is like looking in a mirror, kind of. Being near you is like a warm hug." Or maybe more, but he didn't need to know that. I was a moth to his flame. Would he warm me, or would I get burned?

Lucas was silent for a long moment. "Do you want a warm hug, Andy?"

I blew out a long breath. "I definitely like them." Mustering up all my courage, I glanced at him. He stared at me with an unreadable expression that made my palms sweat.

Change the subject. "Your turn. I have no siblings."

"Wait a minute, you can't answer. That's cheating, I think," he said.

I shrugged. They were made up rules, anyway.

"But I already knew that from the first day of camp," he reminded me.

"What?"

"That you're an only child. It makes a lot of sense."

I didn't know how to take that. "Why?"

He raised his eyebrows.

"What?" I crossed my arms.

"Nothing. Just a vibe."

Liar.

He went back to drawing spirals in the sand. "What's your favorite cereal?"

"Captain Crunch." I shrugged. "What's D&D?" I'd lost a lot of the facts he fed me before the speech, but that piece stuck in my brain.

He held his hand to his chest like I'd shot him in the heart. "You don't know what Dungeons and Dragons is?"

"Sounds… scary?" Dungeons did, anyway.

Lucas rolled his eyes. "It's only the best game ever created."

"Like a board game?"

"Blasphemy. It's so much more than a board game." He proceeded to go into incredible detail about the levels of characters and dice and made-up scenarios until my head spun with all the information. He scooted closer to me, gesturing with his arms as he described fights and dragons and battles. When he finished, he stared at me with anticipation.

It reminded me of a puppy. I hated to disappoint him.

"So, it's for fantasy fans who like to make up stories?"

"You… I…" He laughed. "Sure, Andy."

"What? You must read fantasy books if you like that stuff." I picked up a handful of sand and let it slip through my fingers.

"I don't think you *have* to."

I narrowed my eyes. "Admit that you read high fantasy."

"Gladly. I read high fantasy."

"I knew it." I stuck out my tongue.

"And what do you read, Ms. Know-It-All?"

I straightened my spine. "Historical books. Great works of literature."

"Interesting. I didn't know historical novels had naked people kissing on them."

My face flamed. "You've been spying on me."

"I saw you reading the other day." He grinned. "Admit you read trashy novels."

"Fine. I read trashy novels." I folded my arms. "They're wonderful, and I don't care."

"I love that about you."

My breath caught. He didn't say he loved me, but he might as well have. Even in the low, low light, I could see his face inching toward mine as he stared at my lips like he might…

"My turn," he said, sitting back.

I breathed easier.

On the game went. He'd ask me silly questions. Things that no one cared about. I asked him important things, stuff about his mom and his dog. He moved his hands, as if the words alone were not enough to express himself. His passion flowed into his arms and out his fingers.

When I had to answer, there was no pressure. Who cared what sports I didn't play or what my favorite candy was? It was so fun to be near him. Lucas was so hopeful, so open. His facial expressions varied from ecstatic to depressed to downright dramatic. How exhausting it must be to feel everything so deeply.

After a while, we lost steam on wanting to talk. Of course, he got to that point way after I hit a wall. We flopped back on the sand, shoulder to shoulder. My arm pressed against his, but I didn't move it.

Out here in the country, the night sky felt different than back home. I knew it was the same one, that we weren't far from where my mom and dad continued their lives with me shipped away like a returned shirt from Amazon that didn't fit right.

Unlike home, hundreds more stars shone overhead—some brighter than others. I guessed they must be farther away, or smaller. A teacher once told me they were all suns. I imagined all of them with their own worlds circling around them, finding them as necessary for life as we did.

Lucas was a sun. Even his arm warmed me.

Before I knew what I was doing, the words tumbled from my mouth. "Why do you like me?"

I wasn't brave or sporty or even overly kind. Did he have a white knight complex?

He shifted beside me. "You really want to know?"

No. But now I couldn't take it back. I'd never been able to laugh things off like other people did. So, I waited.

"Because you notice other people, Andy. You listen. Because other people's joy brings you joy, too. Because you're sarcastic, but you're not mean. You stand up for what's right. Because I'm always wondering what you're thinking, and I keep... I keep looking for your reaction when we're together, wondering if maybe you see me, too."

A cloud passed over the moon, and the beach went dark. Crickets chirped as my heart expanded and squished all the air out of my lungs. "I see you."

Lucas braced himself on one arm and looked down at me. "Andy?"

"Yeah?" I squeaked. He was close. Too close.

A sliver of moonlight escaped the cloud.

Lucas lowered his face until it was inches from mine. "You're beautiful, okay?"

I froze. He was going to kiss me, and I'd never kissed anyone before. Would he know? Would it ruin the moment? But I wanted to kiss him. For everything he said, but more for the reasons I liked him. Lucas was the reason people went to camps like this. He was smart, kind, and outgoing. He said I noticed people, but he was the noticer. I'd never felt so seen in my whole life, and for that, I wanted to kiss him. "Okay."

His lips met mine.

Like everything else this summer, he took the lead, and boy, did he know what he was doing. His mouth nudged mine, and it broke me out of my spell. I echoed his movements. I had no time to be embarrassed because all I could do was feel.

My heart hammered in my ears as my tongue touched his. When a soft moan escaped his lips, my confidence surged. I angled my head, taking what I wanted. Why did I ever think I would be terrible at kissing? With Lucas, it was as natural as breathing. What I wanted I took, and he gave. When I pulled, he fell onto his other arm beside my head, bracketing my body. And then, despite the cool breeze from the lake that pushed against us, our body heat merged.

I pulled at his shoulders and tried to get closer to him, though I knew that wasn't possible. We were already attached to each other's faces.

He threaded his hand in my hair, and I arched my back.

"God, Andy." He ripped his mouth from mine, looking down at me with an unreadable expression.

Crap, what did I do? "I um… I have to go," I whispered as I wiggled out from under him.

"No, you don't," he said roughly. "We can stop. We should stop," he muttered.

"Okay." I hugged my knees to my chest. I didn't want to be the girl who ran away from everything, and I liked the way he made me feel. I just… I didn't know what to do with myself and I didn't know I'd react like that, and—

"You're overthinking right now," he guessed. "Don't."

I traced an X in the sand. "It's not that easy."

"I know."

I believed him. But how did he know? I squeezed my eyes shut. "You know the rock wall?"

"Yeah," he said.

"How did you know to do that?"

"To hug you?"

My face heated. "Yeah."

"I don't know. I guess that's what I'd want if I was falling apart." He stared at me, his expression almost sad. "Andy, don't take this the wrong way, but I think people leave you alone too much."

Did they? Kids at school passed over me, but that could be my fault. Brynn definitely was my fault. And I couldn't deal with it. I'd rather read than make an effort to find any new friendships. It exhausted me. My parents didn't leave me alone, though. Mom didn't.

He slid his hand across the sand, and I let him interlock his fingers with mine. "You're shy and I get that, but panic attacks are kind of a big deal."

They were, but I didn't have them often. "I just don't like being forced to do things I'm not comfortable with."

And now he'd to tell me about how life started at the end of your comfort zone or some equally stupid thing this camp tried to brainwash everyone with.

He didn't.

"Did it… Did it feel like I forced you to um…" He gestured to the sand.

What? "No."

"Okay."

"Okay." I could have sat in the sand with him forever, but the darkness closed in around us, and the mosquitos were more than content to munch on our exposed skin, bug spray or no bug spray.

We stood.

"Can I hug you?" he asked. Even when he wanted to kiss me, he'd asked. Another thing he got about me. Asking prepared me and made me less nervous. I needed someone to get me like that.

I sank into his warm chest, and he rested his chin on my hair for a moment before letting go. "See you tomorrow?"

It's not like I had a choice, but now I had something to look forward to. "Yeah."

He looked back for just a second and gave me another megawatt smile before ducking behind the canoes to go to his cottage. I could die. I could die right now and that would be okay. I floated back to the cottage on a cloud of kisses and hugs and compliments until I caught a flash of yellow against dark wood.

The cottage light was on.

Suzie waited for me on the porch, swatting moths away from her face. "And where have you been?"

30

KILLING CURFEW

What did Suzie mean, where had I been? I was... It was... *crap*. I missed curfew—by a lot. I doubted Lucas would get in trouble because his brother was his leader, but me?

Suzie shook her head, disappointment radiating from her normally cheerful face. "This is grounds for dismissal."

My mouth dropped open. *Seriously?* I could have left to read outside after curfew on day one and not go through all this torture? I had finally warmed up to this Happy Sunshine coffee-less camp, and now I was going to get kicked out? She had to be kidding.

The Suzie Smile had disappeared, replaced by a cold glare. "We'll deal with this in the morning, Andrea. Go to bed, please."

Not Camper Andrea. Andrea. I was in deep crap. I tiptoed back into the cottage and climbed into my bed. The sleeping bag rustled as I curled onto my side, hugging myself. Lucas *kissed* me. I kissed him back. And now I might never see him again.

The next morning, Suzie waited outside the bathroom for me, then pointed to the front door. She'd never done anything wordlessly before. I couldn't do anything to make her let me stay. Someone like her couldn't understand someone like me even if she tried.

Paige and Emma watched with confused faces.

I waved them away. If I tried to explain, the truth would cost me more. I didn't want Lucas to get in trouble, too. The circles under my eyes and Suzie's psycho-killer face gave a lot away, anyway. I'd fill them in if I ever escaped her wrath.

It didn't stop Paige from mouthing, *What's going on?* at me as I followed in Suzie's wake out the front door of the cottage. All I could do was shrug and mouth back, *Later*. I hoped there'd be a later.

I had to own that I did something wrong because I did. I shouldn't have broken curfew. But how I broke it? I blew out a breath. It was worth it. The way Lucas touched me, the gentle way he cradled my face. First kisses weren't supposed to be like that. They were supposed to be knocking teeth, too much spit, and weirdness after, but we skipped that. A weight settled low in my stomach that had nothing to do with guilt. No matter what happened now, I would remember last night forever.

Halfway to the main building, Tyler caught up with us. His calm smile disappeared the second he saw Suzie's face, and he took his sunglasses off. "What's up?"

Suzie opened her mouth, then closed it.

"Suze, what's happening? What's wrong?" I'd never seen him so serious.

I was about to put us all out of our misery and tell him when Suzie spoke in a hushed voice. "Andrea missed curfew last night."

Tyler closed his eyes briefly. *I knew it.* He'd totally let Lucas off with a warning.

"You know the rules," she said.

My eyes welled with tears. I wanted to stay for Lucas, for the friends I might be making here, but every task Suzie forced me to do was so hard. It was like chewing rusty nails every time she made me talk. I didn't know how to feel anymore.

He glanced at me, then back at Suzie. With his eyes still trained on her, he said, "Please excuse us for a minute, Andy."

He led the way, and she followed him to the empty basketball court.

I couldn't help but witness the drama that played out.

He folded his arms and rocked back on his heels while she gestured in my direction. I wanted to eavesdrop, but they stood too far away. I did pick up bits and pieces like "flirting with her" and "too much" and "your brother."

By the accusatory glare on her face, I would've guessed she was yelling at him for flirting with *me*. What was *that* about? Apparently, she had enough wrath for both of us.

Oh, God. Did she think Tyler was into me? Sure, he was nice, but he was my mentor, someone to confide in. I never flirted with him. Suzie yelled herself out and stood there, chest heaving. Tyler muttered something and she shook her head. His expression gave nothing away as he continued talking and at one point glanced at me.

Her expression softened. She really did like this guy.

Then she spoke again. He nodded once and pushed his sunglasses back over his eyes. They walked back to me. She was clearly still angry, but I couldn't tell which one of us she was mad at or what thoughts Tyler hid behind his sunglasses.

"Andy, can I talk to you?" he asked.

I nodded at the ground. He was going to report me. I'd be kicked out and Lucas wouldn't be—it was so unfair.

I looked to Suzie for permission since I didn't need any more drama. She nodded.

Okay, then. I followed Tyler to one of the picnic tables and we sat across from each other.

"Andy…" He ran his hand through his hair. I'd never seen him uncomfortable until now.

"I'm sorry I broke curfew," I said. "It won't happen again. I swear."

He pressed his lips together but didn't say anything.

"And okay yes, I was with Lucas, but we weren't doing anything but talking." *Liar.* "We didn't look at the time and we should have."

Tyler sighed. "This isn't about Lucas."

I swallowed. We were really going to do this right now? I wasn't hallucinating Suzie's reaction? Tyler knew better than to think I liked him! He had to.

"There's nothing here. You know that, right?" He gestured to the air between us. "I'm a counselor and you're a camper."

"I know." *Kill me now.* I couldn't gauge if he believed me when all I saw was my desperation and panicked face in the reflection of his glasses.

"If I made you feel like there was more..."

My stomach twisted. "Stop." I couldn't let him continue.

He stopped.

"You stood up for me," I said. "I needed that. This camp is... it's hard for me. I'm bad at this."

He frowned. "Leadership isn't just one style, Andy."

He'd missed the point. "I never thought there was anything between us. I don't care what Suzie says." He had to believe me. I wanted *Lucas*. I'd always wanted Lucas.

He grimaced when I said Suzie's name.

It looked bad when I reached across him for coffee or when we sat too close together under the tree. I got it. "Just because someone is nice to me doesn't mean I like them. Lucas..." Heat spread through my body from the mere mention of his brother. I could still taste him on my lips, still feel the crush of his arms squeezing me at the rock wall. "I swear it won't happen again," I whispered.

"He's different with you," Tyler murmured. Then he frowned. "But I never said that."

I looked away, cheeks burning.

"Suzie won't tell the director, but Andy, it's time to stand up for yourself." Relief washed over me—*I wasn't going home.* He'd struck a deal with Suzie. It looked bad, him stepping in for me and only me during activities. He couldn't be my hero anymore. I swallowed. I wouldn't be sad about this. I had Lucas, and I had... did I still have Emma and Paige? Maybe I needed to figure it out myself. I nodded.

Just then, Lucas sprinted up to the table. "Are you okay?" He panted at me, bracing his hands on his knees. "I swear Tyler, if you—"

"If I what?" Tyler's tone darkened as he stood. "You need to stop this, Luke. It's too much for her."

Stop what? Lucas was too much for me? Just because I was shy, it meant I wasn't allowed to like someone? I frowned. What a bunch of crap. Tyler said he was going to back off, but this was the opposite of that.

The brothers fell silent, and Lucas balled his hands into fists, his chest rising and falling as he tried to catch his breath. Were they going to fight? No, that couldn't be it. I'd been reading too many books. After a tense minute, Lucas looked down at the ground. "I know."

Tyler stalked away. What the heck just happened?

"Are you okay?" Lucas repeated. He slid into the seat beside me.

No. "What was that?"

He ran his hand through his hair in the same way his brother had. Jeez, I was making everyone uncomfortable today. Part of me felt guilty, but the other part of me was glad they got a dose of how I felt for once. How I'd felt every single day during camp.

Take that, you overconfident leadership boys! I wanted to say. I didn't.

"Andy," he started. *Oh, God. Here we go.* He was going to say there was nothing between us, just like his brother. Only this time, I'd be crushed, because there *was* something between us and he knew it. "I'm so sorry about curfew. I should've known better."

Okay, not where I thought he was going with that.

"We both did it." Even though he should've gotten in trouble, too. Why was *I* the victim of Suzie's wrath? *Because she thinks I stole her crush.*

"If it makes you feel any better, Tyler bit my head off in front of all the guys last night."

I wanted to be above it and say it didn't make me feel better, but that wasn't true. I needed it to be fair. I nodded again.

"We cool?"

"Yeah."

He smiled and threw an arm around me. "Wanna get ice cream?"

For breakfast? "Sure."

His arm remained around me as we walked, the warmth of his body leaking into mine. We didn't talk, though he waved with his other hand at a few early risers we passed on the way to the snack shack. It should embarrass me how public he was about us.

But I liked it.

I liked that he didn't kiss me one night then pretend it didn't happen the next day the way I'd heard girls talk about it at school. I liked the protectiveness of his arm around me, caring and comfortable. I liked that for once I was the star in one of my novels. And most of all, I *liked* Lucas.

Maybe too much.

He gave me a playful shove at the snack shack and bought my ice cream sandwich for me. Then we sat together, licking our fingers as the birds chirped in the trees. Was this what it was like to be on a date with a guy? Lucas made it easy. He didn't feel the need to talk unless he had something to say. He'd been great right from the start when he covered for me in that stupid speech assignment. *I'm glad he was my first kiss.*

"So..." he scratched his neck.

I couldn't tear my gaze from his lips. They'd taste like sugar right now. And chocolate. I inched closer to him, even though we were shoulder to shoulder. Everything about my posture said *you can kiss me if you want to.*

He bent his head toward me, then stopped. Pulled back. Shook his head. "The bonfire." His voice broke, and he cleared his throat. "The bonfire is tonight. You'll like it. It's the most chill thing we do. No leadership involved." He gave me a tight smile.

Okay, then. I nodded slowly.

Lucas scrambled to his feet. "I'll see you there?" He didn't even wait for my answer before he sprinted away.

31

WE NEED TO TALK

Emma and Paige left for the bonfire way before I did. I didn't blame them. I'd been kind of MIA, and when I got back to the cottage, I didn't know how to process Lucas's weirdness, so I didn't tell them about the mishap with Suzie. It was so hard to balance them and Lucas now.

I also had no idea what to wear. What looked like *Hey, I like you, but only if you still like me*? Literally nothing. Night brought a bite to the air, so I opted for comfy and threw on a hoodie. I brushed my hair back into a fresh ponytail and passed on the makeup. Lucas just saw me. He knew what I looked like.

I shut the screen door and hopped down the four steps, hugging my sweatshirt close against the wind as I made the trek to the field where the bonfire would be. If Lucas didn't want to kiss me and Paige and Emma didn't want to hang out with me, how early could I leave this thing? I could use the silence of walking alone, but I knew how people saw me when I did that. Like a snob or a girl who needed a friend, needed pity. Nothing was worse than pity.

When I got to the bonfire site, everyone set up large logs to sit on.

"Hey Andy, help me with this one?" Emma called. Apparently, we were talking again.

I jogged over and took one end of the heavy log, and we half carried, half dragged it near the fire. We were sweating buckets by the time we got it placed.

"Oh, hell no," she said when Suzie motioned for us to get another one. "There are guys everywhere. She can make one of them do it. Our noodle arms can go fetch sticks."

I couldn't agree more. Emma pointed to the woods and Suzie gave her a thumbs up. Good, because my noodle arms, as she called them, were not used to physical exertion. We walked to the clump of trees and started picking up sticks.

"I'm not mad at you, you know," she said.

Could've fooled me. I knew I should say something to fix what I'd broken between us by choosing to hang out with Lucas more than her. I willed myself to try.

"I want to be friends," I managed to get out.

She picked up a small branch and plopped it on the stack in my arms. The sun dipped below the tree line, scattering sherbet rays through the branches.

"See, that's just it. Paige pointed out that I was being a jerk, but you had no idea why. Will you sit with us tonight? I have something to tell you."

That wasn't ominous at all. What choice did I have, though? Wander around the fire pit while they glared at me? She said she'd been a jerk, but that wasn't true. I'd been ignoring them, too.

"Okay." I couldn't figure out Lucas right now, anyway. We kissed, then he apologized. We ate ice cream, then he ran away. Maybe the girls would be able to help me, though I doubted they wanted to hear about him.

We walked back to the fire, our arms weighed down with dirty wood. I brushed myself off after we dumped them in a large pile.

Paige waved from the log we'd dragged over earlier, a huge grin plastered on her face. The sun had sunk behind a bank of clouds, and they'd started the fire. It roared, licking up a teepee of logs like it was reaching up to burn the sky. Other campers milled around. Some talked from their seats on the logs, and others huddled in clumps near the huge fire.

I sat next to her, and Emma squeezed in on my other side. Emma opened her mouth, then looked at Paige with a sigh, who rolled her eyes.

"Andy, we need to talk," Paige said.

Yeah, those words didn't make this any better.

"I'm sorry I didn't play tetherball with you guys." I didn't realize she'd be so hurt. Didn't we have fun at cornhole? No one ever wanted to hang out with me back home. Overlapping plans was a whole new world for someone like me.

"Huh?" Emma's brow wrinkled in confusion.

"No. We need to talk about Lucas," Paige clarified.

My face must've betrayed my nerves because she placed one hand on mine.

"We don't want to ruin it for you, and honestly, it seems like he's different around you, but you have to know what he's like. What he does."

Oh, no.

"It's so great being the center of his attention, isn't it?" Emma said. "That's how I felt last summer. Day one and he was already trying to get in my pants."

Oh, no.

"And me the summer before," Paige said, her expression grim. "We went on walks at night to talk and… kiss."

My body went cold. Day one he liked them. And the kissing. They described my exact relationship with Lucas now, minus the walks. But hadn't he asked me to walk with him? We were repeating his previous camp flings. I wasn't special at all.

The flames of the fire before us crackled along the dry bark of the sticks we'd gathered until they surrounded a bigger log.

"It doesn't last. It never does. Andy, he picks a different girl every summer," Emma said in a gentle voice.

I didn't want to hear it. They were just jealous that he liked me instead of them. I balled my hands into fists.

"Andy, think about it," Paige begged, swatting a fly out of her face.

I couldn't help but obey. He liked me the second I stepped foot in camp. That gave him all of camp to get me to like him back. Well, so what? He could be a love at first sight kind of guy. The time I spent with him was so easy. Of course, it would be if he had that much dating experience. Could Suzie have been defending me when she yelled at Tyler? No way. And then he said, *It's too much for her.* They were worried I couldn't handle being dumped. After that, Lucas wouldn't kiss me. Was it out of guilt?

I buried my head in my hands as the pieces clicked into place. "How could I think he'd like me?"

"That's not what we meant." Paige poked her stick into the fire. "He stands up for you, and when you freaked out at the climbing challenge… That was like, whoa. I don't know. Maybe he really likes you. We just don't want…"

"We don't want you to think we don't like you just because we hate him," Emma blurted.

"And we don't want you to get in trouble because of him." Paige leaned toward me. "That's what Suzie was mad about this morning, right?"

"Right," I whispered.

A group of guys walked by, and we all paused until they passed.

"We didn't want you to get super attached to him without knowing everything," Paige whispered so no one would hear. More campers streamed into the fire circle. It was only a matter of time before he showed up.

He's different with you, Tyler had said. But was he? Did this new information change last night? He didn't push me or want to change me. That alone was worth all this drama. No one got me like that, not even my parents.

"Okay," I said, struggling to keep the bite out of my voice. "I need to be alone." I didn't want to talk to them anymore, and I couldn't face Lucas right now. Turning my back on the girls and the fire, I walked toward the cottage with shaky legs.

"Wait, Andy!" Paige called. She cursed behind me, but I was done.

My heart slammed over and over again inside my chest, a deranged bird trying to break free. They'd made cryptic comments from the second I liked him, but I didn't chase them for information. I let it go because I didn't want to know. I still didn't want to know, and I was mad at them for telling me, even though that's what good friends would do. How would I know what made a good friend, though? It's not like I had any. It's not like I had anyone.

It took me longer to make it back to the cottage in the dark. I squinted into the night and groped my way along the path. Stupid camp that didn't let me have my phone. It was my only flashlight!

My knees knocked against the steps of the cottage, and I sighed with relief just as a hand grabbed my arm. I was being attacked!

32

LIKING LUCAS

My hand flashed out and connected with flesh in a sickening crunch.

Lucas groaned. "That's a hell of a right hook, Andy."

"Lucas! What are you doing here?" I could've died. He was the last person on earth I wanted to be near right now, and *ow*. My knuckles throbbed; even in the dark, I knew they'd be bruised in the morning.

I didn't mean to punch him, but I couldn't bring myself to be upset about it. That's what he got after leaving me to find out about his player past from Paige and Emma.

"What are you doing?" I hissed again.

"I wanted to talk, but I couldn't find you."

"Well, here I am." I couldn't believe the anger in my own voice. I was never confrontational.

"Can we—don't punch me again, okay?"

His hand brushed mine in the dark as he led me to the steps of the Beaver cottage. Goosebumps raced up my arms—a total betrayal by my body. He shouldn't be allowed to cause chills for every girl at camp. We sat side by side and stared into the darkness, the far-off flicker of the fire a faint orange behind the trees.

He wanted to talk? Fine. I wasn't helping. I waited.

"I guess Paige and Emma said something," he muttered.

"They're my friends."

"Yeah." He blew out a breath. "I get that."

"I guess they're yours, too." I glared at him.

"Andy..."

When he didn't continue, it became obvious he expected me to interrupt, to yell at him. Why would I bother? I hugged myself, pulling my side away from the warmth of his.

"I like you," he whispered, his voice fragile and thin.

Did he? At least he acted like it, asking me out and kissing me the way he did. And the wall... There were those stupid chills again. No one ever tried to hug me during a panic attack. Everyone gave me space. So much space. I could drown in all the space.

He ran a hand through his hair. "I know I should've... I know they're your friends. I should've said something. It was just..."

"Awkward," I finished for him. I could see that.

"I'm not who I was last summer," he said in a low voice.

Maybe he wasn't. I didn't know who he was back then. Maybe it didn't matter. He didn't care that I knew about what happened between him and Paige or him and Emma, because his relationships with them were over. He was with me. When he couldn't find me at the bonfire, he made the effort to come talk to me.

And who was I to judge his dating past? He didn't judge my lack of one. He never even asked about it because it didn't matter. The girls said he was different with me and so did his brother, who had to know him best.

"I like you, too," I said.

This time he didn't ask if he could hug me. He pulled me into his lap on the porch, and I let him. When I pressed my face against his flannel-covered shoulder, I breathed in soap and campfire and Lucas. He squeezed me, and I hugged him back. It couldn't fall apart if it felt this right.

Something shifted between us the longer I sat on his knees. I no longer wondered whether he should notice someone like me, be with someone like me. He liked me. I liked him. It could be that simple.

The girls treated me like glass the next morning, like I'd shatter at any second. I pushed my sunglasses up the bridge of my nose and breezed by them. It wasn't fair since they were trying to have my back, but I couldn't deal with their judgy comments once they found out I hadn't given up on Lucas.

A nervous energy hummed within me as I headed to the archery field. I needed to do something different. An activity that wasn't typical Andy. I wanted to find Lucas and spend every second with him, but even with my limited relationship experience, I knew that would be too much. At home, I could check socials to make an informed decision about where to be if I wanted to run into him casually, but I didn't have that option here.

This whole camp was so medieval that no one knew where anyone else was. That made it all the more romantic when I walked through the tall grass to find Lucas in worn jeans and a black T-shirt, shooting arrows at a target like a modern-day Robin Hood. His eyes narrowed and his exposed arms flexed as he drew back the bowstring. He let loose an arrow and missed by a mile.

Only Lucas could show so much confidence at a sport he totally sucked at. The arrow had sailed over the top of the target—not even close. It was like... yards above the bullseye. I couldn't help it. I doubled over in a fit of giggles.

Lucas's head whipped around. He did a double take when he saw I was the source of laughter. "Why you little..." He dropped his bow on the ground and started for me, his hands curled into pretend claws. "How dare you laugh at my impressive skills?"

I squealed and ran from him, shocking the other three campers also trying their luck at archery. He caught up to me and pulled me into a bear hug. "Give up?"

"Luke!" the instructor said. "There are weapons out on this field. Kindly take your roughhousing elsewhere."

He released me and I turned on him. "Yeah, Lucas," I taunted. "I'm trying to learn a sport here."

He arched an eyebrow. "Let's see what you've got."

I brushed by him and accepted a bow from the exasperated counselor. He taught me the basic stance, how to string the bow, and where to look.

The first arrow I let fly dropped after about two feet. Lucas snorted, but I wouldn't let him get to me. I wanted to try this. After in-depth coaching from the surprisingly knowledgeable counselor and five more tries, I managed to land one on the edge of the target board. I jumped up and down and high fived the instructor as we laughed together.

Lucas strode up and held out his hand for the bow. "Mine was defective."

"Obviously," I said and slapped it in his hand.

He pulled an arrow from a nearby quiver and notched it into the bowstring. "You might want to get out of the way. There's no telling how fast or accurate this is going to be."

The instructor snorted.

Lucas took extra time lining up his shot, then released the bowstring. The arrow missed the board by so much that it almost hit the target in the lane next to ours.

I doubled over again. "The safest place," I wheezed, "would be directly in front of you."

He gritted his teeth. "You think so?"

I nodded, unable to do anything else when I was dying of laughter.

"That's it."

My feet flew out from under me as he threw me over his shoulder.

Surprised, I screamed. "What are you doing?" I beat his back with my fists, but not too hard. He did fall victim to my brutal right hook last night.

"What are you so worried about? The safest place for you is directly in front of me, right?" he asked as he crashed through the woods, away from the archery field.

"Seriously?" But did I really want him to put me down? Being thrown over his shoulder like I weighed nothing didn't suck. His body was hard and warm beneath mine.

Then he turned down the path to the lake. My gut twisted, and I tasted metal.

"Lucas!" I didn't know what else to put with his name. He wouldn't throw me into the lake, would he?

He adjusted his grip as his feet hit the wood of the dock. He grabbed my wrist and showed the counselor my swimming band. She let him by, chuckling at our antics. He wouldn't chuck me into the water in front of her. He was going to put me down, just like last time. Last time when I pushed him into the lake...

He wouldn't dare.

"Oh, wouldn't I?"

I guess I said that out loud.

"Better hold your breath."

"Wait!" I couldn't swim very well, and he knew it!

"One, two..."

Blood rushed to my head. "If I drown, I'm going to kill y—"

"Three!" He jumped.

The water surged around me, a shock of ice cold. I flailed around for about three seconds before my toes hit the ground. I could stand right up. *Well, that was just—*

I stomped out of the lake, my clothes dripping every step of the way. *Of all the stupid, ridiculous, caveman tactics...*

"Andy!"

"Nope." My shoes squished under me as I stalked up the path.

"Come on, Andy. You could touch the bottom and I was with you. I'm a junior lifeguard, you know." *He was?*

"I don't care." I didn't slow my pace. My feet collected clumps of sand from the beach and made wet marks all the way into the forest.

He wrung out his clothes as we walked. "Calm down, Killer."

I whipped around to face him, my ponytail smacking the side of my face like a wet fish. "Killer? Really? Maybe try not being a neanderthal who throws girls in the water when your precious pride is hurt." My filter glitched around this guy. I'd never say something to someone so hot without planning the phrasing a thousand times first, but he'd ticked me off.

"Sassy Camper Andrea," he teased. "I like it."

I stopped, the tension leaking out of me the way the water now leaked from my clothes. He didn't care that I'd yelled at him? I expected him to roll his eyes, storm off in the opposite direction when he realized I was mad. Not chase after and try to tease the anger out of me. In that moment, something inside me broke. How many times had I replayed what happened with Brynn and wished I'd done something different, knowing that moment had been the beginning of the end between us? I didn't have to pretend with Lucas. He liked me even when I didn't go along with everything he did.

"How can I make it up to you?" His tone was smooth, flirty, but his eyes blazed in a way that made my toes curl and my stomach tighten.

"How do you want to make it up?" I didn't want to play games. We didn't need to do that. Then where did that low, throaty voice come from?

He reeled back, and his eyes searched my face. Did the gruffness of my voice have the same effect on him or was he not expecting me to call him on his crap?

I raised an eyebrow.

"Maybe we shouldn't—"

"Meet me at the canoes tonight," I blurted.

His eyes darted from the archery field to the dock and back to me. Then he looked away.

I rocked back on my heels, a horrible heat blooming in my chest. I was reading this *all* wrong. Time to backtrack. Just because I had this enormous revelation didn't mean his interest matched mine. "You're right. It's stupid. We already got caught once. I don't want to ruin camp for yo—"

"Okay."

"What?"

"Let's do it."

I didn't read it wrong. He was being careful. In the bravest move I'd ever committed in my life, I bent forward and kissed him on the cheek. "Okay." Then I sprinted toward the cottage to change before I was late for the next leadership activity.

33

MOONLIT MADNESS

The rest of the day buzzed by in a blur. I didn't want to talk to anyone. I struggled to answer when they did ask me something. The promise of tonight preoccupied my thoughts.

Last time Lucas and I had talked and kissed. Could I handle that again? What if he wanted more than that? I didn't want to obsess over it, but it was like scratching a mosquito bite. Every time I told myself not to, it just made it worse.

I liked him. A lot. There was no one like Lucas. How safe he made me feel, how I could get mad at him without embarrassment, how I could say stuff I never said to other people. But it was too fast to feel this way, like we were pieces of the same puzzle that fit together perfectly. I didn't want to be that girl who fell head over heels during summer camp, but that wasn't what this was. *Then what was it?* I didn't have an answer, and I didn't want to come up with one either. For once, I wasn't reading what happened to other people. I wanted to live in this moment and believe it would be okay.

When night came, I changed into terry cloth shorts and an oversized T-shirt and sat down to brush my hair. Paige and Emma whispered from one of the bunks, but I tuned them out.

Emma wasn't having it.

"Are you okay? You're acting weird," she said as I pulled against a particularly painful knot at the nape of my neck.

"Sorry," I said as I yanked again. *Stupid knot.*

"Here, let me do that. You're going to rip out all your hair." She took the brush from me and in a complete one eighty of normal Emma behavior began to gently work at the knot. "Are you mad at us?" she asked.

"No," I said. "I just don't..."

"You don't believe us."

I didn't hear judgment in her voice. Just resignation. Did Paige try to tell her about Lucas before they got involved, too?

"I do, actually," I said. "But...." I still liked him, and their history wouldn't stop me. "I don't have a lot of girlfriends," I admitted. I couldn't tell her I didn't have any friends at all. "I don't always know how to say the right thing."

She tugged my hair. "So, you don't say anything? That's stupid. You don't have to censor yourself. Say what you want."

I winced, but it had nothing to do with the way she pulled on a knot. I should tell her. "I'm meeting Lucas tonight," I said.

She finished with the tangle and ran the brush through my now-smooth hair. I expected another lecture, but instead she said, "I'll cover for you," and went back to her bunk.

What? I sat frozen in shock for a full ten seconds before I put my brush back in my bag and settled into a new novel. I couldn't concentrate on the words in front of me, though. Why would she cover for me when she hated Lucas? Was this what real friends did?

At lights out, I tucked myself into bed and waited for the honking of Suzie's snores beneath me and the subtle change in the air that signaled everyone else falling asleep. I couldn't dwell on Emma when every cell of my body screamed for Lucas.

I crept out of the cottage barefoot, the perfume of freshly cut grass surrounding me as I used the moonlight to guide me to where Lucas and I met last time.

I could do this. I wanted to.

He came into view, standing by the water, his hands shoved in his shorts pockets. All at once, the butterflies in my stomach vanished. *He showed.*

His face was still and serious. "Listen, Andy—"

I walked toward him, not breaking eye contact. I wouldn't let him talk me out of it. We both knew why we were here. How much this mattered. For once in my life, I would take charge. I would make something happen.

His Adam's apple bobbed as he swallowed.

Camp would end in a few days, and I was finally letting go. I drew in a deep breath. I wasn't nervous. Since when had that stopped? But I wasn't.

Lucas stayed frozen as I reached him. I could do this. I tugged on his shirt. He lowered his head and our lips met. I took the lead in the kiss, even though I had no idea what to do. He seemed frozen, except that his arms surrounded me, steadying me. He wanted this too.

So, I kissed him harder.

A low groan escaped his throat and vibrated into my mouth. He broke away. "Andy, we—"

"We what?" I asked, breathless. "I want this. I want you."

Silence.

Moonlight spilled over his shocked face. I'd surprised him with my assertiveness, but I was taking Emma's advice. I reached up and circled my hands around his neck. I was done censoring. My skin practically crackled with the electricity between us. Surely, he felt the same way.

We sank to the sandy ground together, and he hugged me gently, reverently. That wasn't what I wanted. I wanted the Lucas who tossed me over his shoulder, the Lucas who teased me and forced me out of my comfort zone.

Then he kissed me, soft and slow at first. He lowered me into the sand, his body a delicious pressure on mine as the kiss became more urgent. His tongue stole its way into my mouth, and I almost died of pleasure. This was really happening right now.

I pressed against his chest. A soft moan escaped his mouth, and I bit his lip as if maybe I could absorb that sexiness. My body hummed with anticipation as his hands played with the hem of my loose T-shirt. Then his fingers stole across my back, warm and reassuring. I wanted those hands in other places, places where no one had ever touched me. Places I was too scared to touch myself. I grabbed my T-shirt and ripped it over my head in one quick movement.

"Are you sure?" he whispered.

Sure about what? I wanted his skin against mine. I might die if I couldn't have that right now.

He pulled back for a moment and studied me. "You're so..."

My chest heaved. I knew how pale I was, how soft I looked. I wore a T-shirt bra, for God's sake. It didn't matter. I wanted him to kiss me in all the right places and show me the fierceness I knew he was capable of. I wanted him more than I wanted anything else.

We smashed together, our teeth knocking as we kissed. It didn't matter. The searing heat of his skin branded mine, tingles exploding all through me. Every place we touched set off an explosion of need. The urge to feel more of him overwhelmed me. I ground against him, my breath catching. A delicious heaviness settled low in my gut as he hitched my leg over his thigh.

Then he broke away from me. "I want you," he said in a rush. "But Andy. You're so—we can't."

"Can't what?" I couldn't even think.

He stared at me a second, then chuckled. "Never mind."

I frowned as he scooted me off him and sat up.

"Did I do something wrong?" I picked my shirt out of the sand and pushed my head and arms back through it. What happened? How did I screw this up?

My heart jackhammered in my chest, beating a frantic message to *run, run, run*. "I'll just go." I pushed to my feet.

He jumped up. "No, don't. I just... I don't want to hurt you." Even in the shadowed dark, I couldn't bear the concern in his eyes.

Of course, he worried he might hurt me. Why wouldn't he be? He saw me freak out before. Poor Andy, too shy and fragile to handle anything, least of all a guy. My eyes flooded with tears, blurring the beautiful, kind boy in front of me who was trying to do the right thing.

"I get it." I started to walk away. *God, how stupid could I be?*

He caught my hand and pulled me back. "I don't think you get it at all. This..." He ran his other hand through his hair. "I've never wanted to... never cared enough to. God, that sounds bad."

I didn't follow at all. He was normally so much better with words, but now he spoke more like me.

"I'm falling for you," I whispered. "Does that count for anything?"

Water rocked a moored canoe against the dock, tapping in the quiet between us.

"It counts for everything," he ground out before his lips were on mine again, frantic and searching.

If a grenade went off two feet from me, I wouldn't have noticed. I would've died happy on that beach, Lucas's hands in my hair, his warm mouth on mine.

When we broke apart, he threaded his fingers through mine under the clear sky. The brightness of the full moon drowned out the stars. Sweat dampened my hand, but he held it in his as we walked back to my cottage. This time we lucked out, and the windows remained dark. Suzie was nowhere in sight.

His gaze was so direct, so earnest when he brought my knuckles to his mouth. "Andy."

I slid through the cracked door, then tiptoed past a snoring Suzie. If she caught me now, I'd get kicked out of camp for sure. I didn't care.

A strange urge to cry overwhelmed me. All the nerves, the happiness, the pain combined themselves into a single tear that tracked down my cheek in the dark. I held my hand to my heart the whole night, the tingling of my knuckles from Lucas's lips soothing me into a contented sleep.

34

IT COUNTS FOR EVERYTHING

With a bounce in my step, I fluffed up my ponytail and dashed out of the cottage the next morning. When Paige gave me a tentative smile on the way to breakfast, I smiled back. What happened between her and Lucas was different than what was going on between him and me. I couldn't fault her for believing otherwise. She was trying to be a good friend. Emma, too.

I grabbed my tray and moved through the breakfast line, piling food on my plate like this would be the last meal before I got stranded on an island with a piece of plastic sheeting. When I reached the end, I scanned the cafeteria for Lucas.

Not here. Huh.

Emma bumped my shoulder. "Hey."

I grinned back at her. "Hey."

She led the way to a table where Paige waited.

"I doubt you sitting with us means you've come to your senses?" Paige said the second I slid my tray across from hers.

Emma and I exchanged a look.

I shrugged, but I couldn't contain my smile.

Emma and Paige stayed silent for a long minute, both pretending that chewing on straws was the most important thing in life.

Finally, Paige changed the subject. "Saw your wipeout yesterday," she teased Emma.

"You guys, it was so painful! I'm not kidding!" She pulled up her shirt, and we both looked at the bright red slap mark on her stomach from the water. "I'm like, dying." She went on to describe in detail the Blob incident where she'd barely managed to keep her footing across the 'big, inflated pillow thing' when a guy at least twice her weight launched her to the moon and back.

Both Paige and I were dying of laughter by the time her over-exaggerated story ended with her as a sopping wet victim who should've gotten carried out of the water on a stretcher. It distracted me for a minute, but when my eyes swept the cafeteria again, no Lucas. Breakfast would end soon, and he loved food. Where was he?

"Hey, Andy. I know that… I know you're still not super happy with me because of the Luke thing, but I'm glad you're still sitting with us," Paige said, pulling my attention back to the table. With downcast eyes, she pushed a cup of coffee my way. Steam rose from the comforting brown liquid. I was beginning to suspect that the lack of coffee here was just hazing. Everyone else got ahold of it, no problem.

"I'm not mad at you." I toasted her water with my coffee and took a grateful sip.

She beamed.

I'd eaten most of my food. Only the canned corn remained. Who served corn for breakfast? I never ate this much, but I had nothing else to do while I waited. No way Lucas had slept this long. He never had before. A chill ran over my arms.

"What's going on?" Concern coated Paige's words. "Andy?"

"Last night, Lucas and I…" My eyes searched the empty tables again.

"Oh, Andy, you didn't." Paige covered one of my hands with hers.

"Not like that, but…" I lifted one shoulder and closed my eyes briefly.

"And now he's not sitting with us," Emma said.

I didn't answer as I pulled my hand away to take a big bite of lukewarm corn.

Paige rose from her seat and a second later, she pulled me into a hard hug. It reminded me of the hug Lucas had given me at the climbing wall. Her body didn't radiate warmth like his, but the pressure was nice.

I didn't need it, though. Lucas skipping breakfast didn't mean anything. I needed to have more faith in him than this. "I'm just being stupid."

To my relief, neither Paige nor Emma said anything as we walked back to the cottage, arm in arm. I hoped and didn't hope we'd run into him. How could he avoid me in a camp this small? Our counselors joined up our cottages for activities all the time.

Then he appeared, like a hero from a romance novel, right in the center of the path. I stopped in my tracks, jerking Paige and Emma along with me. He watched with a small, forced smile. I alternated between panic at being brushed off and the more prevalent hope that maybe he overslept.

"Do you want us to stay or go?" Paige whispered.

"Oh, I'm staying," Emma said.

I didn't know what I wanted.

He jogged up to us. "Hey, Andy." He was the picture of pure innocence. And when his wet hair flopped across his forehead as he trotted over, it made him even cuter. "Paige. Emma." He frowned. "Can I get a second alone with Andy?"

Paige unthreaded her arm from mine and peeled Emma off me, shoving her toward our cottage. The look she gave me before marching through the door might've been somewhere between pity and fear.

Lucas and I trailed behind them until he leaned on the railing of the porch and looked at me. He smiled but didn't say anything.

"You weren't at breakfast."

"Yeah." He raked his hand through his hair and shook water out of the shaggy strands.

"I was tired this morning, too. Did you, um, oversleep?" I didn't want to be the first one to bring up what happened last night. Why was everything between us so weird all of a sudden?

"Andy, I wasn't tired. I was... We kind of rushed into it and like, where do you even live? Can we make this work?" He ran a hand through his hair again.

"I'm like twenty minutes west."

How had we not talked about this? What was he saying? The wet wind whipped through my hoodie like it was a piece of soggy paper.

"I'm not from Vermont," he muttered.

Silence stretched between us as that sank in.

"Where are you from?" Maybe it was drivable. I could get my license. I never needed it since I could walk to everything at home, but for him, I would do it.

"West Virginia." He cringed like he expected me to flip out.

My brain couldn't keep up. *West Virginia?* I tried to do the math in my head, but math wasn't my thing. At least ten hours away. Probably more. Why would his parents send both their kids so far for summer camp? And what did we do now? Could we text? Call? Video chat and like, find a weekend here and there, and...

But his expression mirrored mine. It wouldn't be the same. We'd started this amazing, tender relationship, but so much of it depended on the physical. Not just the kissing, but the handholding, the hugging, the calm of being close.

"Yeah, I used to live here when my parents were together. Now I visit Dad for a couple weeks in the summer before flying home."

I wanted to smooth the line between his eyebrows, tell him it was fine. We'd be fine. Except he lived in West Virginia.

But wait... so, he always planned to dump me at the end of camp?

"Last night when we—" he cleared his throat. "I was going to talk to you about it."

Great. Now I couldn't keep myself from reliving last night. It came back to me in flashes and bursts. All the times he'd been hesitant... he'd even said *we can't* at one point in time.

I'm so stupid.

"So..." He kicked a clump of dirt.

Was he waiting for me to cry? He said we were done. If I could get through this conversation, I could break down later, but I needed to get away from him. This was what I got for letting someone in again. Maybe it was better to not have any friends, any boyfriends. I knew better than to get involved with a guy at summer camp. I didn't think past the ending of this, whether I wanted it to go on or not, and now I knew, in the back of my mind, I wanted more. But life wasn't a romance novel. Not even close. It hurt. So freakin' bad.

Birds flapped in the trees, their tiny screams echoing in the forest.

I started to turn away.

"Andy, don't do this. Don't shut down. This is exactly what I didn't want to happen." He gripped the porch railing. "I can't—I can't believe this is happening." Agony threaded through his voice, a desperate, harsh sound I'd never associate with him.

But I had nothing to say. I wouldn't apologize for what we did. I wouldn't tell him it was all okay when we both knew it wasn't. We couldn't make it work if he didn't even want to come to breakfast, when he led with the fact we lived too far away. I knew the stats on long distance relationships. He didn't have to spell it out.

"Say something," he pleaded. "You can still talk to me." My heart splintered. The way he spoke was so earnest, so real. He had this talent of making me feel like I mattered. But I didn't. Nothing mattered anymore.

Rage welled within me. I was so tired of keeping everything inside, of going along with shit I didn't want to. Everybody told me how different he was with me, but he treated me like every other girl he messed around with. And he wanted *me* to say something?

"What do you want me to say!" I exploded. The volume of my scream felt foreign to my throat. "How is me talking going to make anything better? You dumped Paige the last day of camp! And Emma! Why would I be any different? Way to get it out of the way early." I wanted to claw at my scratchy throat. I *never* yelled.

Lucas reeled back like I'd slapped him. After a moment of his mouth gaping open like a braindead fish, he found his words again. "I—this isn't that, I swear. I love how you stand up for yourself. How sensitive you are. How you see me and not my brother. You're —" He closed his eyes in pain. "I'm sorry I made you yell at me."

"How is this different, Lucas? Please tell me because I am dying to know how this is different for you." My throat throbbed with unshed tears. Screw him for making me feel for even a second that I was special. That he wanted me.

I had to give it to him that practice made perfect. As far as break-ups went, he'd done it in style. He said everything right, did everything right. It was as good, if not better than the ones in my books. It's just that... he was my first everything. First kiss, first hand-hold, first—

"Because I want... Andy, please." His voice broke.

"It counts for everything? It counts for nothing," I said, throwing his words from last night in his face.

His mouth snapped shut as he blinked back the moisture in his eyes, but I couldn't take it back now, even if I was being unfair.

I'd used up all my words. Was I supposed to fling myself on him and cry that I loved him? I didn't. I could have if we'd had more time. Would it have hurt more then? I couldn't imagine anything worse than the pain I felt now. Like a monster ripping through my chest, regret shredded everything in its path. I needed to get out of here before it exploded out of me again.

I turned and walked with shaky legs up the cottage steps.

He didn't call me back.

When I closed the door behind me, somehow Emma and Paige were the only other people in the room. *Thank God.* I slid down to the floor and rested my head on my knees.

"That was epic." Emma said. "You really told him, Andy!"

I didn't want them to see my reaction, but my body betrayed me, and my shoulders shook, anyway.

"Shut up! Look at her," Paige hissed. "Andy, I'm so sorry. I—" She paused. "You're laughing?"

35

THE HEART OF IT

I raised my hands in a helpless gesture and giggled so hard that the tears building up had no choice but to streak down my face.

"She's flipping out like she did at the wall." Emma scrambled to her feet and started toward me.

I shook my head and put one finger in the air. I could control this. I would. I didn't need Lucas to comfort me. I didn't need anyone.

"It's just so perfect," I said when I got ahold of myself.

"She's lost it." Emma made the sign of the cross on her chest. She was Catholic?

I pushed up from the ground, hard. I couldn't do people anymore today. I didn't care what they had planned. I needed space. My fingers tingled, and I flexed them. I wanted my mom. I was a baby, and I needed my mom. I marched to the door with zero plan and pushed it open so hard that it swung wide—

And clipped Suzie right in the face.

"Ow! Mother of Christmas!"

I couldn't bring myself to apologize. I had no words left.

"Hang on, Camper Andrea," she said when I tried to walk past her.

Great. Kick me out. I'm ready.

"We have an activity in a minute," she said, cupping her cheek.

So? She had to let me off the hook. I couldn't be expected to do anything today after what happened.

She bounded over and grabbed my hand. "I think you're going to like this one! It's so you!" She dragged me over to the lake while Paige and Emma trailed after us. The whole way, she lectured me on leadership and Lord only knew what else. My brain couldn't catch up to what was happening. I was being pulled into another activity? I couldn't participate in anything right now. I needed to... but her hand held fast to mine as she chattered on. We crested the hill that led to the edge of the beach—I felt like a kite in a windstorm. The Hippo guys stood on the sand, milling around with most of the Beaver girls.

Of course they were here. They were our partner cabin. I don't know why that hadn't occurred to me. My heart hammered so fast it hurt. Was this what a heart attack felt like? I wouldn't look at Lucas. I wouldn't.

But he gave me no choice.

"Andy," he said as soon as Suzie let me go in the center of the group. His tone was careful, like I might blow up and hit him with shrapnel.

He didn't need to be afraid. *I couldn't...* I didn't know what to do. It was like my brain had shorted out and my body took over what I couldn't. This was so far past a panic attack. This was crippling.

I traced the lines of his face in my mind like it might be the last time I'd ever be able to. The way his eyes squinted against the sun, the start of a tan on his smooth forehead. His mouth compressed with concern. How very Lucas.

"Are we... are you okay?" His voice was like silk. He shouldn't get to have a voice that comforting.

I sat on the ground, even though no one else did. Tyler frowned at his brother and crouched in front of me.

"Andy, hey. What's going on? Do you need to go back to the cottage?"

I turned to him. He had that same voice. Why did I never notice that before?

Suzie squatted down beside Tyler. "Does she have heat stroke? Andy, can you hear me? My face is fine, I swear. No big deal!"

I nodded. *Send me to the cottage.*

"Let's get her back to bed," Tyler said.

Suzie turned to him. "She doesn't need a bed," she said in a scared voice. "I think she needs a parent, Ty."

He rocked back on his heels. "What the hell did you do?" he accused his brother.

My brain buzzed as I picked up bits and pieces of what Lucas said next, his head down and tone sullen. Something about him being sorry. Something about being realistic.

Then I went blank.

When I tuned in again, Suzie and Tyler were arguing, pointing at me. But their words were incoherent. I closed my eyes and opened them to find Emma screaming at Lucas while Paige blocked her from tackling him to the ground.

Tyler yanked Lucas away by his arm. And Lucas's face… I didn't care.

I crawled into the tree line. No one came after me. I wouldn't have cared if they did. A switch had flipped in my brain, freeing me from feeling anything. With four days left of camp, Mom wouldn't come get me. So, I would have to shut down. No drama, no pain… nothing.

This happened to me only two other times. Once in elementary school when I got stuck in the mud, but everyone laughed instead of helping me, and once after Brynn and I called it quits and I realized that everyone had friends, tables to eat at, and I didn't.

Somehow, I ended up back in bed. Through my fog I heard Paige and Emma's voices. The sky darkened. I didn't sleep much. The sun came up. I didn't need coffee. I got out of bed, got dressed, brushed my teeth, and gathered my hair in a ponytail so it wouldn't get in the way of my sunglasses. Not that it mattered anymore.

That was the thing about being numb. It was like living in cotton balls. It felt wrong, but I couldn't move through it, couldn't stop it.

The day went. I don't remember what I did. After dinner I

returned to the cottage and lay on my bed, staring at the ceiling again.

"Oh my God, I can't. I can't!" Emma's voice made it through the fog. "We are not doing this anymore! Why isn't anyone calling her mom?"

"Her mom won't take her home, we know that," Paige said. "Suzie said to give her some time."

"Like time is going to fix anything! They should call her dad. She has a dad, doesn't she? I knew this would happen!"

"It's all our fault," Paige whispered.

It was that whisper that broke me. "No," I murmured. "It isn't."

They'd been good friends, giving me space to be with him, warning me about what that might mean. I ignored them, and now there was nothing. Nothing at all.

"Andy!" Emma vaulted up the wooden slats onto my bunk. Paige followed. Our combined weight might break the rickety bed. I might be okay with that. I didn't have to talk if I was dead.

"I'm so sorry!" Paige wailed. "He's such an asshole! This is all my—"

"No, it isn't," I repeated. "It's mine." I dragged my eyes from the ceiling to their faces.

"Eat this." Emma shoved a granola bar at me.

My stomach grumbled in response. I took the bar and peeled back the wrapper. "I am so over this summer."

They didn't say anything, and I didn't expect them to. I finished the granola bar, then climbed down the bed. I grabbed my duffel and unzipped it, shoving my belongings inside, unfolded. I couldn't be paired with Lucas the next two days and pretend it was okay, and I couldn't float around while we both played the victim. Being numb would make everyone worried—make everyone's camp suckier.

"Hey, now." Paige jumped down and planted her hands on her hips in front of me. "Don't leave. That's crap, and you know it."

I couldn't believe she was calling me out right now. Anger boiled inside me. "Why? Why is it crap? You know what this has been like for me. Victim, Convert? I'm a victim. There's no point pretending I can be anything else." I threw my hands in the air. I'd gone from uncontrollable numbness to being unable to censor myself. "What do you guys want from me? Are we even friends? Why would you want to be friends with the awkward weirdo who just got dumped?" I sank onto Suzie's super-pink bed. "I used to be more than this."

That was the heart of it. Coming here had screwed me up as much as it helped me.

Paige reeled back.

"You're kidding, right?" Emma raised her voice. "No boy can take away your awesomeness. You're hilarious. Your sarcasm is epic, the way you sneak off to read X-rated novels instead of falling into line? You didn't even listen to us when we told you about Luke, because you were so sure you knew better. That's confidence, Andy. You risked everything. You're the most daring one out of all of us! Why wouldn't we be friends with you?"

"Don't fold now," Paige begged. "Don't be a Victim. What about all the stuff we did together? Weren't we a part of your summer?"

I continued throwing clothes into my duffel. It's not like we'd be friends in the real world, anyway. Camp would be over soon, and we'd never see each other again.

"You won a ribbon, Andy," Paige tried again. "You're a leader. Own it!"

"And if you go now," Emma pointed out, "wouldn't that give Luke the satisfaction of making you leave? We heard you out there. You were a total badass."

They didn't get it. They didn't know what I was like with him that night. He wouldn't be happy I left camp, either. We shared the fault in this. I didn't want them fighting with him over me.

I thunked my head against the wooden bedpost and squeezed my eyes shut. "What do I do?" I was so tired of everything. Why else would they have gotten to me? "I don't want to see him anymore," I whispered.

We stood in silence until Paige said, "It's not about him." She placed one hand over mine on the suitcase. "You can ignore him or treat him like a friend, but Andy, it's not about him. It's about you. You've changed."

I hadn't. I was just as awkward as ever. Just as naïve. "I'm still quiet."

"You don't have to be outgoing. We're definitely not going to make you," Emma said.

Paige nodded.

"But you're stronger, Andy," Emma continued. "Like when people ask you things. You don't shrink away like someone's going to hit you."

I rolled my eyes. I never did that. Much.

"Changes don't have to be big and loud to be important," Paige said softly. "You can still be you and rock this. And if you can't, we'll be there. Finish strong. We'll hold you up. We're with you."

Emma nodded. "You've got this."

I let go of my duffel.

36

SCOTT THE SCOUNDREL FROM SCOTLAND

Paige and Emma managed to drag me to lunch the next day, which I was grateful for since my body had decided that a PowerBar wouldn't do.

I loaded up my plate with fruit and greens and even a slice of cafeteria pizza and headed for the table, closely flanked by my protective friends. When I sat, Paige pushed a cup of coffee toward me, steam curling over the lip of the Styrofoam.

I stared at her.

"What? It was here when we sat down, and I know you don't care if it's someone else's."

She's right. Beggars can't be choosers. Never mind the fact that it was a full cup, and I knew of only two people with a history of sneaking me coffee.

I leaned over to view the counselor's table, but Tyler was deep in conversation with Dana, who patted him on the shoulder then skipped up the steps of the platform. I didn't dare make eye contact with Lucas, even though I'd clocked him the second I walked in.

I fingered the edge of the cup. It would be stupid not to drink it. I'd been craving it every second since I got here.

But what if Lucas got it for me?

I picked up the cup and took a long, scalding sip. I didn't care. No one was allowed to ruin coffee for me.

"Okay, campers! It's almost the end of leadership awesomeness!" Dana called through the microphone. Some of the teens cheered, but our table stayed silent this time, eating. Were Paige and Emma burned out from the first two weeks of intense leadership training, or were they that worried about me?

"Those of you returning to us know what that means!"

Paige picked up her pizza and took a big bite.

At the next table, Lucas studied his meal. His hair stuck out everywhere today, like he'd pushed his hands through it a million times, and his face compressed into a frown that wasn't him at all.

"We're going to have a dance to wrap up our leadership experience! This will give you some time to hang out with people you've already begun to bond with. The connections you make here at camp may serve you well in the future." Dana gave us all a rehearsed, professional smile as the cafeteria rumbled with cheers and few whistles.

The people who were psyched were still riding high on their summer fling. The rest of us? I wasn't the only one silent after Dana's big announcement.

I couldn't help myself from glancing at Lucas again. If he'd waited until after the dance to do what he did, would I like him more right now? *He dumped me! Of course, I'd still hate him.* Except it wasn't black and white like that. I didn't hate him.

"I forgot about the dance," Paige said.

Emma turned to me. "I'll stay with you."

Emma would stay with me? Out of the two of them, that surprised me, though I guess I couldn't fault Paige for wanting to spend more time with Marshall. I'd been so consumed by my heartache, I hadn't even asked about him.

I didn't want to go and see how okay Lucas was when I wasn't. If Emma and I stayed back, we'd read romance novels and laugh. The smile that brought on withered. That wouldn't happen. I'd be a wreck the whole time wondering what was happening without me—and missing the dance wouldn't be fair to her.

I wouldn't ruin this for my friends. …I had *friends.*

"I'm going," I whispered. Then louder: "I'm going."

Lucas jolted and looked over at our table. Had he heard me?

But Paige was right. This summer wasn't about him. It was about me. I met his gaze head on, and he blinked.

Paige and Emma walked with me back to the cottage. We had half an hour before the next group activity.

"Alright, let's see those books," Paige demanded, climbing up into my bunk.

"No way. I get to choose first. I want the one with the girl who's about to have a nip slip," Emma complained.

Huh? "What are you talking about?"

"We're reading with you today. Duh," Emma said.

"But… why?"

"All camp we've been asking you to do stuff you don't want to. It's our turn to do something you like." She rifled through my duffel and pulled out the book in question. "Too slow! I get to read—" she flipped it over to the back. "—about the uptight librarian and the sexy scoundrel of Scotland. Ooh, suck it, Emma."

"Looks like she's going to." Emma pointed to the girl on the cover.

"Ew," both Paige and I said.

"Fine," Emma huffed. "Find me the next sexiest one. If I'm doing this, I need something juicy."

I grabbed the next book in the pile.

"The Dreaded Pirate and his Captive Lady," she read from the front flap. "Where do you get this stuff?"

I shrugged and let them lead us out of the cottage. We each found a spot against the trunk of the tree I'd read under the day Tyler found me and cracked open the covers on my dirty obsession.

Ten minutes in and Emma couldn't take it anymore. "I have to read this part to you."

"Ooh, me too," Paige said.

I laughed as we created a small triangle. Soon we were all acting out our favorite parts in dramatic voices.

"You'll stay in this room until I deem otherwise appropriate," Emma boomed. "Who talks like that? She should kick him in the nuts."

"I like my librarian chick. She punches Scott the Scoundrel when she thinks he's perving on her getting dressed. For a scoundrel, he's pretty tame, though. This book is super into alliteration. Scott the scoundrel from Scotland?" Paige snorted. "Listen to this: *Scott's eyes swept over me, and I knew what he was seeing: my chest heaving, my lips parted in askance.* Askance, Andy. They're parted in *askance*." She cracked up.

I couldn't even get mad that they were making fun of my twenty-five-cent garage sale finds. I found them ridiculous, too, and that's why I loved them. Happily ever afters and unbelievable landscapes. Rich words filled with the fantasies of the most outlandish relationships possible. Before camp, everything the heroines in these books did was so far out of my realm, I could have been reading a fantasy with elves and trolls. Completely made up. And now…

"Read us something from yours," Paige said.

I skimmed my page until I came upon a passage. *"How could I ever go back to the way things once were, when all I could obsess about were his hands on my hips, his eyes mirroring my very heart and soul?"*

The girls dissolved into peals of laughter again, and I chuckled bitterly. How *could* I ever go back to the way things once were? Maybe I couldn't. All I could do now was hope the next activity had nothing to do with the Hippos.

37

MAIN CHARACTER ENERGY

The universe really wanted me to know it didn't owe me anything. Why else would it follow such an awesome morning with a group activity Suzie informed us would be "with our partner cottage?" I knew this day would move slow as it ticked down to the dance where I'd have to face Lucas, but not now. Not this soon.

After a steely stare from Emma and a determined nod from Paige, I set my shoulders. I could do this. I wouldn't let anything ruin my last bit of camp.

Ten minutes and a lot of grumbling later, we met up with the Hippo team in a clearing on the side of a hill. I breathed a sigh of relief that I remembered to wear my sunglasses. Seizing the day? Yes. Looking Lucas in the eye? Not a chance.

"Four corners," Suzie said, "is about deciding where you stand on a moral issue. When others defend a decision that's not the same as yours, listen to their side. Be open-minded. Change your choice or resolve to continue with your own decision. There are no winners or losers in this game. We all win if we listen."

Okay, I could listen. This challenge was meant for me. I'd throw myself into it and it would distract me from the fact that Lucas stood ten feet away from me right now.

"When I read a question or statement, you will walk to one of the bases on the ground, whichever aligns most with what you believe." She pointed. "Over here is 'Yes,' there is 'Mostly,' over there is 'Somewhat,' and behind me is 'No.' Once everyone has found their spot, we'll ask someone at each base why they made the decision they did. This might open a dialogue. It might not. That's okay, too." She smiled a watered-down version of her usual grin. Why was she so deflated?

Whatever her issue, I was excited about an activity for once. I didn't have to speak. I could just move.

"The first statement is: Stealing, under any circumstances, is wrong," Tyler read off a card.

Most everyone followed Lucas to the 'Yes' base. I moved to the 'Mostly' base with a few others, including Emma.

"Why is stealing always wrong, Camper Marshall?" Suzie chirped.

Marshall shrugged. "You're taking something that's not yours. There's always another option."

I shook my head at the ground.

"You don't agree, Camper Andrea?" Suzie said.

I could've kicked myself. Why would I react at all? She pounced on me any chance she got. My face burned with embarrassment as I waited for someone to come to my rescue.

Tyler studied the leaves on a nearby tree. Suzie had everyone under her thumb, and it was so—*No.* I could answer a question. It wouldn't kill me. Tyler was right. I could stand up for myself. It didn't have to be big.

"I like to be called Andy."

Suzie reeled back, baffled, like I hadn't told her this a million times. "Okay, Camper Andy. Defend your base," she said, her voice now calm and less judgmental.

I sucked in a deep breath. "I personally don't know what it's like to watch my family starve. If I thought they wouldn't make it, I'd do just about anything to make sure they didn't die, including stealing."

A long moment of silence blanketed the air while most of the group stared at me in shock. A drop of sweat slid down my neck. Was it because I said something, or because they now knew how first world their lives were? All our parents had the cash to send us to a leadership camp, for God's sake.

"Well, that's … great job, Camper Andy," Suzie said. She shook her head, a small smile lifting the corners of her mouth. "If she persuaded you to change your opinion, now is the time to move to another corner," she said to the group.

I ducked my head as three people moved to stand next to me. I couldn't look at Lucas as he crossed the small space between us, didn't want to feel his hand brush against mine, the tingles that raced up my arm when it did. I focused on Tyler, whose smile could be seen from outer space right now. Maybe mine could, too.

"Main character energy," Emma whispered to me.

I nudged her, biting my lip to keep from laughing.

"Okay, the next statement is…"

And on it went. Suzie didn't call on me again, and I didn't volunteer to speak. The whole game I basked in the glow of how maybe the girls were right. When I spoke, people listened. That might be a kind of leader, too. My heart stopped banging a frantic beat when Suzie and Tyler finally called it quits.

Lucas saluted me sadly as I walked away, a heartbreaking, awkward gesture. Though it pained me, I nodded, drawing in a shuddering breath as I joined the girls on the trail.

"Camper *Andy,*" Emma teased as we walked to the cottage. "I almost catcalled you."

I smiled.

"You kicked butt." Paige linked arms with mine. She held out her other arm for Emma.

"Lame," Emma said, but she linked arms with us, too.

"Leadership for the win!" Paige yelled out.

"Survival for the win," I muttered. The words tasted wrong, though. I had fun today. The activity had been in my wheelhouse, and I didn't need Tyler to stand up for me. I did it myself.

When we ate lunch, Paige and Emma penned me in to block my

view of Lucas, and I could have hugged them. Instead, I ate my spaghetti and garlic bread with a renewed appetite.

They herded me out the door seconds after I took my last bite, Emma pulling me by the hand when I had a moment of weakness and glanced over at Lucas's table.

He wasn't there.

During the short walk back to the cottage, the girls shot looks over my head at each other, doing that weird silent communication thing they did when they didn't want me to know their thoughts. Maybe they'd pull me into a three-legged race or another game during free time. Wait, there were three of us. Fine then, a four-legged race. Picturing being in the middle with a leg strapped to each of these Amazons as they forced me forward brought a smile to my face. How ridiculous would that be?

38

TEAMWORK MAKES THE DREAM WORK

I wasn't that far off with my three-legged race idea. Paige and Emma seemed to have a pact to keep me busy all day, probably so I wouldn't lie in bed thinking about Lucas. It wasn't a bad plan, so I was chill when we joined a hoard of people walking down the dirt path.

"We're going to play four-square volleyball, friends!" Dana announced through a bullhorn from the clearing up ahead. I'd almost become used to her voice ruining my eardrums at this point.

I looked from Paige to Emma. Was this a camp-wide activity?

They grinned back at me.

"It's not so much about leadership as it is about teamwork, but you'll have a lot of fun, anyway!"

"Yes!" Emma pumped her fist. "We're going to kick ass."

Paige's lips curled into an evil smile. "They're going down."

It was impossible not to get competitive with friends like mine. "They're going to… lose."

Paige cackled. "We'll work on your trash talk later, but good try."

A few minutes later we stood in the middle of the archery field, but the targets and bows had been removed. In its place, nets in the shape of an X divided the field into four squares.

A large, inflatable clear ball about five times the size of my body sat off to the side. I snorted. No regular volleyball for these people. Everything here was larger than life. Forty-foot rock walls, human pyramids with no training, slip n' slides that rocketed down an entire hill into a lake. I was starting to enjoy that nothing was done halfway. Maybe that was part of their lesson. Don't live halfway.

Suzie herded us to one of the squares. "Okay, everyone. We're up first." She gestured to a board set up at the side of the field with what looked like March Madness brackets drawn on it with a chalk marker. Wow. They weren't messing around. But wait, this couldn't be camp-wide. The freshman cottages weren't here. Was this a last hoorah for the older campers? That kind of rocked.

The sun blazed down on us. I shed my sweatshirt with a couple of the other girls, bouncing on the balls of my feet as I waited for the game to begin.

It took forever for Dana to get everyone in position and explain rotations, brackets, and rules. One of the girls at the back of the Robin quadrant next to us laid down in the grass at one point out of boredom. Bad move on her part because she didn't see it coming. When the front of our team heaved the ball over the net, it fell on her. She squawked and rolled out from under it.

"Why didn't you have my back?" she screeched at her bunk mates.

The other Robins looked away. "Sorry," one threw over her shoulder as she rolled the ball to the front of their square. "Didn't see you there." *Oof.* That was cold.

My eyes skittered over the Beaver group in front of me, glad no bad blood existed between any of us. It would have made this summer so much worse.

"Heads up, Andy!" The jumbo, transparent ball headed right for my head. At the beginning of camp, I might have cowered and expected someone to save me, or at least stepped out of the way, but I didn't want to be like the Robin girls. I liked my fellow Beavers. It didn't take a lot of skill to stand my ground—just guts. I stretched my arms over my head and dug my feet into the ground, waiting for death.

It didn't come. The plastic collapsed around my hands as Paige and Denise stepped in to help me with the weight. At the same time, we all bent our knees, then hurled the ball over the net at the Squirrel team. A couple of girls dove for it, but their hands weren't enough to keep it from bouncing on the ground.

My face split into a wide smile and Paige grabbed my shoulders.

"You did it!" she cheered.

I bounced up and down with her in victory. She was right. I had help, but I did it. Me.

"Score one to Beavers!" Dana said through a megaphone.

"Way to get under it, Andy!" Suzie cheered from the sidelines.

Wait, what? Suzie just cheered for me? I searched the counselors until I found her. She gave me two enthusiastic thumbs up. Hesitant, I mirrored her, then turned to pay attention to the game.

It didn't take long to figure out a strategy with the girls, which was very different from normal volleyball. We all needed to pay attention and at least three or four of us needed to get under the ball each time to have enough power to not only keep it from falling on the ground, but also get it back over the net. We didn't say much except "Got it!" Doing was easier than saying, and soon I fell in love with the sound of laughter and squealing every time the squishy ball fell on our heads.

We won the first game, then the second, and the third. Our streak gave us energy and when the time came to crush the final teams, we were buzzing.

I assumed all three of the opposing teams ended up being boy cottages because the guys had a bit more muscle to push the darn thing over the net. I glanced over at the Bluebirds. We'd just owned them, but now half of them were braiding the other half's hair in the grass. Or the other cottages didn't care they'd lost.

"We've got this, Beavers." Paige bounced from foot to foot. "Do or die time."

"I'm dying," Emma said. She leaned on me, glowering at Paige. "You're not even human."

I laughed. "She's just jacked. We've got this."

Emma rolled her eyes and took her place at the back of the team.

Seconds later, it was on. We sprinted back and forth across the field, Paige harassing Emma when she didn't go fast enough. Emma managed to throw up a middle finger once while the other team reset to serve, but I don't think Paige saw it. If she did, she was too hyper to care.

The counselors eliminated one team after every five points scored. We played hard and managed to knock out one of the guy teams. It put us in a good position because now we wouldn't get as many hits to us. One of the remaining teams would have to hit it diagonally, and that would take way more work. Paige fist-bumped me so hard, she might've broken one of my knuckles. I didn't care. My smile could've passed for Suzie's right now, I was so happy.

"I can't do this anymore," Emma whined. "I'm melting."

She wasn't the only one complaining, but all we had to do now was beat two more teams and we'd win.

During the next play, the clear ball whizzed toward us like a torpedo. The guys who could heave it over our net gunned for us. I tried to ignore the blond head at the back of the Hippo team. I hadn't noticed I'd been playing *him*.

The ball hit the ground beside me.

"Andy!" Paige cried, throwing her hands out in disbelief.

"Sorry!" I'd been doing so well up until now.

The teams rotated players and now Lucas and I were both at the front of the net. But I couldn't check out. I couldn't look away. The Beavers were counting on me, and I'd already cost us one point. If we lost two more, we were out.

I tried to avoid his gaze; I really did. But it was never going to happen. When our eyes met, he smiled a sad smile, and I shrugged. The disappointment on his face made me want to shrink inside myself.

No. No shrinking. Not anymore.

The ball came at me from the back of their side fast and hard. I had no time to grieve over what might have been. This time I got under the clear sphere and with the help of the other Beaver girls, rocketed the thing right at their faces.

Sweat slicked my forehead and arms as I focused on the game.

Run, brace, absorb, and push. We found a rhythm, but no one knew where the ball would go and who would end up with the brunt of it. My ponytail came loose, so I pulled it out and reformed my hair into a messy bun before the ball came my way again.

I felt horrible that it ended up being Paige's mistake when the ball hit the ground the second time on our side.

Marshall pumped his fist on the other side of the net.

Paige mouthed something to him, which may or may not have been colorful swearwords. Then she turned to us. "Come on, guys!" she yelled.

About one minute later, it was over. I don't know if the Hippos were better, stronger, or faster, but when the ball bounced into no-man's land between us, we were beaten.

Dana stepped out. "Beavers, you're eliminated."

"Oh, thank God!" Emma yelled, and a few of the girls laughed.

For a second, Paige's brow creased with anger, but then her expression cleared, and she kicked the dirt and laughed. We retreated to the shade of the sidelines and chugged water like we'd just run a marathon. This time Suzie didn't call me out for lack of participation, and no one had to defend me. For once, I felt like I fit in with the other girls. Was this leadership?

"Teamwork makes the dream work," Emma said with a hint of sarcasm as she knocked her water cup against mine.

After the game, we ate sandwiches and chips in the grass outside the cafeteria for dinner, which felt like a punch to the stomach. We could've been doing this the whole time, away from everyone? I would've been out here every single day! Emma and Paige teased me until my grumpiness faded. In fact, the whole day relaxed me more and more, until I realized that in less than an hour, I'd be at a dance with the boy who broke my heart.

39

GO GET THAT LEG HAIR, TIGER

"I can't do this." I wrung my hands. In the past, I'd keep my feelings inside, but Paige and Emma were my friends. They deserved to know I planned to ditch them.

"Yes, you can," Paige said. "Try to breathe. You're going to the dance."

"I can't. I don't have anything to wear for a dance. I didn't know there was going to be one. All my clothes are dirty and…"

"And you want to look hot for Lucas?" Emma raised an eyebrow.

"No." *Yes.* "I just can't, okay?"

My duffel contained three pairs of shorts, a bathing suit, tank tops, T-shirts, one pair of jeans, and a hoodie. Camping clothes. I made Mom pack for me, and now I regretted it. I dropped my white bra back into the duffel. How could I make Lucas think I was fine if I didn't have anything to wear?

I flopped on the floor. I had a Lucas crisis *and* a clothing crisis. Kill. Me. Now. At least both Paige and Emma believed in being fashionably late. The other girls in the cabin had left twenty minutes ago.

"Hang on, drama queen," Emma said.

I closed my eyes against the glaring light beaming down on me from the halogen bulbs on the ceiling. After a moment, a ball of clothes fell on my chest.

I sat up.

"Sharing is caring." She put on a top that pushed up her boobs until they were basically at her chin.

I sorted through the clothes on my lap. The shirt was meant for longer torsos, but the skirt and dress might work.

"You're taller than me. How is this even…" I held up the black miniskirt.

"Exactly." Emma beamed at me.

"Well, I'm also like… curvy."

"Yeah, you are," Paige said, wiggling her eyebrows.

"You don't get i—oh." I held up the scraps of fabric again. I hadn't considered my hips as an asset to flaunt. I often hid them under baggy clothes.

"Andy, just try them on. If you hate them, wear whatever you brought. It's no big deal." Emma frowned as she uncapped her third lipstick, obviously looking for a certain shade. How much make up did she *bring*?

"Okay."

I shed my clothes and pulled the strapless dress over my head. I liked the cotton candy shade of pink, but the skintight design hugged every part of my body, showing every seam of my underwear and my bulges of back fat. The bottom hem stopped one millimeter short of revealing my underwear.

Emma covered her mouth, but it didn't hide her massive grin. "Maybe that one is a little—"

"Ya think?" I yanked it over my head and turned to the shirt and skirt she'd tossed my way. I pulled the skirt on first, prepared to veto it, but also dreading having to turn back to my sparse clothing collection.

To my surprise, it was super stretchy. It also covered my butt and a bit of my thigh. I walked down to the end of the bunks and back. It stayed in place. "Huh."

Emma smirked. "And the shirt."

I may as well commit to it all. I grabbed the silky green shirt and threw it on. I didn't have the boobs to fill it out like Emma did, but because it had the extra room, it created a draping effect that I could live with. I smiled and looked in the mirror on the door. Big mistake.

"It's too low-cut!"

"It is not!" Emma laughed. "I wear it all the time."

I checked out her outfit again and looked away.

"You better not be judging me right now. I look hot." She folded her arms over her massive chest.

She did look sexy. I twirled in the mirror. It stayed in place. Even though it hung an inch from exposing the bow of my bra, it fit me. It might be the hottest thing I'd ever worn.

"I'm going to re-shave my legs," I muttered.

She pumped her fist in the air. "That's my girl!" she cried. "You are one hot *chica*. Feel free to borrow my stuff anytime!"

I smiled. "If it makes you this happy, I might."

She swatted me on the butt. "Go get that leg hair, Tiger. Don't forget a smokey eye when you do your makeup. We're gonna make you into the badass you are!"

Torn, I scampered off to the bathroom where my razor and makeup bag waited. I wanted to look hot, but I didn't want Lucas to think it was for him. I didn't want to give him the satisfaction.

But I wouldn't let him see me moping, either. That settled it. It was the last night of camp, and I refused to hide anymore.

I was going to get sexy.

40

DANCE WITH ME

It's amazing how a space can convert into something entirely different in no time at all. The cafeteria still smelled like canned peaches and chicken nuggets, but now a disco ball spun above us, and cheesy streamers hung from the ceiling. A DJ had a booth set up right in front of the contraband coffee door, and to his left sat a table with cookies and punch on it.

God help me. I was nervous.

In the end, I cleaned up well. I borrowed high heel sandals from Paige that were a size too large, but I wouldn't admit they were killing my feet. My hair fell in soft waves to my shoulders, and my makeup was professional level. After laughing at my feeble attempts at a smoky eye, the girls had sat me down and gave me a makeover that made me look at least five years older and a thousand times sexier.

When I entered the cafeteria with Paige on one side in trendy ripped jeans and a halter top and Emma in her sexy outfit, it was like a scene out of a cheesy teen movie.

A few campers from the Hippo and Beaver cottages stopped to stare. Suzie's eyebrows skyrocketed until they disappeared into her flaming hair. Tyler winked at me and returned to pouring punch for thirsty campers. And Lucas…

Of course, my eyes betrayed me by zeroing in on where he leaned against the far wall. The air stilled and the pop music faded into white noise. He wore another one of his Henley shirts, this one two shades of blue, paired with dark jeans. For once he'd combed his hair —he looked like a commercial. I wanted to ruffle his hair, to crease his shirt so he wouldn't look so perfect.

Then he noticed me.

For one long second, neither of us breathed. Then his eyes flicked down to the floor and the moment faded.

Heart pounding, I lifted my chin. I didn't need his approval or anyone else's. I pasted a wan smile on my face to hide my nerves, the action so foreign I didn't know if I was accomplishing it at all.

"Let's dance!" Paige squealed when a popular song came on.

I rolled my eyes as she and Emma pulled me out on the cafeteria floor with a bunch of other teens that smelled like deodorant and body spray. They shook their hips and wiggled their shoulders as I stood there.

"At least sway, you lame duck," Emma said, shaking my arm with her hand.

So I swayed. I liked this song. Before long, I moved to the beat of the drums. I even closed my eyes and rocked my shoulders a little.

"That's it, Andy!" Paige said. "Get it!"

I dissolved into giggles, grateful for the bouncing, colored lights that let me be a weirdo in relative darkness.

To my surprise, I stayed out for two more fast dances and got into it more each time until I jumped and screamed the lyrics with Paige and Emma like I was at a live concert. When another quick-paced song came on after all the yelling, I begged off for some punch. Talking made me thirsty, and yell-singing had turned my throat into the Sahara.

I swiped a pre-filled cup of punch from the table.

"Having a good time?" Tyler asked as he ladled another cup to replace mine.

I laughed. Was I even allowed to talk to him without Suzie the vulture swooping down on me? "Yeah, I needed a girls' night," I said.

He smiled at me. "I'm glad."

A slow song started, and I faced the dance floor again. Paige pressed against Marshall in a slightly-more-than sweet way as they swayed, her taller head still the perfect height to perch on his shoulder.

At first, I couldn't find Emma, but then I caught sight of her at the edge of the dance floor talking with a blonde girl as they danced. *Good for her.* I learned new things about my friends every day.

I could no sooner stop breathing than keep myself from looking at Lucas. He stood in the same exact spot. A cute little brunette had bounced up to him, obviously to ask him to dance.

He bent his head toward her with a small frown as he listened to what she had to say, then straightened and shook his head. She walked away, dejected. My body thrummed electric when he looked up, and his eyes locked with mine.

I ran to the bathroom and shut myself in a stall, sitting on the toilet feeling so stupid I couldn't breathe for a second. We barely knew each other. I shouldn't be this attached to him. Why did it hurt this much? I hugged myself and closed my eyes, but I couldn't stay here forever.

I unlatched the stall and went to the sink, washing my hands out of habit. Then, with one wet finger I pointed at the mirror. "Stop being such a wuss." My voice came out calm and echoed loud in the bathroom. Assertive.

Glancing at myself again on the way out, I reveled in the fact I looked good. Confident. Sexy. That should be enough to carry me through. I hoped.

Because fate wasn't kind, I exited the bathroom to another slow song. *Great.* Paige would still be dancing with Marshall and Emma with her new crush.

"Hey, Andy." The skinny kid from the survival challenge stood in front of me. "Want to dance?" He fingered the collar of his polo shirt nervously. Wait, someone was asking me to dance?

"Sure," I said. I'd never slow danced before. *How did I...* I took a stealthy look around, but variations of dancing ranged from the more formal hand in hand to the arms around the hips. *Crap.*

He led me to the center of the room, and we stood motionless for a second until I realized he was waiting for me to decide how we'd dance. I put both my hands on his shoulders, and he followed my lead, placing his respectfully above my hips. We were close. Really close. And he was cute in that geeky, adorable way some guys could be, but he wasn't Lucas.

"You look great, by the way," he said.

"Thanks."

His eyes skated over the low cut of my shirt, and I suppressed a giggle. A boy was actually checking me out.

"Camp is almost over," I said.

"Yeah, tomorrow."

We were terrible at conversation. His glasses slipped down his nose. I reached up to push them back in place for him. Another minute passed where we didn't speak as the music tried to convince us we'd never be in love like this again. Were guys supposed to sweat this much? His glasses slipped down again.

"Uh, maybe this was a bad idea." He pulled his hands from my waist.

"Why?"

"Er..."

"May I cut in?" Lucas asked through gritted teeth from behind me.

"Sure, man. Sorry." The guy with glasses who still hadn't given me his name raised his hands and backed away.

I glared at Lucas. *Rude.*

"Andy."

"Lucas."

He held out his arms. "Want to dance?"

"You couldn't wait until the end of the song?" I asked. That poor shy guy would now likely be scarred forever by Lucas's stupid possessiveness.

He grinned. "No. I couldn't."

"What are you doing? You broke up with me!" I hissed. I would not dance with him if he didn't want me.

"We were never going out," he said.

My mouth dropped open.

"But I wanted to! Of course, I want to, Andy. Come on. And then you walk in here and you look so—"

I waved his unfinished compliment away. "Thanks." I couldn't deal with a jealous Lucas when it wouldn't work between us. I was Strong Andy now, Independent Andy. I swept by him, pretending I had some place that I needed to be. It was true. I desperately needed to be anywhere that didn't include him.

"Wait, Andy." Lucas reached out and touched my arm, his fingers gentle and hot as they brushed against my skin.

I couldn't help turning back.

"I just wanted to... You don't think that I'm... Please dance with me," he whispered.

I swallowed. What could I say when he looked this sad? This was *Lucas*. And just like that, all my resolve disappeared. "Okay."

He led me to the center of the floor and pulled me in close. I leaned my head against his chest. I didn't have to wonder where to put my hands, where he would put his. He took the lead, and it was so natural to curl into him and pretend we were in our own little world.

No one else smelled so good, felt so good. Maybe they never would. All those times he got me, all those moments he kept me going this month.

"Maybe we could make it work," he whispered into my hair.

But we couldn't. He knew it and I knew it. And for this brief, fragile moment, nestled in his arms, it was okay.

41

ANDY THE LEADER

As weird as the whole forcible camp experiment had been, it was surreal waking up the last morning to pack. We trudged to breakfast, sunburned and sore. Exhausted smiles on now-familiar faces littered the cafeteria while we ate.

"It's the last day of camp, my friends," Dana croaked. She looked like she needed rest too with her hair half out of its ponytail and her voice hoarse.

Everyone groaned, me along with them. As much as everything here had pained me, I'd found Paige and Emma. It was nice to have friends for a change, even if they were only camp-long friends.

"We've had a great time with you this year, and now it's time to self-assess."

Campers passed papers and golf pencils in foam cups down the long tables. When the paper came to me, I came across questions about my experience here. They weren't questions like "how was the food" (a solid C-) or "did you like your counselor" (maybe a D+). They focused on us. We had to rate how we'd changed and fill in what we learned about ourselves during camp.

Lots of kids left to complete the survey in their bunks, but I stayed. Soon, my table was empty. I tapped my pencil against the table in a slow rhythm.

What have you learned about yourself that you don't want to change?

What could you do in the future to make yourself more of a leader?

The answers to those questions wouldn't be what they wanted to hear, but I didn't care. I wanted to be honest, tell them once and for all what was going on in my head. I didn't want to be forced to be an extrovert. The girls were right: I was a listener. The world needed people like me, too. I had to learn how to say "no," though. No to doing things that made me uncomfortable, and no to falling apart even when it would have been so easy, especially after Lucas.

I got to work, my pencil scratching my paper, only four or five campers left inside doing the same. For all my sarcasm, this assignment felt real, felt important. When they asked me to rate myself on statements like "I am comfortable with my moral code" and "I have the ability to admit when I am wrong," I could've laughed aloud. Guess I learned more than I bargained for this summer.

After looking over my short answers one more time, I handed my paper to Dana. I walked halfway to the door before she stopped me.

"Andy, wait," she rasped, my paper still clutched in her hand. "I want to talk to you."

Was I in trouble? I twisted my hands together as I jogged back to her. "Okay."

She set the paper down. "I know there were rough patches for you here this summer, but I wanted to tell you that you're a wonderful sort of leader, the kind this camp could use as a counselor next year, if you're interested."

My mouth dropped open. "Me?"

"Yes, you. I've watched you, talked to the counselors. You're a quiet commander of a room, especially in these last few days. It would be good for the campers to see another style of leadership."

I opened my mouth, then closed it. Yet another person who'd been looking out for me, and I didn't even know it. I'd be eighteen next year, old enough to be a counselor. Did I want to lead a bunch of rah-rah optimists who ran their mouths constantly?

She smiled. "Think about it, okay? There will be a sign-up as you leave if you're willing."

I nodded, then left the cafeteria in a daze. Of all the crazy things...

I dragged my feet on the way back to the cottage, not wanting to finish packing because packing sucked, but also not wanting everything to be over. This camp felt... unfinished, somehow. When I reached the cottage and pushed through the door, only a few Beavers remained. Our parents would be here any minute. Knowing Mom, she'd be first in the car line.

Paige and Emma were waiting for me. So was my phone, placed neatly in the center of my stripped bed. I picked it up and slipped it into the side pocket of my duffel, the temptation of opening my social media pages taking a backseat to the faces of my new friends. Ones I might never see again.

"Finally," Emma complained, waving her own phone at me. "Give me your number so I can put you in the group text."

I grinned as I rattled off my number. A second later, my bag vibrated. Maybe we *would* see each other again.

Paige zipped up her bag. "So, what did you decide? Victim or Convert?"

I snorted. I'd been a victim for most of camp, but Dana's words resonated with me. After everything, I didn't feel done here. Not yet.

"Convert," I said. "Definitely. In fact... do you want to do something crazy with me?"

"Who are you and what have you done with Andy?" Emma joked.

"I'm in," Paige said.

"You haven't heard what I want to do."

"True, but I figure if you think it's crazy, it's probably just climbing a ladder or something." She grinned.

I shoved her. "I want to go on the slip n' slide."

Emma laughed in disbelief, but Paige's eyes widened. "Our parents are waiting for us."

I smirked.

"She's serious," Emma said.

"No, she isn't."

"Yes, I am." I grabbed my suit out of my bag. "I'm going to slip and slide, and you can come with me, or you can stay here." But I knew I had them. No way they'd let me do it alone.

"Oh, hell yeah!" Emma cheered and we got dressed in record time. We ran as fast as we could to the lake before the line got too long, our flip flops smacking the packed dirt of the trail the whole way.

When we arrived, we lucked out with only about ten kids in front of us, all younger and on a different camp schedule than us. That's when the nerves set in. The hill rose to a ninety-degree angle before it evened out and launched kids into the lake. How deep was it at the end? What if a rock was lodged under the tarp, I hit it the right way, and it paralyzed me? Okay, fine, that was dramatic, but just because no one had gotten hurt yet didn't mean it couldn't happen.

The sun disappeared behind a cloud, and I shivered, though it had to be at least eighty degrees.

"You gonna chicken out?" Emma asked as the line moved. Now only eight campers stood in front of me. A guy took a running start and dove headfirst onto the mat, yelling until he hit the water with a loud smack.

"No," I whispered. *Stop it.* "No," I said with more confidence. "I'm doing this." I stepped in front of her and Paige to go first. It didn't seem like anyone had to swim far to get to the dock after they hit the water. I could do this.

Sooner than I wanted, I stood at the top of the blue and yellow tarp. Hoses spit water onto the plastic. Was that soap they were using to make it slipperier today? Could they even dump something like that into the lake? A few bubbles betrayed their source as they floated above the slick surface.

Dana manned the slide—she was everywhere. "You okay?" she asked with a kind smile.

"Yeah," I said. I was holding up the line now. *Oh, what the hell.* I got to my knees like I'd seen a couple of the more scared campers do. Then I scooted forward and slid on my butt to the edge of the hill. It was a long way down, and not entirely smooth, either. The slide began with a slight decline and then dropped almost straight down before curving back up, the perfect launch into the choppy water of the lake. I teetered on the edge for a second. I wouldn't die. They wouldn't let me drown. I could do this. I chose to do this.

I pushed off.

My body rocketed down the steep slope toward the water as I screamed. Rough patches of ground poked up under the tarp, but I didn't have time to feel it before I was launched, squawking, into the air, and then plunged into the cold water of the lake. I came up shoulder deep, sputtering and laughing, and scooted to the side for Paige and Emma.

Emma gave a war yell on her turn and did what looked like a sideways cannonball off the end of the makeshift ramp. Paige's descent was more fluid, and the surface of the lake barely rippled as she slid into it, a dive that would make anyone jealous.

Watching my new friends released a hurt inside of me. A bitterness I didn't want to admit I had buried deep down. I always told myself I wanted to be alone at home, but the truth was, I wanted people to try to understand me the way Paige and Emma did these past weeks. Talk to me. Get to know me. A part of me hated that no one else wanted to do that.

I didn't have much left of high school. Just one year. Was it enough time to be the one to reach out? Did I want to change this late in the game? The answers didn't come to me but admitting that I could put myself out there more, stop looking at the floor, and participate in some small, quiet way maybe that was enough.

We sprinted back to the bunks and changed fast. Half-toweled dry, our wet hair slapped the backs of our necks as we ran to the parent pick-up, where a few cars remained. Mom might be mad she had to wait. I didn't care.

And I did want to be a camp counselor. Dana was right: I could be a leader. A different kind, one that selected battles to fight and didn't walk over people. Maybe this camp needed an introverted leader. Maybe I wanted to be that for them, give back a little. They'd certainly given me a lot, whether all of it was intentional or not.

Paige grabbed my arm before I stepped off the wooded path.

"Are you going to be a counselor next year? Please say you are because I already signed up and there aren't enough people and—"

Was she reading my mind? "Yeah, actually." My face heated. I probably looked like a hypocrite considering all my complaining this summer.

Emma stood silent beside us.

"What about you?" I asked her.

She forced a grim smile. "You two don't need me."

Paige rolled her eyes.

"Of course, we do," I said.

"Just tell her," Paige said.

"I'm not coming back to camp," Emma said. "This was my last hoorah."

"But... why?" Without Emma's fiery personality, our trio wouldn't be the same. We needed her sarcasm.

She shrugged. "I'm graduating a semester early and moving to California for college."

"Whoa." I wasn't expecting that. "Congratulations."

She rolled her eyes. "Thanks. Kick some ass next year, and don't pick on the quiet ones."

"I'd never," I joked.

"I know." She hugged me. It was so not Emma, but I guess the end of camp brings out the weird in everyone. "I'm glad I met you both." She heaved her duffel over her shoulder and walked out of the woods and into the sunshine.

"She knows how to make an exit, that's for sure," Paige said as we stared after her.

College a year early. Crazy.

Then Paige turned to me. "So, there's something you should know if you're going to come back to this nuthouse..."

I cringed. I only stood 80/20 on my decision, and I hadn't signed up yet.

"Lucas signed on, too. To be a counselor."

I bit my lip. "Okay."

"Okay?"

"I mean, not okay, that's cool, but okay, I can handle it." I mean, maybe. Probably not.

"Okay," she said, unconvinced.

"Stop saying okay!" I laughed.

Paige giggled. "Okay."

When I asked Suzie for the counselor sign-up at the registration table on the way to parent pickup, her face was priceless. She progressed through all five stages of grief before laughing out loud and forking over the clipboard. I scrawled my name and contact info and handed it back to her.

"I get to drink coffee if I'm a counselor, right?" It was the first time I'd been the one to start a conversation with her all summer, and I hoped she'd notice I was trying. I wouldn't hesitate to pull the clipboard out of her hands if she said no to coffee, though.

She arched an eyebrow, grinning. "Haven't you already been doing that?"

I stared at my feet. "So, I guess I'll see you next summer." I didn't want her to hate me. I never wanted that, and I never wanted Tyler.

Suzie chuckled. Gone was the dentist-perfect, every-tooth-showing grin. This might be the first time all camp she smiled at me for real. "That sounds fun, but I won't be here."

Really? She seemed like a lifer. One of those people who had a normal day job, but then came here in the summer for fun. Ms. Spirit with a capital S, just like Tyler said.

"Why not?"

"I'll be on my honeymoon."

Her what?

"Almost ready, Suze?" Tyler hollered in our direction.

"Yeah, hang on. Andy's the last of them."

My mouth gaped like a large-mouth bass. *No way.*

"I'll keep the car running." He jogged over and kissed her cheek. She beamed as he walked toward the parking lot.

I stared after him, but I couldn't let this go. Not without asking. I ran after him. "Tyler!"

"Oh hey, Andy." He twirled his car keys as we walked.

"What are you—" I gestured back at Suzie, who now used the clipboard to hide her laughter.

He glanced at her, the corners of his eyes crinkling with amusement. "I thought Lucas told you we're engaged."

"But she's so—you can't be serious," I sputtered.

"Yeah," he said with a megawatt smile. "She's adorable."

"So, you're engaged to Suzie?" I asked, still unwilling to believe it.

"Hell yeah, I am." He looked back at Suzie with fondness. Her curls bounced with animation, and her hands flapped around her head like she was trying to swat a fly as she spoke to Dana. "She's all kinds of feisty in the summer." He cleared his throat. "Well. I'll see ya, Andy. Kick some butt next year, Counselor." He winked. And then he was gone.

I blinked. They pretended to be annoyed with each other? It was a game? Was that how they *flirted*?

A familiar honk broke me out of my thoughts. I turned to where my mother's minivan waited in the pickup line. I wasn't sure how to talk to her after I hung up on her earlier, but I could handle it. If anything, this camp had proven I could handle just about anything.

"Andy."

I closed my eyes. *Except Lucas.*

It would be so easy to brush by him, to run to the safety of the minivan, but what good would that do? I'd have to see him next summer. "Lucas."

He took that as permission and jogged up to me. "You signed up to be a counselor next year?" He looked good. Too good. Fitted jeans hugged his hips, and he wore that worn gray T-shirt like he was doing it a favor. He wore his hair parted on the side and slightly messy. He wasn't *my* Lucas anymore.

Except he was never my Lucas.

"Yeah, I signed up."

I wanted him to tell me he was surprised I signed on to be a counselor, that he didn't think an introvert like me could handle that kind of responsibility. It would make it easier to hate him.

Of course, he didn't. He leaned toward me and did that thing he did where he ignored my personal space in public. "This isn't over," he whispered. "I know it's not."

His passion pulled at something primal in me, and every kiss, every touch came rushing back. The way he'd slung his arm around me, the way he'd trusted me with his insecurities about his brother, the way he'd understood when I had enough of everything and wanted to detach from the world.

I drew back because I had to, or I'd get sucked into the black hole of needing him. I didn't want to need anyone. I wanted to want someone.

He held my gaze, his own eyes pleading and sexy all at the same time. The air between us crackled. If this were one of my romance novels, I'd throw down my bag and jump into his arms. We'd find a way to work it out and be together. It wasn't one of my books, though. Life was messier than that. We couldn't live a year apart and bank on not falling for another person in the meantime. Him especially.

As if he could read my mind, he smiled ruefully. He didn't have to say it. Neither of us did.

"See you next summer," I said.

He scratched the back of his neck. "So can I uh… have your number?"

I toed the ground as I recited my cell number, not sure why I gave it to him. It's not like he was going to—

My bag vibrated. I looked up at him and he smiled a sheepish smile. We both knew it didn't change anything. I stepped into his arms the second he opened them. Where his touch usually ignited something deep within me, this time it was like the embers of that fire glowed a little less brightly. My body was catching up to where my mind had already gone — past Lucas.

I turned away from him and took one last look at the camp. The corner of Beaver cottage peeked through the cottonwood trees. A lone basketball sat near the base of the hoop on the court where

Paige had swooned over Marshall, and Lucas and I had played Horse. Though I couldn't see the lake from here, I knew it was just past the trees to the right of my cottage. *My* cottage. Being here had been transformative for me. Mom had been right about that much.

I opened the back hatch of the minivan and pushed my duffel into the space behind the seats, then went to sit silently in the passenger's side. A venti caramel macchiato waited for me in the cup holder, and I sandwiched it between my hands but didn't drink it. I opened my mouth to say something, then closed it again. I didn't know what to say after I yelled at her the way I had.

My mom's body seized up as we turned into the traffic circle, like her breaking point was me not drinking coffee. I mean, it was weird… Her hair frizzed out more than normal, like she'd run her hands through it a bunch of times on the way here. Thankfully, she broke the silence for both of us. "Honey, I've been thinking. I know you didn't want to go to camp, and your dad said…" Her eyes crinkled with concern. "I'm sorry for making you go. I love you exactly the way you are. I don't want you to—" Her voice cracked. "I don't want you to think I don't love you for all that you are. You're so special to me."

After all the pain I went through this summer that she had caused, she couldn't be serious. I threw back my head and laughed.

She flinched against her seatbelt. Her lip trembled, and her voice filled with tears. "Andy—"

I waved her off. "No, it's okay." Then I leaned over and rested my head on her shoulder. "Don't cry, Mom. I had a great time when I tried to."

She sniffled, and I moved back to my side of the car when she drove down the winding roads that would lead us home. As she navigated into traffic, I took my first sip of pure heaven. Maybe Dad had worn her down. Maybe she realized that you couldn't change people. Not really.

Deep inside me, a small piece of my heart stitched back together. Mom didn't want me to be her anymore. She was okay with me being me. I couldn't help the joy that spread through my body and ended up on my face.

Rolling the window down halfway, I stuck my hand into the air rushing past. I didn't want to let go of the smell of lake and pine trees. It would be different when I got home. Less.

"You're so tan," she said after a minute. When we stopped at a stoplight, she looked at me for a long moment. "And relaxed. You really did have a good time?"

I thought of all the moments I wanted to die of embarrassment, of the friends I made. Of Lucas.

"Yeah, Mom. I really did."

She beamed.

42

GETTING A LIFE

For the rest of summer, I took my time doing things.

I sat in the back yard and read the books I wanted to. I did my chores. I went on walks and played horseshoes with Dad. Paige and Emma and I texted a bit, then switched to snail mail because it was a fun, old-school thing to do. I couldn't wait to get to the mailbox. We didn't live too far away from each other and were figuring out a time when we could meet up. A weekend, maybe. It wouldn't be like camp, but it'd still be cool. They were my friends.

Lucas texted me a few times. Nothing epic, just updates about his summer and one this morning that said: *Senior Year, here we come! You've got this, Andy!* But I didn't know what to say back to him. Sometimes I scrolled over his messages to delete them, but I didn't want to delete him. He was a big part of my summer, and my life —*kinda.* So, I let them sit on my phone in limbo after hearting the messages. A contact uncontacted.

The first day of school came quicker than it should have, Mom tsked over how I'd grown as she made me try on new clothes, bought me new shoes, and let me pick out another backpack to truck my many books around. She didn't even cringe as much as normal when I drove us home from shopping. I'd taken my driver's test the previous week and passed with flying colors. After all her harping, I would've thought she'd be happy.

I couldn't help my nerves when I pushed open the door the first day of senior year. The familiar smells of disinfectant and pencil shavings filled my nose, but everything had changed. As students slid past me in the hall, they didn't judge me or feel sorry for me. They had their own lives to worry about, and so did I.

I didn't study the fibers of the hallway carpet like I had last year. I knew them by heart. Instead, I straightened my back and held my head high. It would be much easier not to bump into people if I could see them coming.

Teachers welcomed us in that way they always did the first day of school before we wore them down, standing out in the hall sipping from their coffee mugs. A blonde girl smiled at me when I held a door open for her. I smiled back. Was she someone like Paige or Emma that I never noticed before? Was senior year too late to make a friend? I wouldn't magically become this outgoing girl, but as I walked down the hall, energy sparked within me.

Like last year, Eric's locker was close to mine, and as I walked up, I found him fiddling with the dial. My heart jumped into my throat. I thought I'd spend my entire summer writing love letters in my head to this guy, but I'd been consumed by camp, by Lucas. I didn't even stalk Eric after camp on social media the way I planned to. He must've gotten a haircut over the summer. It showed off his eyes more. Still dark, dark brown. Still that dimple in his left cheek.

He shut his locker after grabbing a notebook and pen from his bag. Sweat slicked my palms. I rubbed them on my jeans. Could we be friends this year? Could I stop being creepy and talk to him instead of his shoes?

As I approached, he looked up and smiled that cute, close mouthed smile the way he always did. "Hey, Andrea."

For the first time, I let myself feel the anxiety, but I didn't let it control me. I tightened the straps on my backpack and took a deep breath. "Hey. New glasses?"

He pushed the newer, darker frames up the bridge of his nose. "Yeah. You like them?"

"Yeah, they're cool." I ducked my head and waited for embarrassment to wash over me.

It didn't.

"Well, Cool is my middle name," he said drily, leaning on his locker to peer down at me. "You know, I don't think we've ever really talked before."

"I know. I'm kind of…" I waved my arm, words escaping me. Eric was talking to *me*. I was talking to *Eric!*

"Quiet. Me too," he said in a soft voice.

I met his eyes, understanding flashing between us. "I know."

He grinned. "Who do you have first hour?"

I inputted my locker combination to give my hands something to do, the numbers muscle memory after three years. "Jefferson."

"Me too. Math in the morning is going to be rough."

I grabbed my notebook and shut my locker, turning to him. I could do hard things. So could he. "We've got this. Do you…"

Eric stood half a foot away from me, his dark eyes searching mine.

Every cell in my body rebelled against asking my biggest crush to walk with me, but I was tired of living in my head one hundred percent of the time. None of the fantasies that I'd perfected in my brain the last three years were ever going to happen if I didn't say something.

"Do you want to walk together?" I asked. Even though it was uncomfortable, and even though my hands were clammy, and my heart had jumped into my throat, I waited for him to wrap his head around it. Waited for him to say no. To maybe say yes.

"We are going the same way, aren't we?" he asked after a moment, his eyes crinkling with a small smile.

"Yeah. We are." Oddly enough, my voice sounded calm, confident.

Eric grinned wider.

I smiled back as we navigated the crowded hall to Mr. Jefferson's class. Our steps fell into sync, and the mingling of hallway banter welled around us as Eric looked down at me the way I'd imagined a hundred thousand times before. Like he saw me, like maybe he liked what he saw. This year would be different.

I could feel it.

CAN'T GET ENOUGH SUMMER CAMP?

Turn the page for a sneak peek of
Andy and the Summer of Something,
an all-new book that puts Andy back at camp Follow the Leader…

…this time as a counselor!

1
FOLLOWING THE LEADER

Riding in Eric's car was a lot different than driving myself. Would I ever get used to the smooth smell of leather and peppermint or the careful way he inched forward at intersections, his hands cemented in a perfect ten and two?

Eric smiled. "You okay?"

I nodded. We'd started dating this past October, and though I'd become more relaxed around him, even after nine months together, chatting didn't come easily to me. I put a lot of effort into matching his mood when I did speak. It was only right, when Eric tried so hard to make sure I felt perfectly comfortable, too.

"Thanks for signing up with me," I said. "You totally didn't have to."

"And miss a chance to spend time with you? Never." He held my hand to his mouth and gave it a brief peck.

Warmth spread through me. Everything was tiny touches, small moments that made me feel special. His hand on my lower back as he guided me to sit down at a restaurant. Fingers threaded together in public. Soft kisses in his car when he dropped me off after a date spent browsing the bookstore or watching one of his favorite action movies. I'd crushed on him for so long that despite my newfound confidence, I couldn't believe this was real. That I had found a way to make this happen.

Eric Phan was my boyfriend.

I touched his dark sweep of hair, tucking a stray piece behind his ear.

His smile expanded, like I'd given him a present. I didn't often get to initiate contact. He always found a way to touch me first. Small kisses, light brushes of his hand against my arm, my face, my hair—he was so affectionate.

"I'm excited to meet the famous Paige," he said.

I turned to the window so he wouldn't see me roll my eyes. Paige called me at least five times this week. He'd gotten a face-full of her perkiness on our last video chat.

"They always need more guy counselors," she told Eric. "You should sign up. And Lucas won't be there, now," she added before I could shush her. "He got recruited for some kind of college swim team and their conditioning is at the same time. Too bad. He would've given you some competition with Andy."

Eric turned to me. "What does she mean by that?"

Paige paled, her eyes darting between me and him. "Just a joke," she said, frowning at me. "He's a hot guy, and you've got a hot girl, there."

Eric chuckled. "You're not wrong about that."

"Are you ready to lead a bunch of Victims, Andy?" she joked, using one of her famous classifications from last year. I imagined her lecturing her own campers on Victims, Converts, and Volunteers this summer. I hoped, for her sake, she got a bunch of Volunteers—kids who actually liked camp.

But I couldn't concentrate too much on that when my heart hammered so hard it might beat out of my chest. I never told Eric about my romance with Lucas last summer. Lucas was the coolest guy at camp, my first kiss, and my first painful heartbreak. He just... never came up. And now I didn't want to dive into my naïve mistakes from last year.

This summer wasn't going to be about me. I knew what it felt like to be forced into activities I didn't want to participate in. I'd imagined about a thousand ways I could make leadership camp more bearable for any Victims that happened along. We wouldn't waste time on embarrassing icebreakers everyone hated. I'd give them way more breathing room than I had. Way more choice.

By the time Eric and I ended the call with Paige, he'd caught the excitement and was ready to sign up.

Eric's car slowed and turned onto a small dirt driveway. I smiled as a large brown camp sign welcomed us to Camp Follow the Leader, which was still a ridiculous name. I could've chosen a more romantic thing to do with my boyfriend than coaching teens, but it would keep Eric and me near each other. We wouldn't have much time in the same zip code once college started in the fall.

I picked at the cuffs of my green UVM sweatshirt as we crunched over the fresh gravel. The University of Vermont was a half an hour away from Mom and Dad. Far enough to make me feel independent, but close enough to celebrate the holidays together. Eric would attend Norwich University a full forty-five minutes away, but he swore we'd make it work. It wasn't that far. Not really.

Part of me wanted to ask him to come with me to UVM, but he'd grown up in a military family. Norwich was in their blood. He never even applied to another college. I couldn't imagine shy, reserved Eric in any branch of the military, but what did I know? All the images in my head came from commercials and movies. And he never questioned it. Not for one second. He was always so sure of everything.

We pulled around the circle drive in front of camp, and I couldn't control my wide smile. Sure, last summer was tough, but magic happened here, too. Camp Director Dana's voice echoed in my head. *"We could use someone like you next year, Andy."*

Eric gave my hand a squeeze after putting the car into park. "Ready?"

Yes. "Let's do it."

He killed the engine, and I opened my door to sunshine and the smell of water and pine. Of course, I was ready. I had everything I wanted: Eric was here, I had a chance to help reluctant campers, and I got to spend my summer at a place that changed my life. What could possibly go wrong?

2
COFFEE REUNION

At least twenty cars peppered the large parking lot. Counselors arrived a day before the campers for training, but by the looks of it, everyone had beaten us here.

"I thought the email said to be here at ten," Eric mumbled. "It's nine-forty. What gives?"

"Maybe some of the people are janitorial and cooking. I doubt it's just us here today," I tried to comfort him.

"Okay," he said though I knew the busy lot had thrown him. He liked to be in the loop and his version of on time was being early.

I went to grab my duffel from the trunk, but he stopped me. "I've got it."

I squinted at him through the harsh glare of the sun. "But you have your bag, too."

"Andy, it's okay. I've got it." He smiled. "Do you want to grab the pillows?"

I picked up the pillows, feeling a little useless.

"Andy!" Paige's scream echoed across the parking lot. "You made it!" She sprinted to us from the door of the dining hall.

I rocked back as she smashed into me and pulled me into a long, tight hug. "Why is everyone here so early?" I asked for Eric's benefit when she finally let me go.

"Oh, half of us are here so far, I think," she said. "You're right on time."

This appeared to please Eric, who dropped the bags and held out a hand. "Hi," he said. "Nice to meet you offscreen."

"Oh my God, Andy, he's so polite. Does he have a brother?" She shook his hand.

I grinned at her tan skin and signature ponytail. It was as if last year never happened. She looked the same, so sporty and outgoing.

"Nope, and he's mine until he leaves me." I hugged his shoulder, gazing up at him.

Eric smiled down at me. "Which will never happen." He kissed my forehead.

"I'm going to die from sweetness overload," she said. "How about you get your man to grab the luggage while we snag some seats in the cafeteria? He can pile them with the other stuff next to the picnic benches."

I dragged my eyes from Eric's, and he gestured for me to go ahead.

"I wish Emma was here," I said as Paige and I walked to the largest log cabin. It wouldn't be the same without Emma's assertiveness from last year. The way she called out Lucas at the climbing wall or yelled at one of the Hippo cottage guys about the obstacle course.

"Oh, I texted her," Paige said. "Guess where she is?"

Knowing Emma, anywhere. I hoped she wasn't cooped up with books trying to do summer classes and work a job or something equally stressful. I shrugged.

"She's studying abroad in Spain. Lucky duck."

I laughed. "Spain sounds like Emma."

Paige sighed. "I miss her, too. But we're going to have a great summer together, and you brought your boy." She nudged me, and I had to windmill my arms so I didn't fall off the path. "I knew you had it in you, you player."

"I'm not a player," I mumbled, my face burning. "Eric is... well, he was my crush at school even before last summer."

"Oh really? Before Lucas?"

I nodded. Should I tell her to calm down about the Lucas thing now that I was with Eric? That should be part of girl code, right?

"I like that," she said. "Fairytales do come true."

I smiled. Maybe I didn't have to say anything. "What about you?"

"Me? I'm flying solo. As you can imagine, Marshall and I didn't last long." She rolled her eyes.

Crap. I never asked her about Marshall when we talked. "I'm sorry."

She shrugged. "It's cool. Summer romances, right?"

"Right."

Lucas's arms around me as we lay under the moonlight. His fingers in my hair, his lips on my neck...

Heat flooded my cheeks.

"I'm not that worried about dating right now. I want to enter into freshman year totally free. Um, not that, you know, it's a thing that you have to do," she backpedaled.

I blinked. "No, I get it."

As we approached the cafeteria, I noticed a few subtle differences in Paige. Her hair was longer, a shade darker. She had on a sedate T-shirt rather than one of the skimpy tanks she'd worn last year. She wasn't looking for a guy now. Maybe people did change.

Wasn't the fact I was here voluntarily evidence of that?

We pushed though the cafeteria doors. The smell of pine and stale macaroni permeated the air. Other counselors and camp staff milled around, freshly showered and energetic, ready to take on the summer. I breathed it all in again, and... *wait, was that the smell of coffee?*

Two large commercial coffee machines sat on a table *out in the open*. Caf and decaf percolated over burners next to a basket of little creamer cups. Last year, they kept the coffee under lock and key like a teenage prison camp.

"Coffee?" Paige asked through her laughter.

"Obviously." I practically floated to the table. I had a cup in my hand and was waiting my turn when a familiar voice rumbled behind me.

"Thought I'd find you here."

Every hair on my arms stood on end.

Lucas.

I turned and our gazes collided. His lips curled into a smile. "Surprise."

For a second, neither of us moved. Last year as a camper, he was all wiry muscle and large, open smiles. He still had all of that, but his muscles were more defined, and he'd shot up at least two inches. My stomach tightened. He towered over me, his jaw more angular, his hair longer, falling in shaggy waves past his ears.

He stared at me, too. Did he see the same girl as last year? Would he notice the subtle difference in my curves, the way my cheeks had thinned a little, or the fact I now wore trendier jeans?

The line jerked forward, and I remembered why I was there. I busied myself pouring coffee, adding creamer. Lucas grabbed a cup of decaf. Why bother drinking coffee if you only wanted decaf? Last summer he said he didn't drink it at all. Not that I remembered every detail about him.

He smiled at me again. "I wanted to—"

"I thought you—" I said at the same time.

He gestured for me to go ahead.

"I thought you were on a swim team."

He shrugged and looked away. "They moved the conditioning dates. Something about pool maintenance."

"Did you get a scholarship?" I asked to be polite. I blew on my coffee.

"Yeah. Full ride. They'll take anyone these days." He chuckled.

It wasn't funny. It was a huge accomplishment to be able to go to college for free. I couldn't think of anything else to say with him looming over me. The way he looked at me with those striking blue eyes scrambled my brain. Last year, he made me nervous. This year…

This year—nothing. I had a boyfriend. I got back in the coffee line.

"You need another cup already?" Lucas grinned. "You didn't drink your first one."

"No, I—" *forgot Eric's coffee.*

Lucas didn't know about him. And Eric didn't know about Lucas because it wouldn't have mattered if Lucas wasn't here. My hands shook as I poured another cup. Now, Eric would find out about him before I had a chance to make it less of a big deal.

I added two sugars to Eric's coffee.

Lucas frowned. "That's not how you take your—"

"Hey." Eric appeared at my side. He grabbed a lid for the coffee and snapped it on. "Thanks for thinking of me."

"Lucas, this is..."

Eric stuck out his hand. "Eric," he said firmly.

Whoa. Why was his voice so low all of a sudden?

"Boyfriend?" Lucas asked me with arched eyebrows.

I swallowed a scalding sip of coffee and nodded, staring at his baseball tee instead of his face.

Lucas peered down at me for a long moment before shifting his focus to Eric. "Well, hey, Boyfriend. I'm Luke. Andy and I—"

"Know each other from last year at camp," I cut in and gave Lucas a warning look. Since when did he introduce himself as Luke?

Neither guy spoke for a long second as Lucas grinned and Eric placed one stiff hand on the small of my back.

"We should find our seats." I tugged Eric forward. "Good to see you again," I threw over my shoulder at 'Luke.'

We settled in next to Paige on the creaky folding chairs. Her eyes were as big as basketballs. *You didn't tell him?* she mouthed as the lights lowered and Dana took the stage.

I shook my head. I knew I was in deep crap for not preparing Eric. I didn't think Lucas would be here, and it didn't come up before because I wanted to keep camp life separate from real life. It was easier that way. Easier to let Lucas go, easier to be with Eric now.

"Heya, Counselors!" Dana called as she ran up the stairs to the cafeteria stage.

"Heya!" I chanted back even though my inner snarky girl rebelled. Eric looked to me in surprise, and I shrugged. I was a Convert, what could I say? And so what if Lucas and Eric didn't know about each other? It wasn't like they'd be in the same cottage. They didn't have to talk to each other. Camp was a big place. Eric and I were dating now, and Lucas was...

...heading straight for the chair beside Paige.

ACKNOWLEDGMENTS

To my husband Andrew, who nodded along cheerfully every time I ranted about characters and who wrangled our kids when I needed a quiet moment to think about plot. You are the love of my life and your support of my dreams makes you the real MVP.

I'd also like to thank my best friend and perpetual cheerleader Nicole Atherton. From listening to fuzzily remembered dreams on the school bus to half-baked ideas about sarcastic girls who like cinnamon roll guys on our walks, I couldn't do this without you.

To my sons Sterling and Samson: I know you're so young right now, but being able to achieve this debut novel took a lot of patience from you. You give me infinite joy. I am so proud of you boys.

To my older sister Valerie, who reads more than I do (and I'm an English teacher) and who enthusiastically dives into every book I send her so she can give me tough love feedback, you are always my target audience. And to my younger sister Stephanie, who is so smart and fearless that I have to stand back and grin. I live to make you proud of me.

To my mom who took me to book fairs and libraries and pretended not to notice the Harlequins I stole from under your bed, you showed me the importance of reading for fun from a young age. To my dad who taught me persistence and work ethic, and how to stop and appreciate the beauty of nature. I love you both so very much.

To Grammy McKenney for your unwavering support and calm presence in my life: I love you deeply, dramatically, decidedly. You get all the adverbs for how you've impacted my life.

Everyone who has met me knows I'd never just spit into the

wind. My writing is only possible because of the amazing alpha and beta readers I have worked with, the Scribophile community, and the Query Warriors. To Sarah Kaminski, Tara Brodbeck, and everyone else who has told me "this isn't quite right yet," you make me better. Thank you.

To my students: you'll never know how much your presence in my life has shaped me. I hope you all read novels and watch movies and go on adventures that make you feel seen. You deserve every happily ever after.

Libraries are the heartbeat of every city and my happy place. To the Portland District Library and the Howard Miller Public Library, thank you for what you provide for your communities and for me. Your impact is boundless.

A big thank you to Michael and Vanessa at Winding Road Stories for accepting my manuscript and helping me shape it into the novel it has become. It is never just one person behind a book, and everyone with whom I have interacted to get Andy's story into the hands of my readers I thank doubly, triply, infinitely. I am so grateful.

ABOUT THE AUTHOR

Jessica K. Foster writes funny, heartfelt Young Adult Contemporary fiction with a dash of romance. She is a middle school Language Arts teacher with a penchant for hot tea and romantic beach reads. Jessica lives in West Michigan with her husband, two boys, and their ragtag crew of rescue animals.

Visit her website at https://jessicakfoster.com for more information.